# The Saga of Sherlock Holmes

## Allan Mitchell

… being a celebration of the life of a most remarkable human being, a life dedicated to the art of deduction, a life of delivering justice, a life of avoiding boredom, a life filled with adventure, a life of willful and uncompromising confidence, a life never actually lived but, yet, enthusiastically experienced by uncounted millions across the nations of the world and throughout more than a century of time.

Paperback ISBN 978-1-80424-304-6
ePub ISBN 978-1-80424-305-3
PDF ISBN 978-1-80424-306-0

Published by MX Publishing
335 Princess Park Manor, Royal Drive,
London, N11 3GX
www.mxpublishing.co.uk
Cover design by Brian Belanger

Dedicated to my fellow

**Sydney Passengers**

with whom I have been privileged to travel
across continents and time
to participate in the
many adventures
of
**Sherlock Holmes**

# Introduction:

The Sherlockian Canon provides us with a discrete collection of tales into which a great many have been immersed to the point of absolute fascination. Perhaps those tales, those stories written so long ago, do not depict the far-fetched high adventures exhibited by the later works of a great many very capable authors, but each of Arthur Conan Doyle's Sherlock Holmes adventures creates an atmosphere of believability in a setting somehow familiar and always readily accessible to those whose imaginations have not been stifled by demands for ever-increasing levels of reality-stretching sensation.

That discrete collection of sixty tales, however, has been augmented massively over the years by a considerable corpus of pastiche tales emulating and building upon the originals. The character of Sherlock Holmes, his persona and his essence, has also entered into language – English certainly, but surely many others as well, his character having widespread international recognition – and carries its own meaning, the name 'Sherlock' automatically invoking notions of deductive superiority even for those who have never even picked up a Conan Doyle book.

Well, in truth, Allan Mitchell cannot help himself – he needs only to sense the merest hint of the character of Sherlock Holmes and his mind is back in Victorian and Edwardian London hot on the heels of the wrongdoer with the man who has long epitomized both the era and the location which Arthur Conan Doyle portrayed so long ago in his many tales of adventure and intrigue. Multiple human generations, immensely destructive wars, great technological changes and huge shifts in human knowledge, outlook and sensitivity have occurred since that author lifted his pen from the pages of the great detective's existence for the last time, though some things have remained changeless throughout. Just as the River Thames, that legend-bearing watery highway, has kept on flowing along through it all, Sherlock Holmes, too, has stayed the course, as has his friend and colleague, John Watson M.D., along with those many characters of lesser mention whose lives were enmeshed with that of the greatest of sleuths ever to grace the pages of the human imagination.

Though not of our own actual experience, the details of those sixty tales have been embedded in, and in many ways, as, our own memories as our imaginations took us along to do battle with murderers, blackmailers, thieves, assailants, and sundry other felonious types depicted in Conan Doyle's paragraphs, or in those later tellings, and more recently in media unimaginable to A.C.D. but beginning to germinate and bud in his time.

It has not been the author's intent, in any way, to attempt to displace, let alone improve on, the writings of the great A.C.D. nor to impose modern notions and sensibilities upon his creation; rather, he, the author, with his peculiar personal propensity to reels of rhyme and rhythm, invites the reader to join him in reliving and celebrating the adventures of a man as modern in his own day as we are in ours and as readers long into the future will be in theirs.

So, beginning at just before the beginning, we must set off to the London of the 1880s to join a recuperating but emotionally drained John Watson just a few footsteps away from an unimagined and spiritually revitalizing destiny.

# Contents:

On the order of the individual sagas, that as presented in Project Gutenberg of Australia eBook No. 0200441 has been followed excepting that 'The Cardboard Box' (pub. 1893) has been placed in its original position in the 'Memoirs of Sherlock Holmes' (pub. 1892 – 1893) and not in 'His Last Bow' (pub. 1908 – 1917) as in numerous later publications.

# *A Study in Scarlet*

### Sherlock Holmes - his limits

| | |
|---|---|
| Knowledge of literature | Nil |
| Philosophy | Nil |
| Astronomy | Nil |
| Politics | Feeble |
| Botany | Variable. Well up in belladonna, opium, and poisons generally. Knows nothing of practical gardening. After walks has shown me splashes upon his trousers, and told me by their colour and consistence in what part of London he had received them. |
| Geology | Practical, but limited. Tells at a glance different soils from each other. |
| Chemistry | Profound |
| Anatomy | Accurate, but unsystematic. |
| Sensational literature | Immense. He appears to know every detail of every horror perpetrated in the century. |

Plays the violin well

Is an expert singlestick player, boxer, and swordsman.

Has a good practical knowledge of British law.

**If ever**, once, a man had been
in need of friendship, true and keen,
it was the one who bore the name
of Watson, John – a man who came
to seek out solace in the streets
of London where those whom one meets
are strangers, all - in millions thronged -
but, with recovery prolonged
from wound of battle, fever struck,
had, wretched, doleful, found that luck
born of the fortune of the fates
had drawn him backward from the gates
of Hell on Earth to find a friend
of former days who'd recommend
a meeting with one of a mind
of true but temperamental kind
who was in need of one to share
a suite of rooms, should he but care,
as, care, he did, and keenly pried
to have the fellow's name supplied.

**Stamford, that friend** of former days
had warned of such peculiar ways
which were a feature of that fellow,
sound but, at times, most unmellow
such that friendship, close, might not
develop once the pair had got
to know each other, though despite
that friendly warning, Watson quite
decided he must meet this man,
this Sherlock Holmes who did but scan
the features, once, of Watson's form
and saw within, a raging storm
of worry and then, by his tan,
knew he'd been in Afghanistan
and was a soldier by his stance,
a doctor, too, seen at one glance,
but one who might be quite content
with sharing costs, should he consent,
and, so, both men arranged to meet
at Two-Two-One-B Baker Street.

**There, Mrs. Hudson**, that next day,
met both - refined, each in his way -
and saw in them, perhaps, a kind
of partnership, a tie to bind
though yet unbound, a vague portent
of promise of immense extent
of things to come, though neither man
had ever entertained a plan
of joining forces with another
closely, as though with a brother,
to venture forth to battle crime,
for this first day was not the time
for such to blossom but, instead,
for sowing, deep, a seed ahead
of distant harvests from a field
of human suffering to yield
delivery from evil's grip
and then, with justice, re-equip,
as Mrs. Hudson, with a grin
of welcome, bade them both "Come in.".

**And in, both came**, and there agreed
those rooms would suit a dual need
of refuge from great London's dangers
and fair premises where strangers
might be greeted and assessed
for what had ailed or distressed
them in their lives, though Watson, then,
sought simple refuge, knowing when
his mind had healed he might retake
his place again in life and shake
off all the horrors of his mind,
replace them with a better kind
of thought and, to a life remade,
proceed in stages to parade
his healing skills upon the stage
of life in light and disengage
with darkness and despondency
and move with great efficiency
back to his occupation, past,
and self-esteem regain at last.

**So, soon ensconced** at Baker Street,
John Watson - settled, yet to meet
his new life as it would unfold
with new adventures, yet untold -
in Sherlock Holmes began to see
a man, obsessed, and yet so free
in mind and thought, though to what end,
such energies, he might expend,
he could not guess, as types diverse
would seek him out and then converse
with him in vocal tones, reduced,
with no perceptive word produced,
that these must be, John Watson mused,
quite private matters, so refused
to listen to such conversation
- his gentlemanly reservation
telling him that he should not -
though, still, he'd try hard to allot,
to his co-tenant, estimations
of his strengths and limitations.

**By chance**, John Watson read, one day,
an article so far away
from common sense, or so it seemed,
'The Book of Life' which simply teemed
with so much 'twaddle', and he thought
that its misguided author ought
to test out on the Underground
claims which he thought to be unsound
about the Science of Deduction
and find out to its subduction
what conclusions might be made
of any single person's trade
for odds against that were immense
and had made Watson rather tense,
though Sherlock Holmes, relaxed, replied
that article was his and tried
to settle Watson, so explained
he had a trade he had maintained
at which he was highly effective -
the world's first Consulting Detective.

**This gave, to Watson**, great surprise
for he, beleaguered by surmise,
had not considered Holmes to be
the ultimate epitome
of all those seekers after clues,
those subtle hidden residues
left by those who were being sought
and, to light, they would have brought,
when, up from Baker Street emerged
and, on the form of Holmes, converged,
a man, all flustered and distressed
in failure, as the man confessed,
insisting that Holmes must proceed
- as well he knew he would, indeed -
though Holmes asked Watson if he might
accompany him that very night
to premises on Brixton Road
and share with him the heavy load
of helping the Police to spot
clues he could see but they could not.

**For Sherlock Holmes** knew he would see
vague patterns of a low degree
then ponder possibilities,
regard all probabilities,
assess what could not be explained
- no speculation entertained -
until those patterns could be seen
for what they were with eyes honed keen
to give their owner such a vision,
void of doubt and indecision,
that he could, from such traces small,
tell what had happened and forestall
a perpetrator's quick escape,
bring him to justice, mouth agape,
for murder, there, upon someone
had, in some manner, dire, been done
and, although Watson's soul was rocked,
his senses weren't unduly shocked
but steeled and focused hard, instead,
upon the victim lying dead.

**A mess of boot-prints** met the gaze
of Holmes who said it would amaze
him if a single clue remained
for none could ever be sustained
for long but, though he thought to scold,
there was a victim, lying cold,
one Enoch Drebber, now quite late
of U.S.A.'s Ohio state,
from whom, when lifted, fell a ring,
a wedding band of gold, a thing
of value which a woman wore
but which, perhaps, a message bore
being placed upon the dead man's form
and when Lestrade, in verbal storm,
found 'Rache' written on the wall
Holmes knew, in fact, this said it all
though some said 'Rachel' was the cause
to which Sherlock gave little pause
because, in German, 'Rache' stated
that 'revenge' was implicated.

**With lens** and measured tape in hand
Holmes, of the crime site, took command,
inspecting all, neglecting none,
until, in time, that job was done
and he could say two men had been
involved as though, himself, he'd seen
them both arrive and one depart
- these being clues with which to start -
though many had been compromised
and others missed as he advised
the constable first on the scene
who'd had the chance to intervene
and catch the murderer that night
who, by a ruse, had taken flight
for he had been the cabbie who
had driven Drebber, hitherto,
and Holmes, with hand held to his head,
said, artfully, 'a scarlet thread
of murder, through life's skein, had run'
and knew The Game had now begun.

**It was discovered**, soon enough,
that Drebber was a type quite rough
and nasty, though his secretary
Joseph Stangerson contrary-
wise was somewhat more subdued
but would fall victim, it ensued,
when killed by knife, his blood applied
as 'Rache' to a wall, which tied
the crimes together, all could see,
and also, near the murderee,
two pills, suggestive, were produced
and shown to Sherlock who deduced
from insight, great - second to none -
poison was present in just one
which, tested on an ailing dog,
soon had it lying like a log,
as dead as Drebber, giving cause
to Holmes to utter, without pause,
he'd proved his case, though back in time
he'd have to delve to solve the crime.

**But Holmes knew well** he must act fast
for there might be a further cast
of victims on some deadly list
and, so, proceeded to enlist
the street lads who, with eyes honed keen,
knew where and why and who had been
about by day and night and could
provide the missing facts which would
lead Sherlock to the unknown man
who'd brought to play a deadly plan
and was the drunk unapprehended
- though, to be so, he'd pretended -
but who was, in fact, the one
who had brought Drebber's life undone
and was the cabbie on that night
who now, to be arrested, might
and was, by trickery, produced,
as Sherlock Holmes then introduced
to face the hangman's waiting rope
the person of Jefferson Hope.

Now, **years before**, along two trudged,
one old, one young, who barely budged
as thirst, fatigue and spirit lost
were mounting to impose a cost
of non-survival for the pair
 - the orphaned Lucy, young and fair,
John Ferrier, last in command -
just two survivors of a band
of hopeful pioneers who'd marched
across America's land, parched,
but who by fortune would be found
by Mormons in their wagons bound
for 'Zion' and who said they could
provide for them if they just would
convert and then live by their code
well knowing what refusal bode
them both, so, given such a choice
they uttered an assenting voice
to live within the forced constraints
and clutches of demanding Saints.

**The forceful Saints,** their Zion, found
 - the plains of Utah, sacred ground -
and set to work to tame the land,
make it submit to their command,
and both the man and girl had thrived
but soon the day John feared arrived
when Lucy, from a child, now grown,
had much attention on her thrown
though she now loved an outside man
 - Jonathan Hope - and so began
demands for her to state her choice
and, in the Mormon faith, rejoice
and wed with Enoch Drebber or,
young Joseph Stangerson, suitor,
but she refused both men outright,
tried to escape in dead of night
to meet with Hope, but found instead
those two men she had learned to dread
would take her back against her will -
John Ferrier they had to kill.

**Within a month** Lucy succumbed
which left sad Jonathan Hope numbed
but, still, he risked his life to see
her one last time and then would flee,
though after he'd removed her ring,
that wedding band to which he'd cling
until, his vengeance, he'd exact,
justice for that most vile act;
but, discontented, Stangerson
and Drebber moved to jettison
all links with Utah and the Saints
and all their dutiful restraints
then travelled overseas at-large
with Enoch Drebber in full charge
and Joseph Stangerson engaged
as secretary while, enraged,
Hope followed them from state to state,
city to city, filled with hate,
until, to London, they were tracked,
the odds against them soundly stacked.

**All this, before death**, Hope related;
Watson, though, felt devastated
when reports, in print, appeared
and hackles on his neck had reared,
for credit all went to those who,
with Hope's arrest, had least to do,
and Sherlock's efforts were down-played
and Watson was indeed dismayed
and said to Holmes he must reply
and, wrongful claims, in print, defy,
but Holmes, disinterested, would not
and, so, acquainted with the plot,
Watson announced, the truth, he'd write
and, then, a Latin quote would cite
as "Populus me sibilat .."
which might, in English, re-format
to "Though the masses might complain
I'll treat complaints with great disdain
and have myself to praise and thank
when counting money in the bank!"

........................................

11

# _The Sign of the Four_

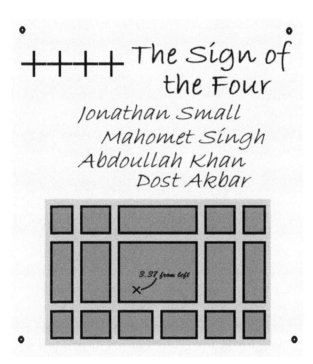

The Sign of
the Four

Jonathan Small
Mahomet Singh
Abdoullah Khan
Dost Akbar

3.37 from left

**John Watson, Doctor** – settled, sound
at Baker Street – felt he was bound
to censure Sherlock Holmes, his friend,
and say that he could not defend
the use of Cocaine to distract
his mind from boredom, such an act
being counter to the elongation
of his life in resignation
to short-term effects produced
but found that he, somehow, induced
his friend to thrust back and to parry
counter words with him to carry
forth the notion that his mind
was of such a demanding kind
that it would perish if denied
the stimulus Cocaine supplied
when challenges of epic sort
were non-existent, falling short
of what a mind like his would need
to carry through each day and deed.

**Watson, unable** to dissuade
Holmes from his Cocaine habit, made
a comment on the case just closed,
a case which opened and exposed
a world of subtle hidden clues,
of small tell-tale residues
and imprints in the softened ground
and how, by all this, Watson found
that he'd been driven to prepare
a narrative, though unaware
of Sherlock's opposition to
and disapproval hitherto
the style he used – far too romantic,
so much so, it drove him frantic -
to which Watson would admit
to some annoyance, and he hit
back saying that his newly written
Scarlet Study had quite smitten
those who'd read it and enjoyed
the skill which Sherlock had deployed.

**But there,** unknown to both, had been
a case of promise - though unseen
by either man – which now approached
and which would very soon be broached
to Sherlock Holmes - so ever gladdened
by those acts which always saddened
others but were hard to solve
and would, a deal of thought, involve -
for, on the stairs, were footsteps, slow,
as Mrs. Hudson, keen to show
upon a salver made of brass
the card of somebody of class
- a young lady, as she declared -
a woman clearly quite prepared
to have uncertainty replaced
with truth to have her problem faced,
as Watson rose, but was restrained
by Sherlock's call and, so, remained
as he was, of escape, deprived,
for Mary Morstan had arrived.

**While Holmes** objectively observed
the lady, Watson was unnerved
a little by her costume - plain
and simple – although, in the main,
he noted sweetness of expression
and was led to a confession
that her face, though plain, defined
a nature modest and refined
and gave a sympathetic look
as, Sherlock's offered chair, she took,
and noted that her hand had quivered
and her lips, a little, shivered
when saying Mrs. Forrester
had stated Holmes had given her
some great assistance in the past
so she'd come to consult, at last,
and Watson once more rose to go
but Mary gestured to him "No!"
which made him, from parting, relapse
and then, into a chair, collapse.

**With Watson startled**, then began
Miss Morstan's narrative which ran
from India - her father's post -
he being Captain Morstan, most
desirous that his daughter - with
her mother dead and neither kith
nor kin in England - should remove
to Edinburgh to improve
her prospects at a school where she
would board till seventeen then be
employed as governess to earn
her living, though she'd often yearn
to see her father, far away,
although, in time, would come the day
her father obtained leave to go
to Britain – some ten years ago -
and had arrived in London but
her great excitement would be cut
short, changing to a grief, unbound,
for Morstan, nowhere, could be found.

**Holmes broke in** and, of her, sought
more details, saying that she ought
tell all, so, though she was dismayed,
she said her father's luggage stayed
untouched at his hotel - a few
clothes and his books - and left in view
were curiosities the man
collected from the Andaman
Islands where he, an officer
in charge of convicts, would prefer
to gather artifacts to sell
or keep for stories he might tell
in later days, but when Holmes asked
about his friends, Mary was tasked
but recalled one who had declared
he hadn't known how Morstan fared
or had, from India, come back
- a Major Sholto, - John, called Jack -
and Holmes found, fully fascinated,
Cocaine's great allure abated.

**Mary continued**, adding more
confusion to what went before
as, four years later, she'd observed
an article quite unreserved
- a newspaper advertisement -
that her address, if known, be sent
and to which she replied and found
a pearl of such size to astound
she then received, and then five more
- one every year - like that before
till she had six, but had no clue
to whom, or why, her thanks were due,
but just that morning in the post
she had received a letter most
intriguing saying she'd been wronged
and justice, to her, now belonged,
so if she'd come that very night
to the Lyceum then she might
receive that justice, so she thought
to ask Holmes if, to go, she ought.

**Holmes, himself**, could not restrain,
so, said unto the lady, plain,
that she should go, but not alone
for doing so he'd not condone
but he and Watson both were free
to go with her, should she agree,
then took the letters she possessed
which he, as was his way, assessed,
and, so, a meeting time to fix,
they set a time, that night, at six
o'clock at Baker Street and then,
with things arranged, she gave both men
an "Au revoir." then walked away
with Watson watching till her gray
and feathered turban disappeared
into a crowd and then he cleared
his throat to utter "How attractive.",
to which Holmes was unreactive,
but, responding, hit a nerve
with "Is she? I did not observe."

**While Mary's image** lingered long
in Watson's mind, Holmes felt a strong
compulsion to check records, old,
The Times kept safe, then saw unfold
the fact that Major Sholto died
a week before someone supplied
a pearl to Mary Morstan, so,
this was a clue with which to go
that night to meet whoever sent
the letter and, perhaps, prevent
some harm which might, to Mary, come
but when Mary arrived she'd some
additional material,
a paper, providential,
in which was penned a cross, ink-red,
a pencilled measure which then led
within its rather small confines
to four strange hieroglyphic lines,
'The Sign of the Four' printed, and then
the names of unfamiliar men.

**Those men** so unfamiliar,
Abdullah Khan and Dost Akbar,
Mahomet Singh, Jonathan Small,
unknown to Mary, four in all,
might be the key, but first she must,
in some unknown person, trust
and so, with Holmes and Watson sped
to the Lyceum to be led
to places unknown through that night
to learn, perhaps, the unknown plight
of Captain Morstan, then were met
by someone bald and strange and, yet,
quite welcoming who claimed to be
Thaddeus Sholto and that he
knew Captain Morstan was long dead
and Mary's disappointment spread
across her face although, within,
she knew the truth and, with chagrin,
accepted she would never see
her father, though this set her free.

**Thaddeus** said his father met
with Captain Morstan , both to set
the details of dividing treasure
such that each man got his measure,
fair, of all its contents, which
would make each man involved so rich
that each might think himself a king,
but, doing so, the stress would bring
death as the Captain, in poor health,
collapsed before the treasure's wealth
could be shared out between them, so,
fearful he'd be accused, Sholto,
the intact treasure, swiftly hid,
and was, of Morstan's body, rid,
but would, before his death decide,
to both sons, confess and provide
the treasure's secret hiding place
but, through a window, saw a face
he feared and, as in terror, cried
loud "Keep him out!", abruptly died

**A single footstep showed** there'd been,
outside the window, someone keen
to hear where Major Sholto hid
the treasure in the house amid
its many Indian effects,
exotic and bizarre objects,
but who had caused the man's demise
before he had time to advise
his sons of its precise location
though they both made indication
Mary Morstan should receive
some payment now and would conceive
the idea that a pearl chaplet
should be dismantled so she'd get
one pearl per year and, then, the three
men and Miss Morstan, keen to see
Bartholomew, the brother, sole,
of Thaddeus to view the whole
treasure, new-found, but were, instead,
all shocked to find the fellow dead.

**A poison dart** had killed the man
and, so, an earnest hunt began
for treasure and whoever fired
the dart, and in time it transpired
two were involved, one rather short
the other needing some support
- a peg-leg - Holmes quickly deduced
on seeing round marks it produced
and which he, to a landing, traced
upon the Thames but found he faced
the problem of finding the launch
Aurora, but with Watson, staunch,
Toby the bloodhound, and a band
of Baker Street boys to command,
the launch was found, so from their base
river police began a chase
upon the Thames with Holmes aboard
and Watson too, after the hoard
of treasure and the men who killed
Sholto – revengeful greed instilled.

**Steam billowed** out from funnels, two,
on launches, each determined to
outpace the other, one to catch
Aurora trying to outmatch
the closing police launch behind
until the smaller man could find
his blow-gun's range and shoot a dart
containing poison to impart
a wound to either stop or slow
the police launch enough to throw
it off the scent, but just before
a second dart flew, gunshots tore
across the Thames, and over went
the small man – to the darkness sent -
but then the fleet Aurora ran
itself aground and, rather than
give up his treasure, long desired,
the peg-legged man, his dream expired,
had thrown away the treasure trove
into the Thames as, on, he drove.

**That man**, Jonathan Small's career
of tea plantation overseer
came to an end when war broke out
in India and, with the rout,
sought refuge in the fortress at
Agra but then discovered that
he must assist two Sikhs to take
a rajah's treasure, though they'd make,
with one more man, a four-way oath
- 'sign of the four' - that all were loath
to cheat the others, but were caught,
sent to the Andaman Isles fraught
with danger but, their treasure, hid
away, though Small began to bid
with two keen officers in charge
who coveted that treasure, large,
- those being Sholto and Morstan
who, on their secret plan, began -
but Sholto took the treasure, found,
then was, to England, quickly bound.

**But Sholto** was a man now marked,
and Small, with friend Tonga, embarked
to take the Agra treasure back,
as did Morstan whose heart attack
and death began a tale of tears,
a tale whose woeful telling clears
as most involved were dead from strife,
though Small, to prison, went for life,
and Scotland Yard, a victory scored,
the matter finished, Holmes was bored,
but, though no folly Watson brooked,
Holmes, to the Cocaine bottle, looked,
in contemplation of the time,
would come his way, a worthy crime,
but Watson, too, found his head turned
by Mary Morstan who'd not spurned
his fond attentions but, instead,
responded knowing that she'd tread,
in time, the aisle, and take his hand
and then, before the altar, stand.

# *The Adventures of Sherlock Holmes*

*A Scandal in Bohemia*

*The Red-Headed League*

*A Case of Identity*

*The Boscombe Valley Mystery*

*The Five Orange Pips*

*The Man with the Twisted Lip*

*The Blue Carbuncle*

*The Speckled Band*

*The Engineer's Thumb*

*The Noble Bachelor*

*The Beryl Coronet*

*The Copper Beeches*

## *A Scandal in Bohemia*

**A tribute** Sherlock Holmes would pay
to someone who would come to play
a part in an intriguing plot,
had been 'The Woman', one who's lot
was sorely tried when, once, the King
of all Bohemia would ring
the Baker Street doorbell in mask
to place, in Sherlock's hands, a task,
quite devious, in its aspect,
and which was that he might detect
and then recover evidence
from one who might, a few days hence,
disrupt his matrimonials
with graphic testimonials
in photo form, for he and she,
a royal couple, couldn't be,
nor would his future in-laws find
his youthful actions of a kind
which they might overlook and, so,
to merge their families, say "No!".

**As women,** as Holmes had expressed,
were of a sex which he'd assessed
to be of traits predictable,
this one should prove evictable
from home and hearth under duress
so he could enter to possess
from somewhere in her residence
that photographic evidence
and then, with satisfaction, bring
that evidence back to the King
who could, in confidence, then wed
another woman who'd been bred
up to a higher station than
she who, those marriage stakes, began
without a chance to win the race
although possessed of charm and grace
and would have made a mighty queen
if only ever she had been
of pedigree and noble breeding
which a King's Queen would be needing.

**So when** this noble in disguise
met Holmes and begged him to devise
a cunning plan to find the image
of the pair, Holmes felt a scrimmage
looming which he'd have to master
so the King's perceived disaster
could, in time, be circumvented
- shameful scandal, too, prevented -
and, so, Holmes forthwith proceeded,
gathering items he needed,
donned his disguise so, in, he'd blend
with 'horsey' people, then to spend
his time amongst them making notes
and gathering curt anecdotes
which might be used to make a plan
of action so that he, a man,
might be admitted freely by
this woman who'd not ask him why
but then, before he could begin,
the lady sent his head a'spin

**But Holmes** discovered more, for she,
- 'The Woman' - had no plans to be
the queen of any king, but bride
to Godfrey Norton, though provide
protection by retaining that
for which the masked aristocrat
would pay a fortune to recover
- proof that he'd once had a lover -
and Holmes stood witness as they wed
- although disguised to look ill-bred -
but still he had a job to do,
a job he was committed to,
for he'd no proof 'The Woman' would
not carry out her threat and could
not take that risk and, so, devised
a plan – perhaps not well-advised -
and thought to fill her house with smoke
which he had reasoned would provoke
her to reveal the hiding place
of that which threatened great disgrace.

**Holmes**, by challenges inspired,
knew plumbers could, if they desired,
make smoke at will and, so, acquired
a plumber's smoke bomb, then retired
into his room for just a while
emerging shortly with a smile
of innocent benevolence
devoid of all malevolence
and all impressions sinister
in costume as a minister
- a non-conformist clergyman -
and then proceeded with his plan
to feign an injury to gain
entry to Irene's home with pain
upon his face and then pretend
to faint, expecting she'd extend
an offer for him to recline
- an offer he would not decline -
and Watson, would, with great aplomb,
through Irene's window, throw the bomb.

**The air** was quickly filled with smoke,
so much that all within must choke
as calls of "Fire" filled the room
and Irene, with portents of doom,
drew back a secret panel but
heard "False alarm!" and slammed it shut
but Holmes had seen it all and left,
though, in his mind, were thoughts of theft
- perhaps that evening or next day -
but heard a passing stranger say
"Goodnight .." - but in a voice he knew -
then "…Mr. Sherlock Holmes." but drew
swiftly away into the night
before Holmes had a single sight
of form or face, and on the morn
the King arrived – not too forlorn -
but, when advised Irene had wed,
his face, of all its blood, seemed bled,
while Holmes called it the best result
for she'd, no more, be difficult.

**To Irene's home** the pair, at speed,
removed but found there'd been no need
for Irene had, that morning, left
and all Sherlock's ideas of theft
went with her, but she'd left a note
which said there was no chance, remote,
that she'd return, though she would keep
the photograph, hide it so deep
the King would never have a hope
of finding it, but he would cope
for she'd not use it unless he,
the King, in any way would be
inclined to injure her some way
but, then, Irene had more to say
and left the King - for him to keep -
her photograph, but she'd not weep
about his treatment of her now
that she'd taken a marriage vow
and wed a man better than he
could hope in any way to be.

**So, there it was,** the King was clear
to marry without any fear
of Irene choosing to expose
their old relationship, then rose
and said that Irene would have been
- had she'd been higher-born - a queen
worthy to bear his noble name
but she just wasn't of the same
level as him, and Holmes concurred
as, rapidly, the sleuth demurred
and said her level differed much
from his – a subtle slight, as such -
and when the King, indebted to
Holmes for his efforts, tried to do
what he thought right - produced a ring
to offer Holmes – Holmes told the King
he'd like the photograph of 'she',
'The Woman', not the ring which he
felt was offensive to his senses,
but kept his thousand-pounds expenses.

••••••••••••••••••••••••••••••••••••••••••••••

## The Red-Headed League

One Jabez Wilson, red of hair,
decided he should tread the stair
of Baker Street, Two-Two-One-B,
and then consult the man whom he
considered might make sense of all
which had combined to have befall
upon him such catastrophe
for that which he had thought to be
a right bestowed by Providence
though now displaying evidence
of being lost in circumstances
inexplicable with chances
such a right might be restored
being very low, so he explored
his options and decided he
had not the skills, himself, to be
off searching, hoping that he'd find
the causes of this act, unkind,
and find out who, with heart so cold,
had made off with his pot of gold.

Holmes interrupted Wilson's tale
- now risen on his interest scale -
when Watson entered but began
to withdraw when he saw the man,
this Wilson, deep in conversation
with his friend whose toleration
of the commonplace and boring
always had that friend deploring
wasted efforts, time misused,
but found that same friend most amused
by what this man, red-headed, stout,
red-faced and pompous, spoke about
so keenly that Holmes said he ought
repeat, in detail, what he'd brought
to be resolved, so Wilson, then,
restarted with the tale of when,
within his shop, a man approached
and for half wages would be coached
to learn the business, something which
Holmes had considered rather rich.

But Sherlock Holmes did not disclose
his great suspicions, simply chose
to listen to the man retell
his story, that of what befell
him when the new man stated he
was wishing his own hair could be
as red as Wilson's, for he saw
an article published to draw
out all red-headed London men,
with details of just where and when
to submit to examination
at a stated destination
to be, there, assessed and ranked
- the rejects all dismissed and thanked -
and one whose hair was redder than
the reddest red would be the man
the grand Red-Headed League would pay
to work, four hours every day,
at tasks an idle man might seek,
receiving four pounds every week.

And at that destination stated
men in droves came to be rated
for the redness of their hair
embellished by means foul and fair
where Wilson's man pushed hard and fast
up stair and landing till, at last,
the hair of Jabez Wilson showed
to the assessors that it glowed
the reddest red that they had seen
and all were, to a man, most keen
to have bestowed on him the post
which all there had desired most
and then instructed him to be
on site each working day so he
could copy out in full the text,
proceeding one page to the next,
ignoring any tedia,
the great Encyclopedia -
the latest of the type Britannic -
with no diversions, mild or manic.

**The time came,** though, Wilson arrived
to find himself, somehow, deprived
of access to his workplace so,
in desperation, thought he'd go
to seek out Sherlock Holmes who might
onto his darkness shine some light
and facts, now hidden, dis-enshroud,
though he and Watson laughed out loud
but took on Wilson's case for he
suspected one he knew to be
of intellect superior
had motives most ulterior
and that an most intriguing crime
full worthy of his skills and time
was now in play and would proceed
without delay and likely speed
to its conclusion very soon,
perhaps that very afternoon
or maybe night, and so he must,
himself to action, quickly thrust.

**For Sherlock Holmes**, was well aware
the man now in Saxe-Coburg Square
in Wilson's small pawn-brokerage
for pay much less than average
which common sense would not condone,
had been, for eight weeks, left alone
and, when described by Wilson, would
alert Holmes to someone who should
not be the least bit under-rated
but who might be incarcerated
if, to a trap, he could be lured
and then, in handcuffs, be secured,
so that a cunning crime well might
be then averted, though, to light,
what crime that was must now be brought,
and so Holmes, as per custom, sought
out clues, directly from the man
and his appearance, of a plan
which must be, by now, well advanced -
a prospect which had Holmes entranced.

**Holmes found**, by tapping with his stick,
the cellar at the rear, then, quick
to think, knew that the bank behind
was what the new man had in mind
to rob, and Wilson's task had been
a crafty ruse, a clever screen,
to keep him occupied each day
and, from a tunnel, well away,
but which, when finished, would provide
access to those who'd crawl inside
that tunnel of some fair extent
and worth the time and effort spent
only for something like a bank,
and that same night would see the prank
fulfilled unless he acted fast
and gathered up a fearless cast
of men to have the felons snared
within the trap which Holmes prepared:
one baited, full, with Gallic gold
and waiting in the darkness, cold.

**A chisel 'clunk'** in dead of night
then, from the strongroom's floor, a light
began to shine until the man,
John Clay, emerged but found his plan
had been discovered and that he
was soon, in custody, to be,
as well he was, but did protest
that he, of noble blood, felt best
provided with some deference
and also given preference
to which Inspector Jones replied
with "Please, Your Majesty" and tried
to keep from laughing loud, and took
the noble criminal to book
then to a cell to contemplate
his likely future gaoled state,
and Sherlock Holmes - his task now done,
the gold secure with losses, none,
and John Clay soon to face the Bench -
said something witty, phrased in French.

**The lady loomed** upon the street
unsteadily upon her feet
and seemed uncertain - hesitating,
wildly wheeling and gyrating -
till, at last, she pulled the bell
announcing that she had to tell
her story, most peculiar, to
one Sherlock Holmes, Detective, who
was, by a friend he'd once assisted
when his help had been enlisted,
recommended as the one
man who could never be outdone
- his powers being so immense
and concentration so intense -
in finding out what had become
of her fiancé, not handsome
but well-disposed to take her hand
in marriage, though before they'd stand
to face the vicar, her endeared
had, for some reason, disappeared.

**Miss Mary Sutherland** had come,
her problem more than troublesome
and worrying - it was bizarre,
as Sherlock's cases often are -
and, when described, it caught the ear
of one who'd need descriptions clear
of those involved and what occurred
if ever he was to be spurred
to action to take on a case
requiring him to start a chase
for facts, reliable and hard
- for false ones, to be on his guard -
but this case, before it began,
Holmes reasoned would involve a man
for he saw Mary oscillate
upon the pavement, not irate
but quite perplexed for if she came
in anger, she'd be all aflame
releasing grievous passions, trapped,
until their door bell's wire snapped.

**But, snap**, that wire didn't, so
there was no inner inferno
but Mary clearly was distressed,
although surprised Holmes had assessed
she was short-sighted and had rushed
that morning, which all left her flushed
and wondering, with just a glance,
how Holmes had reasoned, by her stance
and her demeanor, facts exact,
but Holmes did not let this distract
him from his purpose, so he closed
his eyes and listened, quite reposed,
while Mary told him of her woes
- the pain of going through the throes
of self-doubt and recrimination -
after some strange machination
took, upon her wedding day,
before the church, her fiancé
called Mr. Hosmer Angel who
said, wait forever, she must do.

**She went on** to explain how she
now had a step-father, but he,
being older by a mere five years,
had disregarded all her tears
and would do nothing, for no harm,
he said, was done, and no alarm
was to be raised, then added he,
this Mr. Windibank, said she
should be content within the sphere
of house and home and persevere
and carry on as she had done
and pay no heed to anyone,
and she had income of, per year,
a hundred pounds - which caught the ear
of Holmes – then added that she gave
it all to Windibank to save
the family her own expense
- this making Sherlock rather tense -
and she'd met Hosmer on a day
that Windibank was far away.

**She asked Holmes** if he thought she'd see
Hosmer again when he was free,
but Holmes replied that he feared not
- he did suspect some kind of plot -
and asked for a description, full,
but Mary only had to pull
an advertisement from her purse,
then letters which Holmes saw her nurse
with quiet passion, so he might
see Hosmer better with insight
born of his being able to
focus his mind and make it do
his bidding when he had to sort
out fact from fraud and not support
false notions, but not much stood out
from her description though, about
his letters, even Watson saw
the subtle clue – perhaps the flaw -
in that no handwriting was seen
for every one, typed out, had been.

**This Hosmer Angel**, Holmes could see
seemed sight-impaired to the degree
he needed tinted glasses when
he ventured out in sunlight, then
Holmes learned he'd been sick as a child
and had the quinsy more than mild
with swollen throat glands such that he,
when speaking now, would seem to be
of weakened voice and only spoke
in lowered whispered tones which broke
delivery each time he talked,
and, even more, after they'd walked
and she'd said "Yes" when he proposed,
but added that she now supposed
that Windibank had to be told,
Hosmer had answered slow and cold
that she should never say a thing
until she bore his wedding ring
- a sentiment her mother shared -
but Holmes could see a victim snared.

**Of where he worked**, she couldn't say
although that he, by night, would stay
upon the premises to sleep
- unusual hours he would keep -
and that in offices he toiled
despite his eyesight being spoiled
and that was all she could recall
except it was to Leadenhall
Street Post Office her letters went
when he said they must not be sent
to where he worked for fear he might
be mocked by colleagues, day and night,
then Holmes knew Hosmer was a ghost,
a spectre who'd appear, at most,
when Mary's actions might curtail
that yearly hundred-pounds and fail
to give support to Windibank
and that, perhaps, a nasty prank
on Mary had been being played,
all leaving Sherlock Holmes dismayed.

**To draw out Windibank**, Holmes wrote
to his employers, and the note,
typewritten, Holmes from them received
- proof Mary was, indeed, deceived -
had type features which neatly matched
those in the typed letters dispatched
by Hosmer, and Holmes knew he had
James Windibank at last – the cad -
but when Holmes trapped him like a rat
at Baker Street, he answered that
Holmes could do nothing to him, but
the fellow's mouth abruptly shut
as Holmes picked up a hunting crop
and he ran off and did not stop,
and Holmes said, as the front door banged,
the fellow would, one day, be hanged;
but, as for Mary, sad and low,
she really didn't want to know
the truth of Hosmer, and would stay
true to him till her dying day.

......................................................

**When Sherlock Holmes**, a trifle bored
from gross inaction, had implored
his friend and colleague - Watson, John -
to come and to embark upon
an escapade to Britain's west
for weather there would be the best
while London with its smoky fogs
had weather only fit for dogs,
it had been Mrs. Watson who
told John, with minimum ado,
that Dr. Anstruther would pitch
on in and do a helpful switch
and to his patients, tend, should he
decide to go, for he would be
abroad with Sherlock Holmes for days
and, as he liked the fellow's ways,
it would be good for him to go
as he enjoyed excursions so
and also, as he looked quite pale,
he'd come back heartier and hale.

**The telegram** from Holmes arrived
just as John Watson had contrived
to spend his day with patients who,
with diverse maladies, came to
his door, but, in days, had not seen
a newspaper and, so, had been
quite unaware of trouble out
in Boscombe Valley till the shout
from Holmes to action made him grab
his travel bag and take a cab
to Paddington to meet the man
who always had some subtle plan
in preparation, or in play,
but never gave his thoughts away,
and found him on the platform keen
to be away to places green
and blessed with scenery so fine
and air of quality divine
- which ordinarily he'd shun -
for, there, The Game had just begun.

**The Game was murder**, Watson learned,
and Holmes, for action, new, had yearned
and had read all he could obtain
but finished only as the train
left Reading in its speedy wake
and then felt that he ought to make
Watson aware of all he knew
which was that James McCarthy slew
his father, Charles – it was asserted -
although anomalies alerted
Holmes who sensed not all was right
and rubbed his hands with great delight
as zeal and interest increased
on learning that the dead man leased
a farm from John Turner who'd met
McCarthy in Australia, yet
where Turner was made rich from gold,
McCarthy, it would soon unfold,
had aspirations to exceed
his means, and plotted to succeed.

**The facts**, as Holmes had ascertained
and as the coroner maintained
were that McCarthy had been found
near Boscombe Pool upon the ground
quite badly beaten 'round his head,
though he'd been but a short time dead,
and had gone out – someone to greet
by 'coo-ee' call before they'd meet -
though, near the same time, had been seen
both James and Charles and they had been
arguing like they soon might fight
which gave a witness quite a fright,
thereafter which James came at speed
and told to all he was in need
of help – he'd found his father dead -
at which all raced down, there to tread
in heavy boots, the scene, around,
and foul what footprints might be found
about which Holmes would rant and fume
though still, to gather facts, assume.

**Young McCarthy's** evidence
claimed he'd not killed his father, hence
somebody else was guilty, but
his lips were fastened firmly shut
on why they'd argued, making him
suspicious and his prospects grim,
though, when he said his father's last
words mentioned 'rat', all were aghast
but, what that meant, he could not say
and then his father passed away
so he went off for help but found
himself arrested – prison bound -
and as the door, behind him, clanged
Lestrade declared he'd have him hanged
for willful murder, soon enough,
which Holmes considered far too tough
an attitude for him to hold
so early in the case and told
the police-man to think again
in language definite and plain.

**John Turner's daughter** Alice sought
out Holmes and said she truly thought
James innocent for he could not
kill anyone and that a plot
that they should marry had been cast
by John, her father, seeing vast
resources, once the pair had wed,
transferred to James who had seen red,
refusing bluntly to comply
and would vehemently defy
his father, and would not admit
in court - nor her to say, permit -
their argument was over her
and to be hanged he would prefer
than drag her name into the fray,
but Holmes could see The Game in play
and knew, but could not prove, just who
had killed McCarthy, driven to
such action in his desperation
of a hopeless situation.

**Then notions** of Australian gold
came to his mind and then took hold
and, as he scanned a map, he found
the name he sought, a name profound
for he knew then McCarthy's 'rat'
was just the end of 'Ballarat'
so famous for the fortunes won
- gold by the wagonload, the ton -
but, what this meant, he did not know
but knew, from here, the facts would flow
and then he could collect each one,
examine it until, undone,
was brought some secret, dark and grim,
and Holmes knew it was up to him
to rescue young James from the rope
for there, in 'Ballarat', was hope
and Turner might well, although ill
and nearing death, be able, still,
to shine, upon this matter, light
and save the young man from his plight.

**John Turner**, summoned, came to call
on Sherlock Holmes and told him all,
how in Australia he had been
a bushranger so tough and keen
and brazen in his actions that,
known as Black Jack of Ballarat,
he stole the miners' hard-won gold,
killed guards, but let McCarthy hold
onto his life, but would regret
this, as McCarthy would not let
him live in peace in England, so
he struck him dead; and Holmes said "No"
he'd not report him if he'd write
down his confession – full, contrite -
for Holmes to hold as evidence,
though James - duly acquitted, hence -
was not to know, nor Alice, who
stood by him and had pleaded to
be heard by Holmes so James and she
might, in good time, together be.

**John Watson**, back in Baker Street
- his wife, for now, away to greet
a fond relation - was enthralled
and, deep within a book, installed
- a fine Clark Russell tale told
of seafarers - heroic, bold -
while busy London, vexed and galled
at Nature's anger, grounded, stalled,
would wait out, fearful of its scale,
each equinoctial howling gale
which screamed in fury through the streets
and dashed the windows with great sheets
of water, pressing to come in,
while making an almighty din
which fitted with Clark Russell's themes
and threaten puny humans' schemes
while Holmes, oblivious to all
except a hopeful client's call
to action, heard the sounding knell
of Two-Two-One-B's front door bell.

**Sherlock's conjecture** on who might
be visiting on such a night
was incorrect and proved to be
a client with catastrophe
he'd hope to circumvent, and not
just one of Mrs. Hudson's lot
of cronies as, at first, he'd guessed,
but this man, as Holmes had assessed
at twenty-two years and no more
and had observed the fellow bore
- though high in all propriety -
the weight of great anxiety
and said that he had heard the name
of Sherlock Holmes and, so, he came
despite the storm which raged outside
and hoped the great sleuth might provide
advice - which he would surely do -
and when the great sleuth listened to
a tale of woe, he knew the Law
could not help this John Openshaw.

**Holmes bade** the man come in and took
his coat and placed it on the hook
beside the fire, there to dry
while he, out from this man, would pry
such secrets which he might withhold
- and therefore might remain untold -
and so, without delay, began
preliminaries with the man,
obtained his name and his address,
learned that he was in some distress
with something he could not prevent,
some inexplicable event
which needed background information
so, John started his narration
of how his father Joseph had
seen fortunes looming when the fad
for bicycling was on the rise
and set up a new enterprise
in Coventry for tyres which,
unbreakable, would make him rich

**But Elias**, Joseph's brother,
saw his chances in another
enterprise quite far away
within the southern U.S.A.
and took himself to Florida
and, on its long peninsula,
became a planter and succeeded
but, when Florida seceded,
fought with Jackson and would rise
to Colonel but would then revise
his options with the South's defeat
and, after some years, would retreat
back home to England - disaffected
by the policies directed
to enfranchise former slaves
unshackled from their old enclaves -
and, selling up, would then return
- all contact with most neighbours, spurn -
to Sussex, to a small estate,
to brood and to await his fate.

**His nephew, John**, Elias liked
and, in return, Elias spiked
the interest of John as a lad
of twelve and, consequently, had
his father let him come to live
in Sussex where the life would give
the lad experience and skill
in agriculture and would fill
his life with purpose, though the lad
would sometimes see a vexing bad
side of his uncle when he drank
excessively and when he sank
deep in depression filled with gloom,
retreating to a lumber room
from which all, even John, were banned
- although, to enter, John had planned -
but recently a letter came,
a letter destined to inflame
his uncle for, to his dismay,
it bore three letters – K.K.K.!

**But, more than this**, five orange pips
fell out and, from the uncle's lips,
came "Death! My sins have overtaken
me." and left the man forsaken
of all hope from something dire,
something which seemed to require
surrender of the uncle's life,
some matter dreadful, vile and rife
with great foreboding of his doom,
then from the strong-locked lumber room
the man, a metal box, retrieved
and looked inside - though not relieved -
then burnt the contents in a fire
and said, his lawyer, he'd desire
to change his will, and would leave all
unto his brother should death call
in any way, and that John would
in time – but warning if he should
he might well share his uncle's fate -
inherit his accursed estate.

**Elias, maddened,** then would run
around while brandishing a gun
and call his enemies to show
themselves; but, one day, came the blow
and he was found dead in a pond
of shallow water just beyond
his house, though nothing would suggest
foul play, so he was laid to rest
and Joseph took on his estate
dismissive of his brother's fate
as being more than accidental
or, at most, coincidental,
for seven weeks had separated
death from matters which fixated
and alarmed Elias so,
therefore, to murder, all said "No"
but then a telegram would tell
John of the awful fate which fell
upon his father, in dismay,
for he had, sadly, passed away.

**John said** that he had now received
five orange pips and he perceived
he was to die if he'd not place
upon the sundial every trace
of what Elias tried to hide
and Sherlock said he must abide
by what the letter had demanded
for the Ku Klux Klan commanded
hidden resources which might
strike anywhere by day or night
though Sherlock's warning came too late
and John would succumb to the fate
his father suffered months before,
an outcome, terrible, which tore
at Holmes for he knew, given time,
he could have forestalled such a crime
if Openshaw had come without
delay which caused the sleuth to pout,
depressed, against which logic railed,
but Holmes still felt that he had failed.

........................................

### *The Man with the Twisted Lip*

**Poor Mrs. Whitney**, black of dress,
burst in on Mrs. Watson, less
to be a burden than implore
someone to help her to restore
her missing husband, Isa - who
had gone off days before to do
what he had, long ago in haste,
begun before he'd learned the waste
of life for those who choose to chase
the poppy's promise, false and base -
and it, on Mrs. Watson, fell,
to do her very best to quell
the worries of her old school friend
and offered hastily to send
her husband off to bed so she
and Mrs. Whitney then could be
alone, but searched her mind for names
and, in her fluster, called John 'James'
which did not cause the least ado
to either of those women, two.

**In fact, Kate Whitney** said, instead,
that, for the worst, she feared with dread,
and wanted her old friend's advice
and that it would be rather nice
if Doctor Watson might proceed,
perhaps with her, and he agreed
that he should go, but go alone,
into that vile abhorrent zone
and seek the addicts' reeking den
filled high with ruined pathetic men
to, there, take charge of Isa and
return Kate Whitney's sad husband
from where the man had gone amiss
from family and domestic bliss
to be restored to home in health,
so Watson went, though not in stealth,
and found a place which left him cold
- that dim-lit cave, the Bar of Gold -
and entered bravely, though in dread,
to gaze upon the living dead.

**Despite the reek** within the Bar
of Gold, and unfamiliar
with what he saw – a vision, stark,
of stupefied men in the dark -
the Doctor sought his charge and paid
what debt was owed, and gave such aid
to Whitney to have him removed
outside, while sternly he reproved
his patient for the hurt he'd caused,
but then, in great surprise, he paused,
for sitting on a stool quite near
was Sherlock Holmes who made it clear
to Watson that he wished to stay
alive, so he should walk away
and wait for him, for he would meet
him outside, later, in the street
after he'd had such time to send,
back home again, his sottish friend,
for they must meet, in cleaner air,
a nervous, scared, Mrs. St. Clair.

**As off they went** Sherlock explained
to Watson that he'd been retained
by Mrs. St. Clair who had been
in London where, by chance, she'd seen
her husband, Neville, clear and bold,
above the seedy Bar of Gold
- though only briefly, she confessed -
without a tie or collar, dressed,
and, so, though with police in tow,
went to investigate and show
it was her husband that she saw
look down at her and then withdraw,
but could find nothing of him till
some children's bricks began to spill
out from a box, bricks he had bought,
so further evidence they sought
and found his boots and socks and hat
and watch bundled away, and that
left Mrs. St. Clair mystified
and thoroughly dissatisfied.

**Then blood** upon a window-sill
suggested, recently, some ill
had fallen on her husband, cut
while jumping from the window, but
never, once, this Lascar, vile,
- one never known to ever smile -
on being strongly questioned, would
admit a thing to them, nor could
a crippled and disfigured wretch,
Hugh Boone, a well-known beggar, fetch
the words out from behind the scar
which left his mangled mouth ajar
and tell what happened, though he'd been
within the room and must have seen
the missing man but, being scared
and vulnerable, was unprepared
- he, living by the passing pity
of the people in the city
dropping coins into his cap -
to give, of knowledge, any scrap.

**A further clue** would soon emerge
upon the muddy river verge
for, as the tide ebbed, St. Clair's coat
was visible – it couldn't float,
held underwater by the weight
of coins of value Two-Pounds-Eight -
and, though disfigured, Boone was not
greatly disabled and a plot
to rob and kill St. Clair well might
be carried out without a fight
by him, for what alternative
scenario was there to give
to even half-way fit each fact
available, and counteract
the notion of the beggar's guilt
around which might, in time, be built
a case to prove murder had been
committed though no one had seen
the act itself, for St. Clair may
have, by the tide, been washed away.

**Holmes**, at the St. Clair home had mused
on contradictions, most confused
with what he knew and what he thought
and what, to put aside, he ought,
for Mrs. Sinclair had produced
a letter from which she deduced
her husband was alive and well
though which, as far as Holmes could tell,
may have been sent the day before
his death and, therefore, needed more
deliberation on his part
and, so, decided to restart
the case and clear his mind of all
hypotheses and then recall
each fact and test it in his way
and never let emotions sway
his reasoning, and this being done,
rejected every theme but one
and then moved on - false truths to quell -
to question Hugh Boone in his cell.

**Hugh, in his cell**, sat quiet, meek,
but Sherlock Holmes had come to seek
the truth, no matter how it hurt
Mrs. Sinclair, and then with curt
considered action on his part
gave all around a mighty start
when, with a moistened sponge, he started
bathing Hugh Boone's face - then parted
by a scar – when, with a shout
it fell away, and all about
gazed on the missing St. Clair man
whose face - delivered from the plan
of begging for more cash than could
be earned by other jobs but would,
from now on be impossible
and, for him indefensible -
showed not a blemish or a flaw,
and Holmes knew then he must withdraw
and let the St. Clairs, in their time,
get over Neville's folly, prime

## The Blue Carbuncle

**A battered billycock**, a goose
deceased with long neck hanging loose,
were shown by Sherlock to his friend,
John Watson, hoping he'd extend
his faculties in ways sufficient
to suggest a most proficient
history based on the facts
which observation, keen, exacts
but viewing casually does not,
and Watson tried hard to allot
as best he could, but was assailed
by Holmes, his friend, who said he failed
to notice what was glaringly
in view while he, quite daringly,
picked up the hat, proceeding then
with fine-honed skill and acumen
to read the sad and wretched tale
etched on the hat, and then regale
friend Watson, recently admonished,
leaving him stunned and astonished.

**Both goose and billycock** had been
brought in by Peterson quite keen
to find its owner who had dropped
both when attacked, and had not stopped
to pick them up as off he ran,
and Peterson thought, rather than
keep both himself, he'd bring them to
Holmes who might tell him what to do
which was that he, without delay,
should cook the goose now on its way
to being rather less than fresh,
while Holmes and Watson could enmesh
themselves in mental exercise
and great cerebral enterprise
which put, on Holmes' face, a grin
but brought, to Watson, great chagrin
for he would always miss some clue
so obvious to Holmes who, true
to form, would in detail, minute,
Watson's deductions, all refute.

**Holmes saw** the man had been well-off
but now, though Watson thought to scoff,
experienced some evil days
perhaps for following the ways
of drink, and also Holmes saw that,
because she hadn't brushed his hat,
his wife no longer loved the man
but still he had the sense to plan
for heavy winds and went and bought
a hat-securer which he thought
a good investment - worth the cash -
and, although Watson called it rash,
Holmes said he likely had no gas
laid on at home because, alas,
five tallow stains were clear to see
and - with which Watson would agree -
they'd dripped from candles giving light
within a stairway when, at night,
to bed he would ascend those stairs
and think about such sad affairs.

**John Watson** gave a laugh of glee
and said that he had to agree
but then the door flew open wide
as Peterson burst fast inside
shouting "The goose!", his cheeks aflush,
and then, while trying not to gush,
produced a precious stone of blue,
of brilliant light and striking hue,
which was, as Holmes saw straight away,
the Blue Carbuncle gone astray
and knew the Countess of Moncar
was so distressed she gone so far
as offer a reward of size
- one thousand pounds, a hefty prize -
and Peterson said that his wife
had found it slicing with her knife
into the wayward goose's crop
when, suddenly, she had to stop
for there it was, a thing so quaint
it almost made the woman faint.

**Then Sherlock** concentrated on
the 'Henry Baker' scrawled upon
the billicock's beleaguered band
- exhausting all the clues at hand -
then advertised, advising that
there had been found a goose and hat
and, both, their owner could collect
at Baker Street but should expect
the goose replaced – his was devoured
lest it, as gooses do, had soured -
but all that owner had to say
was that the goose had come his way
from Mr. Windigate who ran
a Christmas goose club and the man
supplied a goose for those who'd pay
him week by week, but could not say
who'd sold the goose to him and, so,
Holmes, to the Alpha Inn, would go
to find the source of Baker's goose
but found some lips were far from loose.

**Stepwise, Holmes** backtracked his way,
back from the goose's final day
when Windigate dispatched the bird
upon December twenty-third,
one of two-dozen bought each year
from Breckinridge who made it clear
that his source was his business, so
Holmes found, by ruse, that he should go
to Mrs. Oakshott who was praised
for fineness of the birds she raised
but, before Holmes could check this out,
there came, from Breckinridge, a shout
of anger to another man,
a man who Sherlock Holmes began
to think knew more of how the Blue
Carbuncle of extreme value
became embedded in the goose
and, loathe to let the man go loose,
escorted him to Baker Street
to have a meeting bitter-sweet.

**James Ryder**, eager to regain
what he had stolen, looked in vain
when Holmes produced the shining stone
and cut the fellow to the bone
by telling him – his look of scorn
then changing to a look, forlorn -
'the game was up' and, though a thief,
Holmes said he'd also given grief
unwarranted when he had made
a false report to help persuade
Police John Horner was their man
who, when approached, at once began
to struggle strongly and protest
but still was placed under arrest
and, though the stone could not be found
- making the case somewhat unsound -
an old conviction said he must
face the Assizes so a just
decision could be made thereon
upon the prisoner Horner, John.

**That day**, to Mrs. Oakshott, ran
her brother – Ryder - where a plan,
quite feeble, he then made to hide
the stolen gem deep down inside
his goose's crop, but it broke free
and then began a crazy spree
which ended with the goose upon
the dinner plate of Peterson,
then Sherlock's venture to assess
and make sense of a confused mess
saw Ryder cowering before
his feet and saying he'd no more
do wrong if only Holmes would let
him go, and that the Court would set
John Horner free in view of no
real evidence - ipso-facto -
and Holmes relented, feeling sure
that this experience would cure
James Ryder's urge to go astray,
then told the man to go away.

**Abed, asleep**, immersed in dreams
Watson awoke and held back screams
on seeing Sherlock Holmes full-dressed
beside his bed and full-possessed
of keenness and determination,
eagerness and fascination,
as one like he was sure to be
when cases came, and he could see
'the game afoot' awaited those
who, to a life of action, rose
and would not lay in bed all day
and waste their beating hearts away;
so, when John Watson did enquire
of his old friend "What is it? Fire?"
his friend said "No - a client waits -
a lady in quite dire straits."
to which John Watson left his bed
and, after having dressed, was led
to find Miss Helen Stoner dressed
and veiled in black and quite distressed.

**As Holmes assessed** his client, he,
John Watson, Doctor, tried to be
- as inobtrusive as he might -
attentive to the lady's plight
while patiently recording all
and being medically on call
should he be needed for his skill
in tending to those hurt or ill
and having need of being cured
or, perhaps, just reassured,
but, when the agitated lady shook,
he looked on as she slowly took
a seat beside the fireplace
- retaining, full, her charm and grace -
and, though she shivered, it was clear
it wasn't from the cold but fear
which sent her rushing to consult
on something causing great tumult
within her as, emotionless,
Holmes sought the source of her distress.

**Holmes saw** that she had come by train
- a return ticket made that plain -
and that upon a dogcart she
had also travelled first, for he
could see, upon her jacket arm
- which gave the lady some alarm -
mud splattered seven times or more,
mud she'd not noticed there before,
all which had served to show that he
had skills, unusual, to be
employed upon a quest to find
the source of trouble on her mind
which he - his faculties alert,
and mind all eager to exert
itself on her behalf - declared
he'd settle if she was prepared
to tell him all and not hold back
for he, thus armed, could then attack
the problem with his usual zeal,
so, nothing, should she now conceal.

**Miss Stoner** was in some despair
- shown by her early-greying hair -
and said she lived in Stoke Moran
with her stepfather, though the man,
once welcomed by the locals, would
refuse their friendship and well could
be violent excessively,
and quite foul-mouthed, expressively,
but was a doctor fully trained
who had, in India, attained
a reputation rather good
- a large practice, she understood -
and had, her widowed mother, wed,
but, anger-filled, the man was led
to kill a servant in a rage
then prison, to him, was a cage
and, when released, back home returned
- ideas of any fortune, spurned -
where, life, they'd hope to re-begin -
her mother, herself, and her twin.

**In London**, Doctor Roylott could
not find success and therefore should,
he thought, move back to Stoke Moran
- his home, ancestral - with a plan,
in time, to succeed there, though he
was not what locals hoped he'd be
and fought and argued violently,
lived off his wife, sufficiently,
but found when, suddenly, she died
she'd left her daughters well supplied
with income should they choose to wed
though Doctor Roylott simply bled
them of that income, but the time
came when the bells were set to chime
for Julia, Helen's loved twin,
and strange things then seemed to begin
- odd clanging doors, whistling at night -
then Julia died, it seemed, of fright
while clinging onto Helen's hand
and crying out, "The speckled band!"

**Holmes theorised**, but he knew he must
use only facts which he could trust
and urged Helen to tell him why
she'd come so far, and clarify
her fear - so obvious to him -
and she proceeded with a grim
face that she, too, was to be wed
but lately, at night, in her bed,
she'd heard a whistle and the sound
of clanging - though no source was found -
and fearful for her life she sought
out Holmes as she was told she ought
by one whom Holmes had helped before,
and Holmes said that he'd help restore
that calmness which she must desire
but that, to do so, would require
that he and Watson take the train
to Stoke Moran and, there, remain
- though keeping Roylott unaware -
and, something evil, find and snare.

**At Stoke Moran** Holmes found the room
where Helen slept was that where doom
descended on her sister, twin,
- and, with that fact, he would begin -
then saw her bed was bolted tight
onto the floor so no one might
move it from where the bell-rope hung
though no bell from it could be rung
for, to the roof, it was attached
but wasn't, to a bell-wire, latched
though, tellingly, the rope hung near
a ventilator, making clear
to Holmes – as it communicated
with, as Holmes anticipated,
the room which had been occupied
by Doctor Roylott – it supplied
access, in some strange manner, to
Miss Stoner's room and had to do,
with beasts, exotic, unrestrained
which Roylott, in his grounds, retained.

**That night**, awake, anticipating
some attack so devastating
it might just kill by fear alone,
the two men heard the softened tone
of something whistling near the bed
- a sound which turned their faces red -
and Holmes, his senses honed and keen,
instinctively knew what had been
the whistle's source and struck a match
and in the dim light he would snatch
a glimpse of something on the rope,
a speckled snake at which, in hope
it could be killed, Holmes struck at hard
and caused the creature to discard
its mission and return to bite
its owner out of fear and spite
and, agonized, a scream he gave
as in both rushed, perhaps to save
the Doctor, but he lay there, dead,
the 'Speckled Band' around his head.

## The Engineer's Thumb

**No longer** calling Baker Street
his home, John Watson now could greet
- in premises, not grandiose
but situated rather close
to Paddington, his new location
on retaking his vocation
of M.D., a Doctor, true, -
his patients who would come on cue
when injured or, by sickness, ailed,
- for he invariably prevailed -
so claimed one loyal patient who,
by John, was cured, hitherto
and now led sufferers to see
'The Doctor' and would guarantee
no patient ever once despaired
for broken bones would be repaired
and wounds, beset by blood congealed,
attended to, would all be healed,
though one such sufferer, quite numb,
consulted him about his thumb.

**Well, not his thumb** but where it used
to be, explained this man confused
and somewhat shocked from loss of blood
which would have been a deadly flood
had not this man - an engineer,
hydraulic, being his career -
assessed his situation and,
upon his much-afflicted hand
applied such pressure as he might
- his handkerchief he tensioned tight
by twisted twig – to stop the flow
of blood enough that he, though slow,
had stumbled to a nearby station
where he'd wait for transportation
to the city, there to find
a worthy fellow of a mind
to offer help and to assist,
though, doing so, he would insist
that Doctor Watson was the best
and only man he could suggest.

**When Doctor Watson** viewed the man,
one Victor Hatherley, a wan
and bloodless face looked back at him -
a face which might betray a grim
and bitter struggle for a mind
distressed – and from which came the kind
of laugh which made the Doctor say
quite forcefully, with some dismay
- as if to pull upon some tether -
to stop and pull himself together
which took some little time, but then
the Doctor himself shuddered when
his patient showed him where a thumb
had been upon a hand now numb
and red, a missing thumb which had
been severed roughly by some cad
who'd made a murderous attack
and, with a cleaver, sought to hack
the man to death for reasons such
as might intrigue Holmes very much.

**As he was** now calm and composed
sufficiently, Watson proposed
to introduce the injured man
to Sherlock Holmes and, so, began
a narrative hard to accept
as anything but false, except
the fellow's thumb was clearly not
connected to his hand, which got
Holmes to remark that there was need
for Hatherley to tell, with speed,
his story, after he had taken
breakfast which might just awaken
memories which he'd suppressed
- a good many, as Holmes assessed -
through shock and injury but might
and would - to Sherlock Holmes' delight -
provide a case of novel crime
which Holmes considered worth the time
for him to listen and to mull
upon a story far from dull.

**Laying back** to save his strength,
Vic Hatherley began, at length,
to say he was an Engineer,
Hydraulic, although his career
was less successful than it might
have been and that, lately, his plight
gave him concern, for failure neared,
but, in his premises, appeared
- with business looking grim and dark -
a man, Colonel Lysander Stark,
whose German accent was pronounced
but in which he clearly announced
there was a job for him to do
requiring that he would swear to
silence, complete, and he should come
for fifty guineas - quite handsome
remuneration - that same night
and that, for sleeping over, might
accept his hospitality
despite its informality.

**At Eyford Station**, he explained,
into the darkness he detrained,
and met the Colonel waiting there
who drove him to 'he knew not where'
for one full hour, maybe more,
and on arrival stood before
a house pitch black, and settled in,
but then a woman made a din
and said to leave 'for heaven's sake'
though, this advice, he wouldn't take
for Mr. Ferguson arrived,
the Manager, who had contrived
for him to inspect and assess
his malfunctioned hydraulic press
for he had Fullers' Earth to pack
down into bricks, though this did lack,
in his eyes, all veracity,
for no one with sagacity
of good extent could think it did
so knew that secrets, dark, it hid.

**The fault assessed** and problem found
the Engineer would now compound
a folly he could not depress
within this counterfeiters' press
which Stark turned on intending to
have him disposed of, lest he do
the honest thing and turn them in,
though Hatherley, cutting things thin,
escaped from certain death, but then
found himself chased by desperate men,
one with a cleaver wielded wild
- his rage and fury far from mild -
which he used to attack the one
who might well bring their scheme undone
and cleaved the thumb off from the hand
of Hatherley who kept command
of faculties enough to hide
then run off to the countryside
like some deranged automaton
then make his way to Paddington.

**Police were called** and then conferred
with Hatherley who then referred
them onto Sherlock Holmes who saw
within their logic was a flaw
suggesting they might look elsewhere,
an area quite close, to where
they all converged and searched around
but found the house burnt to the ground,
the people gone without a trace
and only Hatherley to face
the puzzled questions which remained
unanswered, though what clearly strained
the Engineer was that he seemed
a fool and could not be redeemed
by some reward, though Holmes replied
that his experience supplied
a story of intrigue and strife
which he could now retell for life
though this just struck the fellow dumb,
still minus payment, minus thumb.

## *The Noble Bachelor*

**Poor Lord St Simon** most confused
and quite dejected, unamused,
had written to Holmes to implore
that he'd, all time constraints, ignore
to help in an event pertaining
to his wedding, and explaining
that Lestrade of Scotland Yard
had been called in to be on guard
and display extra perseverance
in matters of the disappearance
of this Lord's new-wedded wife
- a status taken on for life -
for Lord St. Simon, in despair,
had stated that, into thin air,
his bride had vanished just before
their wedding breakfast and, therefore,
against her will had been abducted
- and, from his family, deducted -
but, why this should be so, he did
not know so put, to Holmes, a bid.

**Excitement**, Watson had expressed,
but Holmes was always less impressed
by someone's rank and status or
a person's wealth, but hungered for
a case with interest involved,
resistant to its being solved,
as Lord St. Simon's proved to be
once Watson read to Holmes that he,
St. Simon, had shortly before
been wed and, on the Bible, swore
that he would, to his wedded wife,
stay true and faithful all his life
and she did likewise to this Lord
- both promised of their own accord -
and he, though British, nobly born,
and she, American, had sworn
nothing would tear the match asunder
though it seems there'd been a blunder
somewhere, leaving him red-faced
and her, that day, somehow misplaced.

**With Lord St. Simon** to arrive
that afternoon, Holmes had to strive
to find all that he could about
the situation, so called out
to Watson who read one report
- now some weeks old and rather short
but being all that he could trace -
that marriage would be taking place
between Lord Robert St. Simon,
Duke of Balmoral's second son,
and one, Miss Hatty Doran, late
of U.S.A's great Golden State
of California, which seemed
too brief to Holmes but was redeemed
by comment made, with little tact,
that Hatty's father was, in fact,
a millionaire made rich by gold,
and many English houses old
had mistresses American
with leanings quite republican.

**That same report** went on to say
that, married, Lord St. Simon may
expect a dowry of some size
- six figures, an impressive prize -
would come with Hatty, helping him
redress financial strictures, grim,
which he'd endured for many years,
but then, said Watson, it appears
the wedding actually occurred
- though written before Hatty spurred
away for reasons quite unknown
but which may have been overblown -
and then an article quite new
said that St. Simon's wife, from view,
had vanished, and it seemed there'd been
some altercation in-between
the bride's arrival and the time
she took her leave, and that a crime
of deadly consequence occurred,
and so, to action, Holmes was spurred.

**Miss Flora Millar**, ballet dancer
and, it seemed, an old romancer
of St. Simon, pushed her way
into the breakfast with affray
and was arrested, though she swore
St. Simon had been hers before
Miss Doran came upon the scene
with her great fortune, quite obscene,
and Lord St. Simon was a cad
for dumping her because he had
a need for money, but the time
had come for Holmes to give his prime
attention to the woeful tone
of Lord St. Simon left alone
after his newly-wedded wife
departed, seemingly, when strife
came calling, though the man did say
that as he and his wife made way
along the aisle, her bouquet fell
but it was caught and all seemed well.

**But well, it wasn't**, for the bride
from then on was, herself, beside
and afterwards was seen to talk
with her maid, Alice, then to walk
away, but met Miss Millar in
Hyde Park for some reason, wherein
Lestrade of Scotland Yard, the best
in London, thought he should arrest
the dancer for he did suppose
that, angered, Flora Millar chose
to lure Hatty from the room
to where she was to meet her doom
for, near the Serpentine, was found
a wedding dress and ring, all bound,
so Lestrade had the river dragged
and had expected soon, he bragged,
he'd find a body, though Holmes knew,
for some good reason, Hatty threw
her dress and ring away, then ran,
but hadn't worked to any plan.

**A note** on Hatty's dress was found,
one signed as "F.M.H." and bound
to, Flora Millar, implicate
and have Lestrade declare her fate
although upon its other side
Holmes observed something to provide
the vital clue, a hotel bill
whose prices said F.M.H. will
be staying at just one of few
expensive hotels, and Holmes knew
- as all else he'd eliminate -
a search would help him to locate
the hotel and the man whom he
identified quickly to be
one Francis Hay Moulton, the man
who Hatty Moulton, nee Doran,
had married, though believed him dead
but, just that day, found out, instead,
that he'd been, by Apaches, taken
prisoner, his life forsaken.

**They'd met** and married several years
before - in secrecy with fears
her father would not have approved -
and Francis, seeking gold, had moved
through California and struck
it rich through hard work and good luck
and kept on working till attacked
and captured, but escaped and tracked
his wife to England where he found
she'd been, to Lord St. Simon, bound
in marriage, but managed to hide,
in her bouquet, a note to bide
her "Come at once."; all which resulted
into Holmes being catapulted
into action to deduce
the truth and, in short time, produce
the missing bride, and all was well
except for St. Simon who'd dwell
on how, though wed, he had no bride,
nothing to show but wounded pride.

## The Beryl Coronet

**In all of England** there was one,
a high-born personage, someone
of such nobility and grace
that he need only show his face
to Alexander Holder to
- with little fuss and less ado
in deference to his lofty rank -
unlock the coffers of his bank
and count out to that person's hand
the trifling sum of 'fifty grand'
in notes – each one a thousand pounds -
so much to many that it sounds
implausible, but did occur,
though Holder said it should incur
security because he had
the need to make things ironclad
in fairness to his partner who
insisted things pertaining to
loans of such size they should protect
though, this, their client did expect.

**The high-born personage** concurred
and said to Holder it occurred
to him such matters ought to be
conducted thus, then said that he
had something which would satisfy
his partner who'd then ratify,
without delay, without a moan,
this quite short-notice short-term loan
not just because he'd been seduced
by rank, but by what was produced
- a black Morocco case to hold
a Coronet of royal gold
displaying beryls, thirty-nine -
an artifact almost divine
so much that Holder had to say
he'd have all monies on that day
but added, with all piety,
he doubted the propriety
of one as low as him being let
retain the Beryl Coronet.

**All had gone well** as Holder went
to bed that night, the endorsement
of confidence which was expressed
by one so high in status blessed
his business in Threadneedle Street,
a bank which was prepared to meet
that person's needs, but Holder thought
that, for security, he ought
lock up the Beryl Coronet
where neither bomb nor bayonet
could penetrate, or ever had,
where he, all entry, had forbad
- his dressing room bureau within
his domicile – although when in
the city he'd, right by his side,
keep it in sight and, so, provide
assurance it could be redeemed
upon repayment, and this seemed
the best arrangement he could make
when things of value were at stake.

**But, late one night**, Holder awoke
up to a grim scene to provoke
great anger in him, for he saw,
falling, the last distressing straw
for one who'd gambled and had lost
but could not, himself, bear the cost
as Arthur, Holder's son, pulled on
the Beryl Coronet, upon
which Holder Senior, in his grief,
declared his son to be a thief
and blackguard for, though light was dim,
he'd seen, out from the golden brim,
a corner piece had been removed
for which, Arthur, he then reproved
with great invective and abuse,
although his words would prove no use
but only serve to cause the lad
to stand defiant, though half-clad,
and, to all questions, not reply,
then all threats of arrest, defy.

**Upon that corner** piece detached
had been three beryls quite unmatched
in size and value and which would
fetch thousands each, although they could,
despite young Arthur standing there,
not be located anywhere,
then Holder's niece and adoptee,
Mary, rushed in and she could see
her cousin Arthur, uncompliant,
standing there and most defiant
with, in hand, the Coronet
which made her visibly upset
such that she started there to sway
and then she fainted dead away
as Holder Senior summoned the
police so that Arthur could be
arrested and placed in a cell
at which point Holder rushed to tell
to Sherlock Holmes his woeful tale
of disgrace on a massive scale.

**Holder explained** to Holmes, Arthur,
his son, had met a man, a cur
called Sir George Burnwell who had led
the lad astray and who had bled
him dry of funds by playing cards
at gambling clubs filled with blackguards
who took advantage of his son
who'd never learned nor ever won
but now had taken beryls, three,
so that he might, of debt, be free,
and though, from this, he wouldn't budge,
Holmes would be far less quick to judge
and knew there was more to be learned
so said to Holder that he yearned
to see himself where had occurred
this so-called crime, and then he spurred
to Holder's house to look around
upon the recent snow-clad ground
and gather facts, for he could tell
the crime involved Sir George Burnwell.

**Holmes looked about** for any clue
the snow retained, and then gave due
consideration of the facts
the snow revealed about the acts
which had occurred the night before,
but would not comment on that score
but did tell Holder Senior he
might well consider it to be
a possibility that his
son Arthur was, and therefore is,
quite innocent for he could not,
in silence, have put such a lot
of force upon the Coronet
and not be heard, and he would get
the missing jewel if he'd agree
to pay expenses - and a fee -
for its return, then disappeared,
his mind, of doubt, now all but cleared
to which Holder gave thanks, profuse,
while Mary looked on most obtuse.

**With Sherlock's** knowledge and contacts
it took no time to sort the facts
and to locate and to return
the jewel to Holder, taciturn
on learning Mary, that day, fled
with Burnwell, and that she'd been led
to take the Coronet, but had
been seen by Arthur who, though clad
in only shirt and trousers, fought
with Burnwell, as a good son ought,
and, it being twisted in the fight,
Arthur had tried with all his might
to straighten up the Coronet
quite unaware that he had let
Burnwell break off his golden prize
with beryls of substantial size,
but Holmes was soon upon their track,
young Arthur was to be begged back,
poor Mary, with George, ran and hid
and Holmes took home a thousand quid.

··············································

## *The Copper Beeches*

**Miss Violet Hunter** entered in
to Baker Street, devoid of grin,
and sought out Sherlock Holmes, the one
who she'd been told might bring undone
the reservations she began
to feel and which, around, all ran
within her mind to bring her grief,
and it might offer some relief
if Holmes might offer some advice
- if he would be so kind and nice -
which he would be, for he deplored
the awful state of being bored
and moaned to Watson that he'd been,
of late, besieged by ladies keen
to get advice for lives in tatters
- although never for those matters
of the heart of which he knew
so little – and perhaps might view
with such a great mind in his head,
the fates of pencils made of lead.

**Miss Hunter had**, some days before
- her lack of funds hard to ignore -
sought new employment such that she,
a useful governess, might be
and at an agency run by
Miss Stoper had sought to apply
for suitable positions when
a man much stouter than most men
with smiling pleasant face and who
looked once at her and said "She'll do!"
and stated the remuneration
she asked for in her vocation
was too low and said that she,
one-hundred-pounds per year, should be
expecting, and produced a note
of Fifty-Pounds which would denote
an advance of fifty percent
of yearly salary which sent
Miss Stoper reaching for a pen
and shocks through Violet's abdomen.

**Holmes listened carefully** and thought
the salary far more than ought
to be expected, so there must
be something more to this, but thrust
such thoughts aside and listened while
Miss Hunter, quite without a smile,
said that Rucastle added, then,
- her interest obvious – that when
she, to the Copper Beeches, came,
she'd be expected – though a shame
for one like her, of funds distressed,
and with her future well expressed
as bleak – to cut her hair quite short
to which she gave a sharp retort
of "No!" but re-evaluated
how her funds were situated
and when she was offered more
- an extra Twenty Pounds – it wore
her down - she yielded to ambition
accepting Rucastle's condition.

**Alas, Miss Hunter** should have known
that all due caution had been thrown
into the winds, and that the bid
of Rucastle, great menace, hid
and there had been evil intent
within his offer to be sent
westward as governess to one
who had redeeming virtues, none,
- a child of such malignant mind,
to helpless creatures so unkind -
and simply was a horrid rort
of such a cruel and callous sort,
and she would, with her short-cut hair,
sit meek and still upon a chair
and wear a dress of special hue
- a vivid and electric blue -
and then face this way and then that
as her employers bade, and chat
as though she was upon some stage,
unknowing of Rucastle's rage.

42

**Before a window**, on her chair,
she'd sit - blue dress and shortened hair
and always told to face away -
but saw a form upon one day
reflected in a mirror shard,
a young man trying very hard
to catch her notice, but was told
to turn and give to him a cold
look of disdain and then to wave
away this brazen upstart knave
- to know why, she was at a loss -
but later she would come across
a door, once locked but now unlatched,
and, being curious, she snatched
the opportunity to find
such secrets as might lurk behind
and so crept to a further door
and heard footsteps upon the floor
beyond and, frightened, turned and ran
but met Rucastle's looming span.

**Miss Violet Hunter**, scared, confused,
found Rucastle was not amused
- he said he'd throw her to his hound
if she, beyond that door was found
again - so, she, to Sherlock, made
a call which, his assistance, bade,
and he came willingly for he
knew that Miss Hunter had to be
in danger and suspected more
than could be seen – he'd not ignore
the possibility that she,
a decoy of some sort, must be
as, so, she was, for one so much
like Violet Hunter was in such
dire need of rescue and had been
kept from that young man she had seen
and Holmes felt, what this meant, he knew
as, all boredom, he overthrew
and then, with Watson's help, began
to formulate a hurried plan.

**With Watson's** old revolver, placed
inside his pocket, both men faced
the unknown dangers of a brute
whose manner might well constitute
a manic fury unrestrained
if loosed - one not to be contained
unless by force – proceeding fast
to Winchester where Holmes, at last,
would join Miss Hunter, then proceed
with caution, though not without speed,
to reach The Copper Beeches, there
- Rucastle known to be elsewhere
and hound being kennelled safe away -
to enter and, that very day,
find who was hidden, kept within
the secret room, and enter in,
but found its occupant had fled
away, from Copper Beeches led
by one who sought her freedom, long,
that young man with a passion, strong.

**Rucastle's daughter**, Alice - kept
against her will - in silence, crept
away to claim her funds by will,
funds Rucastle had use of till
she wed - so he locked her away,
kept her husband-to-be at bay
and found a look-alike to take
her place so, monies, she'd forsake -
but, on returning, roared and raged
and had his savage hound uncaged,
a hound kept starved, a beast untamed,
which saw the man for whom it blamed
its callous treatment, then attacked,
and Watson, though he clearly lacked
great sympathy, dispatched the hound
by bullet-shot, then dressed and bound
Rucastle's wounds, and Sherlock mused
on two young women, badly used,
who now were free to go their ways
anticipating better days.

# The Memoirs of Sherlock Holmes

## *Silver Blaze*

**For days** there had been on the mind
of Sherlock Holmes a case of kind
quite undefined and so unsorted
that the great sleuth had retorted,
suddenly, that he must go
- and, if he would, Watson, also -
to Dartmoor, way off to the west,
to King's Pyland, one of the best
horse-racing institutions where
a valued racehorse, premiere
- listed to run the Wessex Cup
and which all bookmakers marked up
as favourite - had disappeared
just days before, and it was feared
that it may well have to be scratched
unless were found those who had hatched
some diabolic evil scheme,
a scheme now growing more extreme
for, out upon the moor, found spread,
had been its trainer, lying dead.

**The Wessex Cup** would still be run
for preparations had begun
long months before, as through the years,-
but it would bring Britain to tears
if Silver Blaze should fail to start
so Holmes said they should play their part
and, starting off at Paddington,
both Holmes and Watson stood upon
the platform, there to board the train
to Exeter, and would obtain
the latest newspapers to take
upon their journey, though would make
quite certain that the news they read
was true and genuine instead
of pure conjecture on the part
of journalistic types who'd start
without confirming facts before
they'd write their stories and explore
those ways by which – being so adroit -
the gullible, they might exploit.

**With Reading passed**, those papers read,
a deal of travel still ahead,
Holmes thought to count poles passing by
and time their intervals, then cry
out loud to Watson that their speed
of travel - if that fact he'd need -
was fifty-three and one-half miles
per hour, breaking into smiles
as he made mention of the dead
man, Straker, struck upon the head,
and of the owner, Colonel Ross,
who, panic-stricken by the loss
of Silver Blaze, was very keen
for Holmes to trace a fellow seen
at King's Pyland – a tout he thought -
a fellow who felt that he ought
offer good money – cash, hard cold -
for information – not too old -
from anyone there who'd endorse
the winning prospects of the horse.

**Inspector Gregory** – cold, hard -
was also sent from Scotland Yard
and had begun investigations
looking at the indications
that the crime was perpetrated
by this tout who'd infiltrated
King's Pyland but was seen off
but was described to be a toff
and in possession of a stick,
a Penang Lawyer, very thick
- upon its end, a heavy knob -
and of Ned Hunter with the job
of guarding Silver Blaze by night
who was discovered at first light
unconscious in the horse's stable
- not much help - being quite unable
at that time to say who'd doped
his dinner plate, as had been hoped,
but Sherlock Holmes knew well to seek
more facts and never to be meek.

**Quite readily**, Holmes saw a clue
which Gregory did not pursue
which was, that night, an incident
occurred with features evident
to Holmes who saw a furious
large dog and thought it curious
that it did nothing, not a thing,
and had not barked at all to ring
alarm bells when a stranger prowled
- it neither barked aloud nor growled -
for, certainly, that the dog well knew
the culprit, being no stranger new
to King's Pyland, but was well known
- perhaps one of King's Pyland's own -
then Holmes desired to inspect
Straker's belongings to detect
anomalies and saw a knife
identified by Straker's wife
but which Watson said was, in fact,
the type to treat a cataract.

**A dress receipt** was also found
- a dress, expensive - to compound
suspicion in Holmes' mind, but he
thought, on the moor, he ought to be
- where trainer Straker breathed his last -
for he knew now he should act fast
and had deduced Straker, somehow,
was implicated, so he'd now
look all around, the tracks to find
of Silver Blaze and, though once blind,
his eyes were opening to see
that Silver Blaze somehow broke free
and roamed the moor until someone
had found the horse but had not done
the honest thing and led it back
to King's Pyland but took a track
away to somewhere else close by
- and Holmes could guess the reason why -
and sought to search the countryside
for all the clues it might provide.

**The nearby Gypsies** were assessed
but they were innocent, Holmes guessed,
for such a horse could not be hidden
by them, nor could it be ridden
freely without being seen,
but Holmes well knew that he had been
correct in his suspicions, and
went to a nearby stables, grand,
at Mapleton, where Silas Brown
declared to Holmes he'd knock him down
if he persisted and came near
but Holmes just whispered in his ear
and Silas Brown, now cowed and scared,
looked back at Holmes and then declared
that he would do as Holmes advised
- a threat, as Watson had surmised -
and Holmes and Watson then returned
to King's Pyland where strongly burned
the lights, as Colonel Ross suspected
Holmes was not as he'd expected.

**Holmes, though**, said to go ahead
as if the horse was there instead
of missing, to which Colonel Ross,
deciding not to cut his loss,
agreed, and when the Cup was run,
it seemed a stand-in had begun
the race in Ross's colours and,
in an exemplary manner, grand,
had won, but Sherlock simply washed
the forehead of the horse and quashed
the Colonel's worries as he showed
a Silver Blaze upon it glowed
and then explained the trainer had
- he being a conniving cad -
great money troubles and had sought
to lame the horse which duly fought
back killing Straker, but was found
and led to some nearby compound
till Holmes had - not being led astray -
deduced the truth and saved the day.

...................................................

47

**Holmes**, on one blazing August day,
his mind, as normal, far away
from mundane matters - deep in thought -
saw Watson leaning back and sought
to deduce what was on his mind
so he observed his friend to find
the matters likely, at that time,
to occupy that brain, sublime,
and said "You're right! It does so seem
preposterous that we might deem
to settle disputes in that way."
to which his friend was led to say
"Yes, most preposterous." before
realizing that he'd done no more
than think the thoughts his friend relayed
back to him and, somewhat dismayed,
asked how he knew his private mind
and Holmes explained – a tad unkind -
he'd read his features – smile and frown
and eyebrows going up and down.

**Whenever Holmes** addressed his friend
in such a way, such quips would end
with Watson flabbergasted and,
expectant of some new and grand
adventure about to commence,
Watson – Holmes' favoured audience -
waited, then heard his friend declare
a Croydon lady had a scare
at which the lady shook and shivered
violently, when was delivered
in the post, a cardboard box
which held, to Holmes, a paradox
but which to her, Miss Cushing, posed
great horror, for she found enclosed
and packed in coarse salt, what she took
to be a prank before a look
much closer brought her to the brink
of screaming and, from reason, shrink,
for inside, bringing her to tears,
she saw a pair of severed ears.

**Holmes hastened** off to Croydon keen
to view what evidence had been
preserved untouched, for, though the best
man Scotland Yard could send had zest
and passion, his imagination
Holmes would treat with indignation
though would find, when he arrived,
the box, despite his fears, survived
and was, to Miss Cushing's distress,
still in her house, and she'd express
the need to have 'the things' removed,
an action of which Holmes approved,
and which, when done, had need to be
inspected by the sleuth till he
might render to those standing by
the possible 'who', 'how' and 'why'
which he could see - but, others, not -
perhaps some inkling of a plot
which need testing and support,
though he might risk a brief report.

**"The package** tied with naval knots
was filled with salt which, thus, allots
the sender to a merchant ship,"
said Holmes, "a ship back from a trip
perhaps with hides which salt preserves,
and there's the wrapper which deserves
our time for, on it, the address
of 'Croydon' showed someone careless
or unfamiliar with the place,
for 'i' to 'y' was changed, and trace
that coffee smell, and I would think
the sender used a low-grade ink
applied with a broad pointed pen,
a 'J' type probably, and then
it's obvious a man addressed
the package, and would be assessed
as limited in education."
then Holmes, maintaining concentration,
set all his faculties to clear
and studied, close, each severed ear.

**Though journalists** had speculated
that the ears were separated
by a student in a prank,
Holmes, from this supposition, shrank
and said that no preservative
was used and, more informative,
was that the ears were not a pair
but from two people, and a fair
deduction was, as it was small
and fine and pierced, one had the hall
marks of a woman, unlike those
the other ear had to disclose
which were that it was quite sunburned,
heavily tanned, and pierced, which turned
Holmes' thoughts onto a man who'd been
a seaman as, too, he had seen
in clues the package had disclosed,
and then, on Miss Cushing, imposed
more questions, but would chance to see
a portrait group of sisters, three.

**Miss Susan Cushing**, as portrayed
with Sarah and Mary, displayed
a close resemblance, though beside
this portrait was one to provide
Holmes with a line of thought to test
for Mary, in her Sunday best,
stood with a man, a man she'd wed,
a ship's steward who'd now been led
back to his drinking habit by
the meddling Sarah who'd supply
disharmony on being spurned
by him, Jim Browner, and who'd turned
Mary against her husband and
had left their home on his command
though had returned when Jim had been
at sea - with Alec Fairbairn keen
to keep time with Mary who would,
in turn, see Alec all she could -
all which filled Browner up with hate
and threatening a savage fate.

**One of his ears,** Jim said he'd send
to Sarah should Fairbairn offend
again, and then returned to sea
on issuing this threat – a plea
no less from one with heart so wild
he had no time for manner, mild -
and who, when through an accident
at sea and with fond yearnings, went
back to his home, he was to find
his wife and Fairbairn of a mind
together to go off and take,
to New Brighton, a train to make
free with their time for, Jim, they thought
to be away at sea, still ought,
though Jim, behind then, followed keen,
enraged by all that he had seen,
and as the couple oared a boat
from Brighton, Jim, behind, afloat,
caught up with them as, out, they cried,
for on Jim's face, their deaths they spied.

**Fairbairn** took a stance defensive
while Jim, taking the offensive,
struck a blow across his head
and, in an instant he was dead,
and Mary, too, suffered like fate
while Jim, now in a savage state,
cut off from each an ear to send
to Sarah so she'd comprehend
what she had caused, but wrote an 'S'
upon the package's address
for 'Sarah', though 'Susan' received
Jim's message, though, never deceived,
Holmes deduced all and found how Jim
had motive to commit the grim
ear-slicing crime, and had the skill
and opportunity to kill
Alec and Mary on their jaunt
away, which they would freely flaunt,
all which left Holmes, the sleuth, to pose
questions of why such things arose.

## *The Yellow Face*

**Quite under protest** on a walk,
a jaded Holmes refused to talk
and yearned for mental exercise,
his demons, grim, to exorcise,
and all his energies conserve
despite the Spring having the nerve
to show its early verdant face
which anyone alert could trace
in London's parks which he and John
Watson, M.D., had gazed upon
with different eyes, and, on returning
back to Baker Street and spurning
further physical exertion,
found that during their desertion
of their Baker Street abode,
and which caused Holmes to near explode,
their page-boy said a gentleman,
a client, or perhaps a fan,
had been and gone but would return,
which caused the brow of Holmes to burn.

**Quite grumpily** and quite annoyed,
and quite unfairly, Holmes employed
a tone approaching disrespect
toward his friend who could detect
frustration rising which defused
when Holmes remarked, a tad bemused,
their visitor had left behind
his pipe which seemed to Holmes the kind
of well-loved pipe its owner kept
repaired and possibly had wept
when it was damaged, but deduced,
from clues the valued pipe produced,
its owner was left-handed and
quite muscular and had a grand
strong set of teeth, was well-to-do
though careless, and who burst into
the room without notification
by knock, or other indication,
though seemed a true apologist
to Holmes, the criminologist.

**The visitor** was Grant Munro
a man unsure of how to go
about expressing his desire
to tell about a pressing dire
grim domestic situation
full of fearful speculation
to a stranger, but proceeded
forthwith, telling Holmes he needed
help and guidance in a matter
- less the former than the latter -
as, of late, his married life
has suffered, for his loving wife
Effie was acting ever distant
- to his questions, quite resistant -
and, in Atlanta where they'd met,
she'd been a widow although yet
just twenty-five, after a wave
of yellow fever, to the grave,
had sent her daughter Lucy and
one John Hebron, her late husband.

**Though not Empire-shaking**, this,
as Holmes often made emphasis,
was such a case which might provide
a challenge to his skill and pride
and, though never emotional,
Holmes saw at least a notional
intriguing case about to start
and so decided to depart
for Norbury - to where Munro
had been distressed and worried so -
there to assess such facts as might,
investigated, come to light,
for Munro had, with too few facts,
decided that his wife's odd acts
stemmed from the possibility
that she'd committed bigamy
and someone, of that truth, had known
and to the lady's home had flown
intent on money to extract
from her - a blackmailer, in fact.

But **Holmes** did not rise to that bait
and told Munro he'd have to wait
until he'd had time to assess
the source of Grant Munro's distress
which started recently when she,
Effie his wife, asked him if he
could give to her one hundred pounds
and not ask her what were the grounds
of such a question – after all
it was her money which she'd call
upon if needed – to which he
agreed, though was upset when she
had visited a house nearby
and he'd begun to wonder why,
as jealousy began to grow,
why such an interest she'd show
and then decided to inspect
the house himself, to which effect,
saw from a window, high and black,
a yellow face was looking back.

**Deciding then** to look inside
to find what clues such might provide
he climbed the stairs and found a room
full-curtained but could, in the gloom,
see on the mantlepiece, a face,
a portrait of his wife to grace
the room, it seemed, and then returned
- the sight, into his memory, burned -
and, so, thought he might make contact
with Sherlock Holmes for, if he'd act,
Holmes may observe where he'd just seen
and then determine what had been
the wife's motive for each event,
some secret, dark, which might prevent
her taking into confidence
her husband, for the evidence
seemed to suggest an amorous
intrigue which, though unglamorous
and difficult to contemplate,
suspicion just would not abate.

**Holmes thought** about the problem, long,
when, back at Baker Street, a strong
and pleading message was received
from Munro, and so Holmes perceived
that he and Watson should attend
which they both did, there to extend
their help, and to the house approached
with Munro, all the time reproached
by Effie, when the yellow face
appeared, though it was hard to trace
its features so, Munro, incensed
entered the house, enraged and tensed
- with Holmes and Watson following -
but stopped, for in the room, that thing
changed to a child, expressionless
but yellow-faced, without distress,
and Holmes, a yellow mask, removed
- though Effie strongly disapproved -
and there a dark-skinned girl appeared
and Munro's anger disappeared.

**Effie's first husband**, she explained,
was African, a lawyer trained
and well-respected, though his dark
skin, at that time and place, would mark
their marriage as being most unwise
but she'd accept no compromise,
but he had died, although their child,
their daughter, took the fever mild
and did recover and was brought
to England where Effie had thought
to keep her hidden till the day
her new husband would bid her "stay",
and then, with kindness, Grant Munro
picked up girl and said they'd go
back home, and kissed her on the face,
- of anger, showing not a trace -
and Effie joined them as Sherlock,
to Watson, still somewhat in shock,
said they should go, their case was solved
and they were no longer involved.

........................................

**John Watson**, now contently wedded
and his doctor's mind embedded
deep in a periodical -
the latest British Medical
Journal – had heard the strident tones
of Holmes which, down into his bones,
shook him, for he'd not seen his friend
for ages, so stood up to tend
the hand of welcome, biding him
"Come in!" while wondering what whim
had caused the man to venture out
and his reclusive nature flout
but, first, commenced the ritual
- always, with Holmes, habitual -
in which Holmes told Watson where he
had been and likely would soon be
and know, as if read from a book,
such details from a single look,
and, after being frolicsome,
told Watson why he'd really come.

**Watson, good-natured**, took it all
in, knowing Holmes had come to call
with something brewing on his mind,
though he knew it would be unkind
to stop his friend from exercising
all those talents so surprising
to those uninitiated
until he had dissipated
each pent-up, frustrated urge
and let the matters brewing surge
forth, letting Holmes – always prepared,
and feeling Watson had been snared -
to ask the Doctor if he might
go forth – as if some errant knight -
with him; for Holmes had come that day
to ask if he might come away
with him and one – a clerk adrift -
and if so, himself, he must shift
and, with his needs, his satchel, cram,
then travel up to Birmingham.

**The Doctor**, primed and ever ready,
stalwart always, ever steady,
had, with colleagues, organised
to substitute when one advised
the other of the need to be
away, and so told Holmes that he
was, for such moments, well equipped,
his satchel packed, its handle gripped
as out he rushed into the street,
a waiting client, there, to greet
- Hall Pycroft – then to be away
- no time to waste upon that day -
to catch the train to Birmingham
with little time to even cram
a breakfast morsel, although sound
within their carriage, outward-bound,
Holmes said they had an hour-plus
for Hall Pycroft's discourse and, thus,
Watson, in full detail, would hear
the client's story, strange but clear.

**Watson observed** the man and saw
a type he liked, a Cockney, raw,
smartly attired, though perturbed
about some matter which disturbed
his native outwardness and placed,
upon a countenance, once graced
by beaming smile and confidence,
a frown denoting reticence
to admit that he'd been deceived
but, as the fellow had perceived
from Holmes and Watson not a hint
of judgement, he would use this stint
aboard the train to tell that he,
a clerk, accounting, used to be
but markets crashed and left him out
of work for months but, then, about
two weeks ago, an offer came
from one, Arthur Pinner by name,
at pay more than the standard rate
if, northward, he would relocate.

**Perhaps he** should have smelled a rat
but, short of funds, considered that
a great increase in earnings might
make up for times when funds were tight,
so he'd accept, despite the fact
that he would now need to retract
acceptance of an offer made
by Mawson's, though Pinner forbade
him doing so, for Mawson's had,
he said, spoke of him as some cad
who they had rescued from the gutter
which Hall Pycroft called an utter
insult, so agreed he'd not
write his retraction, and then got
his job with Pinner who'd entranced
the fellow greatly when advanced
one-hundred pounds – a fortune, small -
and told him that he was to call
upon his brother Harry to
be shown precisely what to do.

**To Birmingham**, Hall-Pycroft went,
the fellow most excited, bent
on proving Pinner's trust was not
misplaced, so, eagerly, he got
to work by making lists, complete,
of Paris hardware stores, replete
with contact details and address
of each, but then had to confess
to Pinner that he'd need more time
to finish off this listing, prime,
but then was told to carry on
and given more to work upon,
but there was something he'd report
- a strange coincidence of sort
which could not be, but was – for he,
in Arthur Pinner's mouth, could see
a set of teeth – as, Holmes, he told -
one being badly stuffed with gold,
but Harry had, to his dismay,
the same tooth filled the self-same way.

**Identical**, the brothers seemed,
and, even though Hall Pycroft deemed
this strange, Holmes knew he had a case
of worth to ponder and to chase
then called on Watson to drop all
and join with him to pay a call
upon this Harry Pinner who,
with brother Arthur, needed to
be closely scrutinized, for he
the sleuth of sleuths, knew it to be
most likely that they were one man
then came up with a simple plan
to say that they sought work within
the Pinners' enterprise and spin
the line they were accountants who
were out of work and keen to do
whatever Pinner might assign
but found some malady malign
had caused the fellow so much strife
that he would try to take his life.

**Two brothers**, Beddington, had posed
- one as two Pinners, Holmes supposed,
the other as Hall Pycroft at
the firm of Mawson's where he sat
and waited till the coast was clear
to break into the safe with near
one hundred thousand pounds within -
alas, a watchman had come in
and came on Beddington red-handed
but the felon quickly landed,
on the watchman's skull, a blow
which, though being meant to lay him low,
had killed him, and then, in a panic,
the other Beddington went manic
just as Sherlock Holmes arrived
and had him, in short time, revived,
then came the time, Hall Pycroft knew,
for him to ascertain, in view
of such an underhanded deed,
if Mawson's, of him, still had need.

....................................................

**A wistful Holmes** in mood to please
- as much as it might serve to tease
his colleague, Watson - sought to tweak
the Doctor's interest on a bleak
cold Winter's night, relaxed beside
their Baker Street flat fireside,
by showing him a tattered note
upon which was a cryptic quote
which made no sense unless one knew
it was encoded with a view
to being read only by those
few confidants the writer chose
to hold the key to its translation
to release the information
held within; but, as he sat
relaxed at home, it happened that
a Justice of the Peace felt dread
and later died when he had read
that cryptic quote and understood
the message boded him no good.

**That J.P.** – Mr. Trevor - dead,
appeared to see some evil thread
of danger looming, although he
was known, in Norfolk's Broads, to be
a man of charity who would,
to those convicted, where he could,
be lenient; and Holmes, who knew
this old but robust man, could view
within his mind a case to solve
which naturally would involve
Victor, the dead man's son, a friend
on whom Holmes always could depend
in College days when friends were few,
their friendship being that which drew
Holmes, injured, to his home to stay
and convalesce one month away
enjoying hospitality
and, with his specialty,
such secrets as he might, obtain,
to, Mr. Trevor, entertain.

**The note** told of 'rising supply
of game and then, to Hudson, fly
paper on order must now be
received and that catastrophe
to hen-pheasants he should avoid'
though this was, of all sense, devoid
to all but Mr. Trevor who
had obviously hastened to
his death on reading such obtuse
and muddled words of little use
beyond, it seemed, distressing those
who understood the mangled prose
and saw within a threat to life
and limb to come with storm or strife
although no one who knew the dead
man, Mr. Trevor, and who'd read
the note could guess why he so feared
its content, so Sherlock had cleared
his scheduled tasks to make his way
to find some puzzling "J.A.".

**But Holmes**, before, "J.A.", had seen,
on Trevor, tattooed, which had been
in part removed, though when observed
by Holmes it left the man unnerved
so much that, to a faint, he fell
and, therefore, had a tale to tell
which wasn't told but later would,
when Trevor died, tell Holmes he should
look at the note again and try
- his mental faculties apply -
again, then found a message hid
- a cypher message - deep amid
words otherwise nonsensical
revealing the hysterical:
"The game is up. Hudson told all.
Fly for your life." which seemed a call
sent by some Beddoes that some 'game'
beset by unsaid guilt or blame
had been revealed, and each and all
was destined for a grim downfall.

John Armitage – J.A. – had been,
for others' money, far too keen
but, caught, had found himself transported
to Australia, but consorted
with Evans when they, aboard
the 'Gloria Scott', heard that a hoard
of cash was hidden by a man,
John Prendergast, who then began
to make a plan to seize the ship
and circumvent their southbound trip
to servitude, but all went wrong,
the Captain putting up a strong
defence, though he and many men
quite loyal would be killed, but when
deciding what they ought to do
the victors were persuaded to,
by Armitage and Evans, let
themselves and those alive be set
adrift within a longboat, sound,
so they, for safety, could be bound.

**Things went** from going wrong to dire
for, in the Gloria Scott, a fire
among the powder kegs, fast spread,
a great explosion leaving dead
all but the scheming Hudson who
was picked up by the longboat to
be rescued from a fate, unknown,
when fortune saw the Hotspur blown
toward them on its way, at speed,
to Sydney, then, with them, proceed
- each changing his identity
to hide each man's complicity,
whereafter Armitage became
Trevor, and Evans took the name
of Beddoes, each then making way
out to the gold fields till the day
- now quite rich men - each could return
to England - former ways to spurn -
to live with great civility
and new respectability.

**All had gone well** until arrived
this Hudson who, with malice, strived
to coerce Mr. Trevor to
give favour to him and to do
whatever he might choose to ask
but Victor Trevor took to task
his father, though this had aggrieved
Victor, that son, who had believed
that Hudson had some fiendish hold
upon his father, still he told
- his blood, in fury, set to burn -
Hudson to leave and not return
and he begrudgingly complied
- though not in manner dignified -
to seek out Beddoes to apply
blackmail to make the man comply
as Trevor had, but Beddoes wrote,
in fear and dread, that cryptic note,
then one would die upon that day,
though who, no one could truly say.

**Police thought** Hudson, in a rage,
killed Evans but then thought to stage
the death to seem that he was dead
but Holmes, the opposite, had read
and thought, though evidence was thin,
that Evans had done Hudson in
and, with as much cash as he could,
removed to some place where he would
be safe, to change his name once more
then go on as he had before
or take on some new enterprise
in hope no one would compromise
his new existence, so the case
fell quiet, with few leads to chase,
and Police sought Hudson in vain,
Holmes, of boredom, would complain,
Watson had a tale to tell,
Beddoes went elsewhere to dwell
- perhaps out west, perhaps to sea -
while Victor went off planting tea.

## The Musgrave Ritual

**Although the workings** of the mind
of Sherlock Holmes were of the kind
to organize all data gained
in ways which he had once explained
to be in many ways compared
unto an attic where was spared
no space for thoughts extraneous
nor data deemed superfluous
but allocated all to serve
each neuron and each vital nerve
existing only for perfection
of the science of detection,
Sherlock could be quite the bane
of those around him when mundane
domestic chores of any kind
imposed upon that tidy mind
so much that each neuron and nerve
contrived to help their owner swerve
away and, for excuses, look
to somehow get him off the hook.

**Watson admonished** Sherlock hard
and told him that he must discard
a major portion of his mess
but, this was, to the man, duress
too hard to countenance, so he
thought that the only way to be
excused from cleaning duty might
involve some object of delight
which Watson might well write about
and, so, Holmes dragged a tin box out
from underneath his bed into
their living room, proceeding to
undo its latches, lift its lid
to show, within, old files long hid
away; and of a box of such
corroded metal that not much
could be identified, Holmes then
said, once all adult Musgrave men
made use of it, habitual,
for their grand Musgrave Ritual.

**Its riddles** held a truth long lost,
perhaps of promise, or of cost,
for full eight questions would be asked
with every questionee being tasked
with answering without a flaw
- no chance to repeat or withdraw -
starting "Whose was it?" to which all
would answer "He who's gone." not stall
nor stammer, then say "He who'll come,"
when asked "Who'll have it?" onto some
more questions on the time of year
- the month, precisely - then show clear
awareness that the sun would shine
"Over the oak." whose shadow, fine,
was "Under the elm." and then proceed
stepwise as per the written creed
by North, then East, and South, and West,
swear to sustain this noble quest
"For the sake of the trust.", and give
"All that is ours." long as he'd live.

**What truth** this held, no one could say,
though it brought back the fateful day
the last Musgrave to bear the name,
to visit Holmes in London, came,
- a problem heavy on his mind,
a problem of perturbing kind -
for, of his staff, considerable,
for reasons quite imponderable,
two members, in one single day,
had, for some reason, gone astray,
they being Rachel Howells, and
one Richard Brunton in command,
till recently, of house affairs
- he being butler - though his airs
caused Reginald Musgrave to hand
the man his notice and demand
he leave his house, though did allow
him to remain one week, though how
he might explain his fall from grace
was something left to him to face.

56

**That butler** and the maid, mislaid,
were lovers till the former paid
attention, too much, to Janet
Tregellis, making Rachel get
- distraught, rejected – fighting mad
though, mostly, quite forlorn and sad,
while Brunton who had been, till just
before he disappeared, a must
for any master to employ,
for all who knew him would enjoy
his talents, but the time did come
he was to show he harboured some
unpardonable and strange desire
- above his station to aspire -
when he, with some malign intent,
withdrew a private document
- the Musgrave Ritual, in fact,
a treacherous, unfaithful act -
and studied it in great detail,
himself, of secrets, to avail.

**So sly** and underhanded had
the butler been, and such a cad,
that he was dismissed there and then
although this would be tempered when
he begged permission to remain
some little time and so maintain
his dignity and save some face
and not be sent off in disgrace,
so, to his duties, he returned
although the fires in him burned
as strong as ever that he sought
out Rachel, saying that she ought
assist him in an escapade
by telling her that he had made
a great discovery which would
make them both rich if she just could,
one night, assist him in a quest
and treasure, from the Musgraves, wrest
though when the dark of night had cleared
they both had, somehow, disappeared.

**Holmes, when summoned** by a friend
like Musgrave, dropped all to attend
and hear how Rachel, raving, mad,
to bed rest for her safety, had
been sent, but then could not be found
despite folks searching all around,
and then, summoned, the butler could
not be located, Musgrave would
call for police to intervene
and, at the Musgrave house, convene
to find where either might abscond
and drag the river and the pond,
though Holmes, insightfully, could see
that Brunton wanted to make free
with Musgrave secrets, then he saw
the Ritual was meant to draw
attention to some treasure hid
upon Musgrave's estate, so bid
to read, more closely than before,
the Musgrave Ritual once more.

**With line and ruler**, Holmes began
and, through the Musgrave Ritual, ran
- tree shadows trailed, distances paced
until a flagstone he had traced
deep in a cellar underground -
below which - lifted, propped - he found
a crumpled form, a sight to dread,
for there was Brunton lying dead
- presumably by Rachel's hand
as much as Holmes could understand -
when she had pulled away the prop
and let the heavy flagstone drop
to seal the fickle butler's fate
then from there, herself, extricate,
all leaving Holmes to say, deep down,
he'd found the King of England's crown
left for safekeeping centuries past
though not retrieved by him, at last,
for Civil War was raging hot,
all which the Musgraves just forgot.

......................................................

## The Reigate Squire

**The Spring of Eighty-Seven** brought,
to Holmes, great fame he had not sought
but was unable to evade
because of inroads he had made
on crime of such a scale it must,
if left unchecked, completely bust
the treasuries of nations which
had, up till then, been rather rich,
bankrupting them and bringing to
those nations, wealthy hitherto,
great ruin for people high and low
but Sherlock Holmes stepped in to show,
just in the nick of time, how they
- if they might listen and obey
all such directives he might give -
avoid financial death and live
and prosper when the danger passed
with wretched criminals outclassed
and scattered wide, or else detained,
all leaving Sherlock Holmes quite drained.

**John Watson**, in Afghanistan
had treated, in the field, a man,
one Colonel Hayter, who'd insist
that Watson one day might enlist
his London friend, by fame, adept
at solving puzzles, and accept
his Reigate hospitality
in true conviviality
whose house was open to his friends
to come and go to meet such ends
as giving Sherlock Holmes the rest
he needed, meeting each request
for help by saying, simply, "No!",
so Holmes agreed that he would go
and meet the Colonel who displayed
his Eastern weapons full arrayed
and, as there had been an alarm,
said he thought that he ought to arm
himself against potential scares
and not be taken unawares.

**And, being drained**, Sherlock could not,
Watson advised, hope to allot
the days ahead to anything
but utter rest so he might bring,
from depths so gloomy, deep and black,
in time, his mind and body back
and regain health of former times,
and not go chasing after crimes
of choice and challenge, but submit
to good advice and to admit
that even he, if broken, might
not ever mend, and such a plight
would be far worse than meeting death
and giving out a final breath
for one like him, both blessed and cursed
with talent – something to be nursed
and nurtured should it start to fade -
so if, for now, he'd find some shade
and rest awhile away from light,
he'd soon be stronger for the fight.

**Watson enquired** of what had been
the circumstances, when the keen
though weakened mind of Holmes awoke
and he then, from the sofa, spoke
declaring that police should make
something of matters if they'd take
the evidence at hand and see
the obvious, but such degree
of interest Watson curtailed
by telling Holmes his health had failed
and needed time and ample rest
and it was truly for the best
for Holmes to remain uninvolved
and that the case would soon be solved
by others, but Fate intervened
and, Watson's orders, contravened
as, in – with Holmes a little crushed -
the butler, shouting "Murder!", rushed
while yelling in a voice quite shrilled,
that coachman William, had been killed.

**For, through the heart**, he had been shot,
this coachman William in a plot
to rob the Cunninghams nearby
by whom he was employed, though why
this happened was put down to be
the fellow's loyalty which he
displayed when he had taken on
the armed intruder, whereupon,
though Holmes agreed he needed rest,
Inspector Forrester, the best
the local Force had to deploy,
asked Sherlock Holmes if he'd enjoy
to join him in investigating
such a crime, thus devastating
Watson's warnings for the health
of his old friend who had a wealth
of knowledge which he might impart
and which he was so keen to start
deploying on the case at hand,
and then, the murderer, remand.

**The burglary**, original,
though obviously criminal,
was such that little of value
was taken – in itself a clue -
and that Acton, the victim, had
been at a loss to name the cad
who'd broken in, but this seemed small
compared to that which would befall
the Cunninghams' coachman who died,
though Holmes could see somebody lied
when there was found in William's fist
part of a note whose veiled gist
was at "quarter to twelve" there'd be
some incident, the one which he
perhaps had interrupted when
he lost his life, the killer then
absconding quickly, although he
left no impressions which could be
identified or even seen
to show the sleuth where he had been.

**Investigations** then moved to
the Cunninghams who seemed to do
no more than not get in the way
of Sherlock Holmes who'd cause to say
the junior Cunningham could not
have seen the murder, and some plot
had been afoot, then used a ploy
which Watson would in time enjoy
for he could see Holmes on the track
as he feigned sickness and dropped back
upsetting fruit stacked in a dish,
sneaking away - as was his wish
as all the others cleared the mess -
to search the room without duress
from either Cunningham, to find
a damaged note, the strangest kind
with alternate words written by
each Cunningham to, thus, deny
the other freedom to declare
that he was, of it, unaware.

**Holmes,** by the junior man, attacked
but rescued by Watson who lacked
no courage, said the note had been
prepared for William as he'd seen
them breaking into the estate
of Acton who had tried, of late,
to regain lands he said belonged
to him and of which he'd been wronged,
the coachman, to blackmail, resorting
systematically extorting
money from his employers
who turned into his destroyers,
and Holmes, seeing no residue
or powder burns on Williams due
to close assault, knew he'd been shot
at distance in an evil plot,
and all who witnessed Sherlock's skill
declared it was the greatest thrill
as Holmes, to Watson, said in jest
that he'd enjoyed his few days' rest.

......................................................

## The Crooked Man

**The ring** of Watson's front-door bell
at close to midnight seemed to tell
the tired Doctor 'duty called'
which left the weary man appalled
but also ready to respond
and rise to action far beyond
that offered by his colleagues, rich,
but was part of that calling which
he had accepted, so arose,
prepared to act and diagnose
his patent's illness to ascribe
its nature and then to prescribe
a draught, medicinal, to take
which would, if taken timely, shake
off maladies both slight and grave
and patients' lives and well-being save
and, so, to his front-door, proceeded
finding, indeed, he was needed
for, there, out in the dark and cold,
stood Sherlock Holmes, his friend of old.

**Watson -** stunned a little - muted -
stood there while his friend saluted
him apologetically
then entered energetically
as Watson found his voice and bade
Holmes "Enter!" knowing his comrade,
for idle chit-chat, hadn't called
but Watson's question was forestalled
as Holmes began his customary
scrutiny, preliminary
to asking Watson if he'd care
- and if he had the time to spare -
to venture forth and seize the day
at some location far away
where Holmes, observant and efficient,
would upstage the police deficient
in the skills which he possessed
and which the man himself assessed
as unsurpassed by any measure,
to which Watson said, "With pleasure!"

**In Aldershot** it seemed there'd been
an incident, and Holmes was keen
to observe, for himself, the scene
before police could intervene
and upset any clue which might
give him, with his innate insight,
the basis of some theories which
might form hypotheses quite rich
in promise which, when tested, would
explain the matter and then could
be used to have the crime rebuilt
in Holmes' brain attic so guilt
could be apportioned to the one
who had, the deed of murder, done
though, in this case, the clues as yet
collected by the blue-clad set,
such as they were, all pointed to
the dead man's wife, a lady who
yelled "Coward!" at him followed by
"David" though nobody knew why,

**Holmes had** some basic facts to share
with Watson, though he would not dare
make rash conjecture at that time
nor did he know, indeed, a crime
had, in fact, even been committed,
though it had to be admitted
that the Colonel, James Barclay,
was dead and that his body lay,
or had, upon the tiled floor
within a room whose heavy door
was locked and that its key had been
removed and nowhere could be seen
and Barclay had been rendered dead,
it seemed, by some blow to his head
and Mrs. Barclay, nee Devoy,
Nancy by name, did not enjoy
some act committed by some man
called David, though when she began
her tirade, most felt she was loyal
to Barclay of the Munsters, Royal.

**James Barclay**, Colonel, veteran
- Crimea, Mutiny - began
as Private and, a musket, bore
but rose in rank and, in time, wore
the scarlet of an Officer
to which his comrades would defer
but, as a Sergeant, took a wife
- Nancy Devoy – and led a life
of military duty mixed
with social disadvantage, fixed
upon promotion to the rank
of Colonel with the swish and swank
of high command which he would earn
though Holmes, from officers, would learn
he went through deep depressive moods,
the type where one withdraws and broods
on some dark secret of the mind
though no one ever guessed what kind,
and, so informed, Holmes then approached
the death room and, on clues, encroached.

**Homes, in that room**, determined that
some carnivore, though neither rat
nor climbing cat, but bigger, ran
up drapes to where its form might span
the distance to a bird, cage-bound,
and, judging by the clues he found,
thought it was of the weasel kind
and so knew that he had to find
its owner, but before he could
the sleuth determined that he should
seek Mrs. Barclay's closest friend,
Miss Morrison, who in the end
told Holmes that Nancy chanced to meet
an old friend on a darkened street,
a friend of crippled crooked form,
right after which it seemed a storm
descended on her, so returned
back home, where fury in her burned
and sought the Colonel in a rage,
the man, in anger, to engage.

**That man**, once Private Henry Wood,
had with his Sergeant, Barclay, stood
but loved and was loved in return
by Nancy who would, Barclay, spurn,
but, came the day when closely pressed
by rebels, Barclay, self-possessed,
sent Wood upon a mission grim
for reinforcements, placing him
in line for capture by the bands
of rebels, sent into their hands
by, of all people, Barclay who,
for Nancy's hand, conspired to
- as David in the Bible story
sent Uriah to a gory
end, then claimed Uriah's wife -
deprive poor Henry of his life,
but Henry, maimed and tortured, came
to Aldershot, crooked and lame,
and told his Nancy of his fate
though it was now, for him, too late.

**Holmes tracked** the man to his abode,
a crippled man whose only mode
of living was to entertain
with mongoose Teddy as his main
attraction, and admitted to
being in the room prepared to do
what Barclay, with his secret, vile,
did to himself, for all the while
he lived in livid fear and shame
until his retribution came
and he fell back and cracked his head
and, in an instant, he was dead,
no more the king of his domain,
but all Holmes efforts were in vain
because, before Nancy came 'round,
the coroner's inquest had found
for "apoplexy" as the cause
of death, Holmes giving no applause
for in a case so full of pain
there was no winner, none who'd gain.

...............................................

## The Resident Patient

All who could had long deserted
London's stifling heat, diverted
to the breezes and the shades,
the verdant waving cooling glades,
of Hampshire's green New Forest or,
intent on ocean breezes, for
Southsea and all its coastal reaches,
there to sit on shingled beaches
watching waves break on the shore,
the drudge of labour to ignore,
while Watson, by such thoughts seduced,
found that, for now, with funds reduced,
in London he would have to stay
and work each dreary day away
while Sherlock Holmes, no friend of trees
or Nature's treasures – short of bees -
sought out the country only when
some miscreant took flight and then
gave chase, though thinking it a pity
preferring the busy city.

While mental contests might ensue
between the men, Holmes would subdue
his friend with logic - knowledge, facts -
and, on occasion, artifacts
from cases past – simple, profound -
but Watson held the higher ground
when medicine came to the fore
and he could even up the score,
so when Doctor Trevelyan
arrived, the mind of Sherlock ran
amok and scanned his coach and pair
and instruments which gave a fair
account of what the man might be
though, what his troubles were that he
should come to consult, he had not
the least suggestion to allot
but Watson, hearing once his name,
knew of the Doctor's work and fame
with obscure nervous lesions, and,
of first discussions, took command.

Dr. Percy Trevelyan came,
aware of Holmes' deductive fame,
to Baker Street upon that day
but was impressed, he had to say,
with Dr. Watson's knowledge, wide,
and how his presence could provide
what was required to understand
Trevelyan's problems there at hand
for though, in training, he had shown
great promise, he, on being thrown
into the world had less to show
and it had come as quite a blow
that, in his speciality,
he'd had to face reality
and settle down and hope in time
- ten years or more - to gain a prime
Harley Street spot – the goal of some -
but recently a man had come
called Blessington, one now distressed,
and of some morbid fear possessed.

But that first day, one could not see
any distress, and he seemed free
of all concern and talked as one
who possessed worldly troubles, none,
and had a plan to invest in
Trevelyan's future and, therein,
obtain an income of some size
while offering the tempting prize
of moving to a prime address
with no outlay beyond prowess
in nervous lesions of a sort
which would cause patients to exhort
an expert's treatment rather than
not living out a normal span
of healthy years, and, though surprised,
Trevelyan did what was advised
and felt his new life then begin
while Blessington, living within,
became, as now was evident,
Trevelyan's Patient, Resident.

The heart of Blessington was weak
and often he just wouldn't speak
but, to his rooms, retreat and rest,
though at each evening request
to see the books, examine them,
split takings as per a system
of three-to-one, the larger to
the benefactor, strange, but who
looked after premises and all
the staff and, any problems, stall,
then, for each patient's Guinea paid,
see Five-and-Thruppence each day laid
before Trevelyan – quite handsome
remuneration - an income
far better than he thought to earn
when, unestablished, he would yearn
for better days and recognition,
unaware a proposition
soon would come, an offer which
would make the Doctor rather rich.

But Blessington, as time went on,
became obsessed and, whereupon
he'd formerly been confident
and businesslike, he often went
into a great depressive state
in which he'd worry and fixate
on matters criminal around
the city, saying thieves abound
and that somebody had been in
his room, for he had kept therein
a strongbox, soundly locked and latched,
and that, against him, had been hatched
some plot to rob him, and accused
- leaving Trevelyan unamused -
a Russian patient of intruding
on his privacy, alluding
to those traces left behind
and which Trevelyan called unkind
but saw, when peering through the door,
strange footprints left upon the floor.

With that, the Doctor hastened to
see Sherlock Holmes on what to do
about his Patient, Resident,
to which Holmes thought it provident
that he should go that very day
and see the man without delay
but found the frantic fellow armed,
prepared to shoot and quite alarmed,
but Holmes began to question him
but found the fellow sullen, grim,
and quite evasive such that he
caused Holmes to think the man to be
not Blessington but someone who
was hiding some past act to do
with some betrayal on the part
of this strange man, so, to depart,
Holmes rose, then left the fellow's room
- perhaps with portents of his doom -
the morning bringing only dread
for Blessington had been found dead.

The man had hanged himself, it seemed,
but Holmes, observant, quickly deemed
the matter 'murder' when he saw
cigar butts which had helped him draw
a quick conclusion that three men
had been involved and added, then,
the page boy must have let them in
- for he could not be found within -
though all had rapidly departed,
but Police had soon imparted
news that Blessington was known
to them as Sutton who had sown
his seeds of death when he informed
on fellow thieves whose gang had stormed
a bank and killed an employee
and now, from prison, were set free
but never would be apprehended
for, it seems, their days were ended
when the Norah Creina sank
and Sherlock's interest quickly shrank.

**Their lingual sparring** left aside,
rambling discussions would provide
John Watson with no end of scope
for frank discussions in the hope
that he might match, perhaps exceed,
the mind of Holmes in depth and speed
of recall of such varied facts
of how the Sun on high attracts
the Earth to cause obliquity
- observed from deep antiquity -
of the elliptic; changing then
in subject to just how and when
are peoples' attributes imposed
and, in their characters, reposed
for Holmes said his ancestors, old,
bequeathed to him the keen and cold
deductive skills he'd further hone,
and said, in flattened monotone,
on that one point and to the letter,
his brother, Mycroft, was his better.

**Surprised, perplexed**, taken aback,
John Watson briefly seemed to lack
a sound response, but then declared
that he'd been truly unprepared
for news like this, and asked just where
in Britain had this premiere
majestic mind been hiding and
before he could, on that, expand
Holmes said he worked in Government
and, though he was omnipotent
in logic and in mental strengths,
he'd never venture to the lengths
required to investigate
with energy, and circulate
among the city's millions, squashed,
and, criminality, have quashed,
but then called Watson to his feet
for if, his brother, he would meet
they'd find this mental Hercules
at lunch at Club, Diogenes.

**There, at the Club,** no one could speak
and if one did, a warden bleak
would cast a look of disapproval
leading to a swift removal
if it happened more than twice
- apparently, quite good advice -
and when Mycroft himself appeared
and greeted Sherlock, Watson feared
his seal-flipper of a hand
but very soon would understand
what Holmes had meant about his mind
- a mind of most uncanny kind -
which matched itself as in a game
with Sherlock's own when onward came
a stranger whom both would assess
by observation, not by guess,
just what he was and what he did
then, to each other, make a bid
of history and occupation
to John Watson's fascination.

**Words of wonder** and rebuff
by Watson would then call their bluff
but he found they, indeed, were right
to his amazement and delight,
and Mycroft said he had a case
which was too much for him to chase
but which Sherlock might like to hear
about and, as he lived quite near,
had Mr. Melas summoned to
ask Sherlock what he ought to do
about a very strange event
- perhaps a murder to prevent -
and Mr. Melas, on arrival,
said he feared for the survival
of a fellow Greek detained
against his will, he'd ascertained
by virtue of his plastered face,
though where this was he couldn't place,
and by the threats he had received
by those who drove him there, deceived.

**That tortured man** refused to sign
a document, clearly malign,
by which his sister, Sophy, might
be married, for he thought her plight
would be dishonour and disgrace
- a fate which he'd not see her face -
and Mr. Melas was engaged
against his will and, though enraged,
was forced - himself, a London Greek
interpreter whom one would seek
to translate for those with the need -
to make the tortured fellow heed
his captors' questions and demands
and follow their evil commands
but Mr. Melas, as he asked
those questions which he had been tasked,
had added extra questions such
that extra information, much,
in secrecy might be obtained
and his abductors' aims explained.

**Melas learned** that the man was called
Kratides and had been appalled
that Sophy's large inheritance
- in trust to him – might soon enhance
the coffers of these evil men
and, so, refused to comply when
asked to accede and to comply,
and all he would do was defy
them all by saying to them "No!"
although, his life, he might forgo,
but then, surprised, a lady cried
"My God, it's Paul!" and he replied
"Sophy! Sophy!" as, in, she came,
her face awash with fear and shame,
but, quickly, she was pulled away
and Melas heard his captor say
he now must leave but not reveal
what he had seen, for that would seal
his fate, and then, into the night,
was cast to return as he might.

**Back home**, forthwith, he advertised
- though this was surely ill-advised -
to find if anyone might know
this man Kratides and could show
where he was held, but he would learn
that all this did for him was earn
the vengeful hatred of those men
who violently reacted when
they found they'd been betrayed, and so
Holmes knew it was now time to go
with information he'd received
to Scotland Yard for he perceived
he'd need more help, for Melas now
was missing and Holmes must, somehow,
find him before both men were killed
- a prospect which had left him chilled -
but, finally, they came upon
the house, deserted, whereupon
Holmes entered quickly but discovered
Kratides could not be recovered.

**The man was dead,** but Melas, not,
so Watson, on his patient, got
to work and found they'd been in time
to save him from this evil crime,
but his abductors had departed
- bound for unknown parts they'd started
leaving wheel ruts in the road,
signs of a rather heavy load -
and nothing further Holmes could find
for, not a clue, they'd left behind
though Holmes felt that, in time, he'd hear
some news to celebrate or fear
and this prediction came to be
some few months distant after he
received from distant Budapest
a notice which would put to rest
the matter, for two Englishmen
had both met death together when
they stabbed each other in a fight -
and that the lady'd taken flight.

**A chemical** investigation
proved a source of fascination
for the challenge it presented
and the fact it represented
freedom or the hangman's rope
though Holmes was never one to mope
about the outcome of a test
- it always was about the quest -
but 'death' announced itself this time
- the subject guilty of the crime -
and Holmes could say with confidence
he had conclusive evidence
and proof to offer, fast and hard,
and said the same to Scotland Yard,
but then asked Watson if his letter
offered something even better
than the case which he just solved
and Watson, keen to be involved,
told Holmes he shouldn't be so fickle
for Tadpole Phelps was in a pickle.

**Young Percy Phelps**, Watson recalled,
had been with him, at school, installed
though two full classes in the fore
and rather easy to ignore
except that Lord Holdhurst had been
his uncle though this wouldn't screen
him from the jibes and schoolyard pranks
which saw, attacked, his lower shanks
which left him bruised upon the shins
by cruel and puerile assassins
who'd called him 'Tadpole' for his size
despite him winning every prize
on offer by schoolmasters proud
who showered him with praises loud
and saw him win a scholarship
to Cambridge which would then equip
the lad, when grown, to fill the space
arranged for him – an envied place
his uncle contrived to allot -
a Whitehall Foreign Office spot.

**Holmes read** the letter and could see
its writer was, he'd guarantee,
not this man Phelps but was, in fact,
a woman of some grace and tact,
but further he could not proceed
and, first-hand facts, said he would need
and they should waste no time at all
to answer Percy's desperate call
and, fast to Woking, took the train
for Holmes could feel the woman's pain
and met with Joseph Harrison,
the woman's brother, whereupon
all went to Percy's room to speak
with him – though he was rather weak -
and Annie his fiancé who
stood by him and attended to
his needs, for Percy - to his cost -
a vital document, had lost,
and Sherlock sensed a challenge, meaty,
for, missing, was a secret treaty.

**His senses honed,** Holmes listened hard
and not one fact did he discard
as Percy told him of the night
fate placed on him the dreadful plight
of letting down those who, in him,
had placed great trust before the grim
reality of what transpired
- the loss of papers which, acquired
by certain foreign powers could
result in war, and likely would -
he'd realized, then saw before
him shame, dishonour, so much more
than such a mind as his could stand
- forever he would wear the brand
of one unfit to ever walk
through Whitehall's corridors or talk
with those who brook no form of error -
and with that grim prospect came terror
such that he broke down on the train,
collapsing from a fevered brain.

**Lord Holdhurst** saw the need to ask
of Percy to take on the task
of copying a document
so sensitive it might foment
a major war should others see
its contents, so he must agree
to work alone upon his bench
at night and copy out in French
a Naval Treaty made between
Britain and Italy, both keen
to know just how Britain's defiance
of a strong Triple Alliance
might affect each party to
the Treaty and what each might do
should France surpass the naval strength
of Italy but, with its length,
Percy had found the task demanding
so sought out an understanding
employee for coffee which,
his faculties, would re-enrich.

**Alas for Percy** who, returning,
found his innards sickly churning
on his finding that, although
so fleeting had been his furlough,
the Naval Treaty wasn't there
nor could he find it anywhere
but someone certainly had been
there who had come and gone unseen
but rang the bell before he beat
a sneaking silent quick retreat
along a corridor where not
a rat could hide, and as a blot
to Percy's record loomed upon
his troubled mind, his horizon
appeared quite bleak unless he found
the missing Treaty, so he'd hound
all those who'd been at work that night
and anybody else who might
have been involved but, beaten, had
a fit, and felt a hopeless cad.

**Ten weeks** went by before he sent
for Watson hoping he'd consent
to asking Sherlock Holmes if he
might help in something which might be
not just a case, for Holmes, in fact,
would, in the national interest, act
and, if successful, would prevent
a war of enormous extent
from breaking out, and also save
Phelp's sanity and catch the knave
who took the Treaty should Whitehall
want such a thing announced at all,
and Holmes assented making no
assumptions, rushing to and fro
to check on this and rule out that
although it seemed to others at
a distance he was quite confused
and, though Joseph was unamused,
his sister, Holmes thought, was a type
endowed with charm, devoid of hype.

**Holmes ruled out** things impossible
and, though at first improbable,
he had the case details set
within his mind and hoped to get
the missing Treaty and his man
so, with indulgences, began
to bait his trap to catch the rat
who stole the Treaty leaving flat
and mentally debilitated
- on his future fate fixated -
Percy Phelps who, breakfasting
with Holmes and Watson saw something
upon his plate and gave a yell
of thanks, for now his days of Hell
were at an end, for Holmes had found
the Naval Treaty, safe and sound,
where Joseph hid it weeks before
and Percy Phelps could now restore
the document to Whitehall and,
of his life, retake command.

## *The Final Problem*

**The heavy heart** of Watson beat
in subdued tones when, on his seat,
he sat to render, one last time,
a sad account of such a prime
inspired mind which now was lost
for he'd been left to bear the cost
of separation from a friend
who met his sad heroic end
in battle with an evil master,
one which ended in disaster
for the world at large and for
friends left behind who'd now abhor
the vacuum in their lives which could
never be remedied and would
remain and, perhaps, not be filled
in their lifetimes when he was killed
along with Moriarty who,
an ex-professor, wanted to
be rid of all restraints at last
and rule an evil empire, vast.

**As Watson struggled**, he thought back
to weeks before a vile attack
on Holmes' reputation came
from one who shared the evil name
of Moriarty and, in fact,
wrote abject lies which would detract
from Moriarty's loathsome shame
and Sherlock Holmes' well-earned fame,
then recalled when his friend arrived
within his rooms and there contrived
- two knuckles burst upon his fist -
to ask, though he would not insist,
if, for a week, Watson might care
- of course, if such time he could spare -
to go abroad somewhere upon
the Continent, to which Watson
- as Holmes had closed the shutters tight -
asked what was causing him such fright
which had him, to his quarters, driven,
and "Air Guns", in response, was given.

**In haste**, Watson prepared to go
upon this trek, though to and fro
he looked for Holmes upon the train
but all his searching was in vain,
though, once away, a priest spoke out
- Holmes in disguise and not about
to let his enemies know he,
in foreign parts, was soon to be -
but learned that Moriarty had
evaded capture and the cad
had, in his rage and fury, tracked
them down and they would be attacked
unless they changed trains quickly and
made way, in time, to Switzerland
and rest awhile and see the sights,
enjoy Englischer Hof delights,
hike up to view Reichenbach Falls
though Watson soon would hear the calls
which beckoned him with pleading breath
to help a woman nearing death.

**So, back to base**, Watson then rushed
but had his noble spirit crushed
on learning nobody at all
was ailing, and the urgent call
for help was just a wicked ruse
which Moriarty's man would use
to lure the Doctor well away
from Holmes so that, upon that day,
two men could meet alone to draw
their battle-lines beside the maw
of Reichenbach, and one would win
- the other, lose and stay within
the depths below the mighty Falls -
and Watson, fearing that his calls
to action were to be too late
and Holmes might meet a deadly fate,
rushed onward, though when he arrived,
could find no one who had survived
and, though a frantic search was made,
Watson's bright hopes were quick to fade

**The horror** of the situation
filled Watson with trepidation
as he looked around in vain,
the spray like tiny drops of rain
surrounding him as he sought out
a clue, a hint, to tell about
the unwitnessed catastrophe,
the battle which occurred while he
was on that errand, false and base,
that errand which caused him to chase
a phantom patient, nowhere found,
his rush to help now quite unsound
in hindsight, leaving Holmes alone
to face a man whose every bone
within him screamed of vengeance for
defeat, which the ex-Professor
could not believe but had to face,
but Watson, now, could only trace
two lines of footprints in but not,
a single outward one, could spot.

**Prostrate**, he peered over the edge
hoping in vain that, on a ledge,
his friend might have clung on in hope
of rescue, though to straws he'd grope
and cling to before he'd accept
his friend was gone and had been swept
beyond all help, then rose to find
if Holmes had left for him some kind
of message, then against a rock
he saw, leaning, an alpine-stock
then something small reflecting light
- Holmes' cigarette case shining bright -
and, underneath, a paper square
explaining that, too well aware
that he might die, he asked if he
might leave a note which proved to be
a testimonial of sorts
- what must be done and where reports
might be located – and then bade
Watson 'farewell', his life to trade.

**Sherlock Holmes**, he knew, was dead,
but Watson also knew, instead
of giving in to evil's wiles,
Holmes went those gruelling extra miles
and sacrificed his life for those
who, straight and honest living, chose,
and Moriarty's evil stain
upon the Earth would not remain
for Holmes' legacy would be
that he had rid the world of the
most infamous, despicable,
and evil man conceivable
who'd never drawn an honest breath
but who'd been rendered safe by death,
and though he had been horrified,
Watson felt sadly satisfied
that Holmes' life had been fulfilled
and ended as the fellow willed
with virtue's soldiers standing tall
and evil's henchmen made to fall.

**"The best** and wisest man I've known!"
Watson declared, quite overthrown
by grief and sense of loss that he,
Holmes' chronicler, would cease to be,
though he might, in the future, write
of past adventures to invite
his readers to recall a man,
remarkable, and who began
long years before to battle crime,
a man of action, yet sublime,
who had declared he'd suffer death
and offer up his final breath,
- the favour of the Fates, entreat -
if, Moriarty, he might beat
by, in the battle, giving all,
but found the Fates had come to call
for payment due upon that win
by having both the men fall in
that roaring chasm, there to stay
till Gabriel's call on Judgement Day.

..................................................

# The Hound of the Baskervilles

# Baſkerville Hall
## 1742

On the origin of the Hound of
the Baſkervilles there have
been many ſtatementſ, yet as
I come in a direct line from
Hugo Baſkerville, and as I
had the ſtory from my father
who alſo had it from his, I
have ſet it down with all
belief that it occurred even
as is here ſet forth. And I
would have you believe, my
ſons, that the ſame Juſtice
which punishes ſin may alſo
graciouſly forgive it, and
that no ban is ſo heavy but
that by prayer and repentance
it may be removed. Learn then
from thiſ ſtory not to fear the
fruits of the paſt, but
rather to be circumſpect in
the future, that thoſe foul
paſſions whereby our family
has ſuffered ſo grievouſly
may not again be looſed to
our undoing.

**When Charles of Baskerville** crept out
in dark of night and looked about,
someone to meet, who would have thought
that he'd confront a hound which sought
his brutal death as once foretold
within a document so old
which told to all who bore the name
of Baskerville it was their shame
that forebear Hugo of their line
had seized a maiden, truly fine,
who managed to escape from strife
but fell dead running for dear life
from hounds and from a vile band
of men who could not understand
the spectre which they now could see
and from which they'd be forced to flee
as glow, it did, an evil sheen
and which they would declare they'd seen
to tear out evil Hugo's throat
and leave his body there to bloat?

**Could those** upon the Moor that night
forget the sounds of fear and fright
as men accustomed to the hunt
were too afraid to bear the brunt
of something vile and obscene
sent straight from Hell to intervene
in Earthly matters as it ran
from Satan's realm to seek the man
who called upon the Evil One
to have his wickedness be done
upon that maiden, scared but bold,
who'd clamber out onto the cold
and darkened Moor to find escape
in death whose mantle came to drape
itself upon her as she braved
the ire of those men, depraved,
who now were fleeing or, instead,
were, as was Hugo, lying dead,
their vile souls to Hades taken,
hopes of Paradise forsaken?

**Well, all** who had survived that night
declared that they had seen a sight,
a spectral hound of massive form
which like a mad and frenzied storm
ran through the dark of night with flame
aflickering until it came
upon its quarry, white with fear,
and, whereupon, on coming near,
cast evil Hugo from his horse
and killed him there without remorse
as ripping fangs tore flesh and bone,
a fitting ending to atone
for non-fulfilment of his pledge
to Satan who'd push to the edge
contracted terms made on that day
and drag Hugo to Hell to pay
for having let the maiden slip
away, her soul lost to his grip,
and there to dwell forever more
as Satan settled up the score.

**But as the centuries** dragged by
Hugo's descendants wondered why
an ancient superstition should,
and how at all it ever could,
affect, in an enlightened age,
a Baskerville who read the page
on which was written down the lines
about a legend which defines
the fate decreed so long ago
for males descended from Hugo
that there would come a vile hound
in fire which would leap and bound
and take the life of those who saw
the savage teeth and felt the raw
and savage snarling heated breath
which heralded the coming death
of those that foul satanic maw
had come from Hell to kill then gnaw
on bones of Hugo's tainted line,
and, on their souls and entrails, dine.

**When came the time** for Charles to face
that fate he feared, he chose to place
himself in danger for a friend,
perhaps to face a grisly end,
and wait for that friend to appear
but who did not, so, gripped with fear,
Charles persevered with courage bred
of generations, long, kindred,
who bore with pride the noble name
of Baskerville, then saw the flame
of fate approaching through the dark,
at first no brighter than a spark
but then increasing to disclose
a spectral hound which, tail to nose,
was glowing - evil set alight
to bring to Baskervilles the blight
of Hugo – as his heart began
to pound as he turned back and ran
until in terror, fear and dread,
Sir Charles of Baskerville was dead.

**Though sorely missed** by folks around,
an heir for Charles would soon be found
and, found, he was across the wide
Atlantic Ocean where, beside
a cabin, humble, he received
the news he never had conceived
that, his life, now, he must forsake
for Destiny said he must take
his late departed Uncle's place
at Dartmoor, there to live and trace
a chapter, new, within the book
of Baskerville, a task he took
to be a duty, therefore he
returned to Baskerville to be
known as Sir Henry, baronet,
Lord of his Manor, once beset
by crushing debt, the gentry's blight,
but now with Fortune smiling bright
for Charles saw through a venture, bold,
which filled his coffers high with gold.

**James Mortimer**, doctor, once friend
and confidant of Charles, would wend
his way to London, there to meet
Sir Henry whom he'd freely greet
as friend, declared and newly found,
but keep the legend of The Hound
of Baskerville a secret, yet,
until advice he'd been to get
from one called Sherlock Holmes, a man
who some said that, if any can,
it would be he one might approach
and Hugo's legend, with him, broach,
though it would be curtly disdained
in language blunt and unrestrained
for Holmes regarded legends, such,
as fairy tales, and then with much
anticipation of a crime,
declared that he might spare some time
to meet Sir Henry and to find
if, for The Game, he was of mind.

**Holmes had few facts** beyond the one
that said Sir Charles had come undone
in circumstances, strange, but which,
the Devon man being grandly rich,
caused Sherlock's mind to sense a plot,
the nature of which he could not
at this time ascertain or guess
but which, by instinct, would assess
as being quite malevolent
and, having been quite indolent,
was keen to be upon the trail,
to check each feature and detail
and then begin to formulate
hypotheses appropriate
to facts established, not presumed,
on which he might act, quite consumed
by something novel, something new,
his brilliant mind again askew
until it could set things a'right
and, in the darkness, shine some light.

**Holmes, then**, with Watson rushed along
to meet Sir Henry, one whose strong
and forthright character impressed
them both, although he'd not assessed
the danger to him at that time
while Holmes, suspicious of a crime,
took note that Henry was upset
about a missing boot he'd yet
to wear and said he'd been surprised
to find a note which had advised
him, for his life, to stay away
from Dartmoor and, such plans, belay
and, though Holmes tried, he failed to find
who wrote the note but knew some kind
of criminal adventure loomed
which may well see Sir Henry doomed
and when another boot - one old
and black - went missing, this had told
to Holmes, his mind and soul aflame,
that soon, Afoot, would be The Game.

**That Game**, afoot, was danger-filled,
a prospect which left Sherlock thrilled
and keen to gather facts which might
shine, on the mystery, some light
while keeping Henry in the dark
until, at last, Holmes could embark
upon a quest to meet the Beast
of Baskerville and show, at least,
that there was something else behind
Sir Charles' death, an evil mind,
and murder was, somehow, involved
and he would have that murder solved
for, when he learned of Henry's wealth,
he felt somebody, in great stealth,
had gone to great lengths to employ
that legend, ancient, to destroy
the heirs to Baskerville and clear
the way for someone, standing near
but unsuspected, to demand
Sir Charles' fortune, truly grand.

**Sir Henry chose**, on Dartmoor's wide
expanse, to Baskerville, to ride,
accompanied by his friend, new-found,
James Mortimer, who laid the ground
for his protection and explained
that there had been a tale which strained
all reasoning, though it persisted,
of a Hound whose form resisted
any explanation given
as it was, from Hades, driven
forth to fulfil Satan's Curse
upon the Baskervilles and nurse
a manic fury till the day
all Baskervilles would fade away,
though Henry would refuse to run
from any danger which his gun
could render harmless - maimed or dead -
and Holmes would help, although, instead
of coming down himself, he'd send
John Watson, doctor, soldier, friend.

**But this** was just a subtle ruse
designed to muddle and confuse
those who might do Sir Henry harm,
though Watson would raise an alarm
should any threat to him arise,
while Holmes sat nearby in disguise
upon the Moor collecting facts
and watching for suspicious acts
while Henry, badly smitten by
Miss Stapleton, though forced to cry
about that lady who had turned
his head but, though attracted, spurned
his best attentions as her brother
wanted her to love no other
than himself because, in fact,
the two were married and could act
in secret as, to life, they brought
the legend of The Hound and sought
to kill off Henry, heir of late,
then, from afar, claim his estate.

But **Sherlock Holmes** was not deceived
for, from intelligence received
and portraits from the paintings hung
high in the Hall, all doubts he'd flung
away for, Stapleton, he'd found
to be a Baskerville whose hound
had been, in fact, the beast which walked
the Moor at night, and now had stalked
and killed a convict who'd escaped
but was, in Henry's clothing, draped
as Holmes and Watson, nearby, saw
a thwarted Stapleton withdraw
as they purveyed the news to all
at Baskerville's beleaguered Hall
and then Sir Henry's man revealed
a clue – 'L.L.' – which he'd concealed
and Watson found it had to be
a lady - Laura Lyons – and she
had sought to meet Sir Charles the night
he'd fallen to his foretold plight.

**These facts** undoubtedly surprised
John Watson who was then advised
to utter nothing at that time
for Holmes could not yet prove a crime
but must interrogate someone -
L.L. - to whom great wrongs were done,
and Laura Lyons, much appalled
at what Holmes said to her, had called
for proof of what she had been told
and Sherlock Holmes, in manner bold,
with Laura close to lamentation,
showed, to her, documentation
proving no mistake was made
- their friendship was a cruel charade -
which she accepted then agreed
to do whatever Holmes would need
to bring to justice such a man,
so Holmes could formulate a plan
most intricate in its inception,
to foil this master of deception.

**The plan** which Sherlock had prepared
required that Sir Henry dared
to trust in him completely and
walk on the Moor at his command
while he and Watson would pretend
to take the London train, but wend
their ways back to the Moor in time
to frustrate Stapleton's great crime
for Holmes knew he would try, that night,
to, poor Sir Henry, kill by fright,
while Scotland Yard sent down its best
with warrant held for the arrest
of Stapleton with whom would dine
Sir Henry at the stroke of nine
while Holmes, Lestrade and Watson hid
in ambush, all the rocks, amid,
until Sir Henry bade "farewell"
then stepped, as though cast by spell,
in hesitation, through the door
to bait the hound upon the Moor.

**The three men**, crouched behind a rock
in darkness - each gun at full cock,
prepared to shoot - gave out a yell
when first appeared that Hound of Hell
and poor Sir Henry shrieked with fear
as, close, the glowing Hound came near
but heard the guns discharge and kill
the Hound whose form went limp and still,
a form he would no longer dread
- the Curse of Baskerville was dead -
and run, would Stapleton, for life,
abandoning his battered wife,
and, panic-stricken, rashly storm
onto the Moor's unstable form,
Sir Henry's old black boot, discard,
then stumble forward with regard
for nothing but escape until
that Curse he would, himself, fulfil
by meeting Death, in manner dire,
within the depths of Grimpen Mire.

# _The Return of Sherlock Holmes_

*The Empty House*

*The Norwood Builder*

*The Dancing Men*

*The Solitary Cyclist*

*The Priory School*

*Black Peter*

*Charles Augustus Milverton*

*The Six Napoleons*

*The Three Students*

*The Golden Pince-Nez*

*The Missing Three-Quarter*

*The Abbey Grange*

*The Second Stain*

'**Sherlock Holmes**, my friend, is dead'
went 'round and 'round in Watson's head
for two longs years as, yet, it would
as Watson pondered if it could
somehow be true Sherlock survived
and had, indeed, somehow contrived
to clamber from the deadly Falls
of Reichenbach and climb those walls
so slippery and, so, escape
the thundering and dreaded gape
of such a chasm, though, deep down,
he knew his friend of great renown
was gone, not ever to return,
and he should, such a notion, spurn,
but stumbled on a group discussing
and, indeed, intently fussing
over how Ronald Adair,
the Honorable, to much despair,
had met his death, their theories all
outlandish, Watson would recall.

**Retreating**, Watson then collided
with a bookseller provided
with obscure books and who,
with much invective and ado,
received the books Watson retrieved
with little grace, still much aggrieved,
and went his way, while Watson mused
upon how all were most confused
about the death of young Adair,
well-liked and rather debonair,
by bullet-strike, though met his doom
within a second-storey room
locked from within, when Watson, now
back in his study, found, somehow,
that bookseller had tracked him down
and, with remorse shown, and a frown
upon his face, apologised
to Watson and then criticised
his bookshelf in such terms unkind
that Watson turned to look behind.

**Watson turned back** but, there, instead
of that bookseller, straight ahead
stood Sherlock Holmes, alive and well,
and Watson found he could not quell
a fast-oncoming dizzy spell
and fainting, to the floor, he fell
which gave to Holmes a heartfelt shock
though Watson, steady as a rock,
rose asking if it truly could
be him, and Holmes felt that he should
be much ashamed to treat a friend
in such a way, and would commend
a little brandy to his lips
though taken in quite tiny sips,
and after Watson had regained
his senses, fully, Holmes remained
quite mortified but knew he must,
to keep the friendship and the trust
which Watson held, fully explain
his absence and, good faith, retain.

**In detail**, Sherlock Holmes told how,
as fortune and fate might allow,
at Reichenbach's majestic Falls
as he, too vividly, recalls,
he'd mastered Moriarty's bid,
at last, to be of himself, rid
and had seen, fall, this evil man
and, with him, his most evil plan
to ultimate obliteration,
but, instead of exultation,
Holmes felt only satisfaction
of a job done, though a fraction
still remained, for someone seated
high above, his chances cheated,
swore to finish off the one
who'd brought his master's plan undone,
and sent that master to his death,
so summoned up the deadly breath
Von Herder's air-gun would expel,
a lead projectile to propel.

**Poor Watson**, as his friend was dead,
or so he thought, was left to tread
a sad trail home, his spirit crushed,
while Sherlock Holmes, to safety, rushed
and saw an opportunity
to act with full immunity
to finish off what he'd begun,
though mourning friends at home to shun,
and also for him to pursue
a host of tasks long overdue -
explored the Arctic with the name
of Sigerson attracting fame
then visited, in full disguise,
the head Llama, so very wise,
in old Lhassa in high Tibet,
in Khartoum, the Khalifa, met,
and, facts to Whitehall, would advance,
then tested coal tars deep in France
but rumours, vile, began to churn
so, homeward, knew he must return.

**The murder** of Ronald Adair,
its mystery and deadly flair,
suggested that Colonel Moran
was back and so Holmes formed a plan
to trap him and put him away,
contacted Watson whose dismay
fast turned to eagerness when he
saw how determined Holmes could be
then watched his dummy form appear
on Baker Street's window, so clear,
as both stood in an empty house
- each man as quiet as a mouse -
then through the darkened hours, wait,
until Moran would take the bait,
his air-gun, ready, prime and cock,
and load and, at the window, chock,
prepare and take his deadly aim
at Sherlock's form, his life to claim,
and then, while holding back a howl,
pulled on the trigger with a scowl.

**The sound** of shattered glass announced
a window's breaking as Holmes pounced
upon the unsuspecting man
who then discovered that his plan
had gone awry, but still he fought
and, to death, throttle Holmes, he sought
but Watson, with his gun butt, struck
his head and showed him that his luck
had run out as the piercing trill
of Sherlock's police whistle, shrill,
called reinforcements to the room
and Colonel Moran saw his doom
as Lestrade and policemen, two,
came running in with great ado
and took the prisoner in-hand,
compliance from him, to demand,
and, to Holmes, heard the man repeat,
in utter and complete defeat,
"you clever fiend" for well he knew
that, to its end, his life now drew.

**Lestrade**, for charges, then expressed
'Attempted Murder' but confessed
surprise when told by Holmes he had,
in custody, the evil cad
who'd foully murdered young Adair
by bullet fired through the air
in silence by that air-gun used
that very night, as Watson mused
on Sherlock's actual death had not
the sleuth seen through Moran's foul plot,
then listened as his friend explained
that Moran was a man disdained
who made a living cheating those
who, playing cards for money, chose
but was uncovered by Adair
who, being honest, playing fair,
had threatened Moran whose composure
could not countenance exposure,
making plans, malign, though clever,
silencing Adair forever.

......................................................

**When Holmes**, his mind rested and slack,
said that he might well welcome back
Professor Moriarty so
that he, with such a mind, could go
to battle, for he felt the urge
to find a case which well might purge
the boredom which infused his mind,
Watson declared it was unkind
to hope that such an evil man
- that diabolic artisan -
might return just to entertain
Holmes' underused majestic brain
when peaceful protests were replaced
as, flustered-madly, reddened-faced,
burst in John Hector McFarlane
announcing he was near insane
and most unhappy, but should not
be blamed as he, by some strange plot,
had, with a warrant, been invested
and was about to be arrested.

**With great surprise** and some confusion
at this sudden loud intrusion,
Holmes and Watson, mouths agape,
each took a little time to scrape
together a response sufficient
to this gentleman deficient
in formality, but who
had raced in desperation to
the one man whom he knew would try
to help him, when he'd explained why,
and Holmes, delighted but restrained,
took all in as the man explained
in hopeful clinging desperation
that his looming situation
"I'd endure if I just knew
that Sherlock Holmes would take a few
moments to listen, not ignore,
my story, baffling." before
Lestrade, in fear he'd go astray,
in handcuffs, led his man away.

**Lestrade, indeed**, was on his tail
presuming that he would prevail
but took some time to track his man
to Baker Street, and so began
McFarlane's narrative, confused,
until Lestrade, most unamused
- of London's criminals, the bane -
with warrant held for McFarlane
grasped resolutely in his hand
and who, in loud voice, did demand
McFarlane, to him, to submit
and, to a murder, full admit,
which he did not, but by request
of Holmes was freed to tell the rest
of what he'd earlier begun
- confession of the crime to shun -
while Lestrade sat - impatient, fuming -
watching McFarlane, assuming
guilt - no thought of innocence
of this foul murderous offence.

**McFarlane started** to tell all,
of how a man had come to call
on him, and that "This visitor
had need of a solicitor
in drawing up a will that day
and was, of course, willing to pay
the standard fee - and he who came
was Jonas Oldacre by name,
a man whom I had never met
but knew my mother who might fret
if told about the will in which
- Oldacre, well-off, rather rich
and having no relations, close,
and, on this point, rather verbose -
I would, with great priority,
inherit the majority
of property the man possessed,
to which I certainly expressed
surprise and incredulity
and questioned its propriety."

"**That night**, prepared, I travelled thence
out to his Norwood residence
where we worked on Oldacre's will
till late – not being finished till
near midnight whereupon, without
my walking-stick, I ventured out
but, in a Hotel, stayed that night
but found, arising at first light,
Oldacre was reported dead
by murder and that on my head
was placed a warrant of arrest
for there were some who could attest
that I was there and stood to gain,
the police thinking it quite plain
I'd placed him in the timber fire
which blazed just like a funeral pyre
and then there was the blood found on
my walking-stick." and whereupon,
as fires in his mind were stoked,
Sherlock's suspicions were provoked.

**McFarlane's fingerprint** in blood
was found and certainty would flood
through Sherlock's mind, for then he knew
his man was innocent, and flew
at once to Norwood, out to where
he seen no fingerprint was there
the day before, and he could sense
a plot and, so, a new intense
inspection of Oldacre's house
he'd start so not the smallest mouse
would be ignored, as Watson took
to hidden files and found a book
revealing all – then Holmes, returning,
mind afire and blazing, burning
with desire as, then, he called
Lestrade who was a tad appalled
as Holmes set gathered straw alight
and watched the smoke rise with delight
then had a burly police throng
yell "Fire, Fire" loud and strong.

**This call of "Fire"** Holmes invoked,
in short time had, through fear, provoked
a series of events which proved
McFarlane's innocence and moved
Lestrade to anger and to pounce
- less so, his error, to announce -
for, in a far wall, there appeared
a door from which, as smoke had cleared,
a horror-stricken man came out,
a man the fuss was all about
who was, in fact, Oldacre who
had convinced all he'd succumbed to
the violence of McFarlane,
though Sherlock's faith was not to wane,
and who stood there for all to see,
nowhere to hide, no way to flee,
and said it was a simple joke
at which Lestrade's great temper broke
and made him say, "A joke? Be danged!
You almost had this man here hanged."

**McFarlane's face** glowed bright with joy
and Sherlock took time to enjoy
Lestrade's admission of defeat
though Watson had thought it a cheat
that Holmes would take no credit in
the matter and Lestrade would win
the accolades, but Holmes would say
he got the glory, in his way,
for Oldacre, importantly,
had failed, as he, apparently,
was set on vengeance for he'd been
spurned by McFarlane's mother, keen
to wed one so much better than
the builder – though a poorer man -
and from Oldacre's secret file
enough was found to wipe the smile
right from his lips, and all could trace
his fear on learning what he'd face
was prison time for being rash,
as creditors took all his cash.

. . . . . . . . . . . . . . . . . . . . . . . . . . . . . . . . . . . . . . . . .

## The Dancing Men

**Watson, intent** upon some task,
looked puzzled as he heard Holmes ask
a question of him which implied
that he'd unconsciously supplied
his inner thoughts from deep within
his mind, for Holmes had, with a grin,
declared, in query form, that he,
his friend, was not inclined to be
drawn to investing hard-earned cash
in something he considered rash
which Holmes said were South African
securities which caused this man,
this doctor, soldier, to demand
that Holmes explain how, out of hand,
he could have known that such had been
upon his mind and he, less keen
to act than he had been before
was negative upon that score,
agreeing with Holmes' mental amble
that it was too great a gamble.

**Thus, did Watson**, of a mind
to question Holmes, set out to find
the nature of Holmes' thought process,
- unless it was a lucky guess -
which led onto the conclusion
no pecuniary infusion
would be coming forth, for now
or ever, though he knew, somehow,
that Holmes would have it all explained
in terms so simple that it pained
a brain like Watson's, though indeed,
that brain worked at a faster speed
than did most others of its day
as work with Holmes was not child's play,
though what he showed the Doctor next
was not a message sent in text
but crafted using 'dancing men'
which Watson would, in haste, liken
to simple drawings from a child
which sent Sherlock a little wild.

**But Holmes**, though wild, did not intend
that Watson's mind would have to bend
to see the figures on the page
for what they were, and would engage
with him in one more escapade
which, certainly, for Holmes would bade
good tidings of a case to solve
but which for Watson might involve
more thinking than Holmes felt required
or that which Watson had desired,
for, with his mind cleft right in two,
was coming, Hilton Cubitt, who
had need to have a puzzle solved,
a puzzle which, of course, involved
the 'dancing men' but, too, his wife
Elsie whose mind seemed filled with strife
of which she had refused to speak
and, although Cubitt tried to tweak
the details from her, she remained
mute as, some secret, she retained.

**Cubitt, a Norfolk man**, and proud
and hardy, stalwart, never loud
but softly spoken till the time
he sensed, toward his wife, a crime
born of her native U.S.A.
though she, to him, refused to say
just what it was which gave such fear
for, when they wed, she'd made it clear
that there'd been things in her old life
she'd put behind her as his wife
though they weren't things of which to be
ashamed, just things of old which she
had cast aside – left in her wake
when, Cubitt, she agreed to take
in matrimony – but these men,
these dancing figures, plagued her when
they had appeared, and Cubitt knew
great trouble had been on the brew
and that his wife, Elsie, though scared,
knew who, to draw these men, had dared.

**Holmes looked** at samples of these 'men',
these dancing figures, and knew then
that they were messages in code
and he would have to learn the mode
of their decipherment before
he could tell Cubitt any more,
so asked, if further 'men' appeared,
he'd copy them before he cleared
them all from view, and send them on
to Baker Street and, thereupon,
Holmes would construct a table to
decode this 'writing', making do
by substituting letters for
each type of 'man' without error,
which was proceeding well until
a message came, one to instill
in him frustration and regret
for he, focused on codes, had let
his client down, for he'd been shot
to death in some obscure plot.

**The death of Cubitt** sent Holmes out
to Norfolk where he heard about
the wound to Elsie Cubitt's head,
a wound which should have left her dead,
and that this wounded wife had shot
her husband there upon the spot
and, should she live, would answer for
a crime which most folk would abhor
- her husband's murder coupled to
a suicide attempt to do
what Justice would itself impose
when she would hang, all might suppose -
but Holmes perused the murder room
and saw that Cubitt met his doom
not from a bullet Elsie fired
but from the party which conspired
to do harm to her but, instead,
that party shot poor Cubitt dead
and Elsic, as her life she'd shun,
upon herself, had turned his gun.

Holmes, with his insight so profound,
saw, Hilton, in his home, had found
the one who'd drawn the dancing men
and came for Elsie Cubitt when,
enraged though very apprehensive,
Hilton fired but, with extensive
skill with firearms saw him
- that man of Elsie's secret, grim -
all danger to his person, spurn,
the bullet, dodge, and then return
the shot, in quick time, leaving dead
the Norfolk man and, then, instead
of taking Elsie, safety sought,
and Elsie, seeing all, had thought
to end her life for all was lost
- her secret, well she knew, had cost
the life of Hilton – for the man
who'd killed him, although not to plan,
was one whom she'd been promised to
but spurned - Abe Slaney - hitherto.

**Abe Slaney,** deep immersed in crime,
Holmes would identify in time
and set a trap to snare his rat
and use, for bait, those drawings that
he had decoded, then decoy
this killer back, and fast deploy
his handcuffs, and reveal to be
near death the very one whom he
had come to claim back as his own
- despite the fact Elsie had shown
complete contempt for him and had
regarded him an evil cad
and taken to a better man -
and Slaney, now distraught, began
to wail and beg it wasn't true
- unable to, his grief, subdue -
but was, for murder, then detained,
and Elsie, though she lived, remained
in Norfolk living out her days
remembering her husband's ways.

........................................

**Miss Violet Smith**, most graceful, tall
and rather queenly, came to call
on Sherlock Holmes who'd been engaged
to end the persecution waged
against John Vincent Harden and
identify the cruel brigand
who'd perpetrated acts so vile
that Holmes would go that extra mile
and not have logic set awry
nor ever be distracted by
another case but, though fatigued,
by Miss Smith was, in fact, intrigued
and at her had begun to look
and read the lady like a book
whose cover might provide a clue
which well might help him to construe
her circumstances, and one glance
toward her shoes helped him advance
- the roughness of their soles, as such -
the notion that she cycled much.

**Miss Smith explained** her father died
impoverished, and she had tried
her best to make her music pay
by taking pupils, but the day
came when the lady was alerted
that an advertisement inserted
in The Times said to contact
a certain lawyer for, in fact,
in far South Africa had died
her Uncle Ralph, so she complied
and met two men, each one a friend
of Uncle Ralph who, at his end,
asked them to notify his niece
about his passing, though this piece
of information fell on ears
of one who really had no tears
for one whom she had never known,
but one man was quite overblown
in manner, for his constant gaze
toward her set dislike ablaze.

**That fellow**, Mr. Woodley, had
not acted like some callous cad
but put Miss Smith at great unease,
the other, though, seemed keen to please,
he being called Carruthers who
was older, polite, given to
agreeable behaviour which,
although not noticeably rich,
made her accept an offer made
to her, with pay at twice the grade,
to teach his daughter music in
his country home and live within
throughout the week, although on each
weekend she'd cycle off to reach
the railway station, there to take
the train, just for her mother's sake,
and stay for two days, then return,
but found, in time, she'd have to spurn
advances from Woodley who'd come
to stay - his manner, unwholesome.

**Red-moustached**, Woodley was not
a gentleman, boasting a lot
about his wealth and how he could
give Miss Smith diamonds if she would
agree to marry him, to which,
despite his claims to be so rich,
she turned him down without a thought
but he, insisting that she ought
to reconsider, roughly grasped
the lady, and then as she gasped
for help, Carruthers pulled the man
away, but Woodley then began
to fight and knocked Carruthers down
cutting his face, then with a frown
Woodley skulked off, not to return,
Carruthers seeming then to burn
with awkwardness, but promised he
would never permit her to be
accosted such as she had been
and, for her to remain, was keen.

**Miss Violet Smith** stayed on in spite
of her experience, but quite
a strange occurrence caused some small
alarm - an incident to gall -
for, as she cycled as per plan,
behind her she observed a man
with full beard covering his face,
who, all the way along, kept pace
slowing when she did, speeding when
she raced along the road, but then
would disappear, but he was not
someone she knew nor would allot
to being Mr. Woodley who
she'd recognize, nor could she to
the one to whom she was engaged
- one Cyril Morton – but, who'd staged
this most confronting escapade,
she couldn't say, but then she made
comment Carruthers may have been,
upon her, just that bit too keen.

**Holmes then** had Watson crouch beside
the road to watch the lady ride
on by and see the bearded man
but things would never go to plan
for he would disappear before
Watson could catch him, and this wore
on Holmes' patience, so the sleuth
decided he would get the truth
himself and found Woodley and one
called Williamson had somehow done
a deal with Carruthers - who
Miss Smith rejected hitherto -
for marriage, and then would forsake
his house - a horse and trap to take
down to the station - keen to wed
her fiancé, though Holmes saw red
after he was, to meet her, late
and in a very rattled state
when Miss Smith, for her safety bound,
was simply nowhere to be found.

**Unknown to her**, her Uncle had
been very rich, but when the cad
Woodley and friend Carruthers learned
of this, they had together yearned
to both inherit, so one would
marry Miss Smith so they both could
share in that wealth, but she defied
them both and, so, Carruthers vied,
- though smitten quite sufficiently
to cycle solitarily
disguised with beard to follow on
each time Miss Smith embarked upon
weekly excursions for the train -
but all his efforts were in vain
for Woodley, using force, would take
the lady for his wife and make
the union legal, so he thought,
and, to the wedding venue, brought
Williamson in his vicar's smock,
the lady's wishes, there, to mock.

**But Williamson**, defrocked of late,
had no right to officiate
in wedding ceremonies but,
to all objections, simply shut
his ears, as he and Woodley then
abducted Miss Smith, although when
Watson and Holmes had come upon
her empty trap, Carruthers on
a rampage threatened both but changed
attention, going quite deranged
on hearing his beloved was wed
to his ex-partner when he shed
control and, with his pistol, shot
Woodley, though Holmes said he had not
been wed in any legal sense
and, though the parties still were tense,
he had defused the situation
stopped a cruel abomination,
of riches, felons, had deprived,
now waited till police arrived.

·······················································

**Dishevelled, somewhat** - out of breath -
also in spirit, near to death -
one Doctor Huxtable - first seen
as large, majestic – must have been
near his wits' end at Baker Street
where, Sherlock Holmes, he came to meet
for he, on entry, fell upon
the floor before Sherlock and John
who jumped, surprised and very shocked,
their calm demeanor soundly rocked,
and rushed to help this ponderous wreck
of human flesh and loosed the neck
of clothing by a rapid pull
at buttons, whereupon this full-
grown massive man began to rise
and, in his shocked red-faced surprise,
looked up at Holmes and Watson, then
asked for – this most distraught of men
but clearly of the learned ilk -
a biscuit and a glass of milk.

**Recovering**, this man who'd sought
out Holmes was clearly overwrought
and said that he, though now a wretch
in his appearance, came to fetch
one with the skills and bid him come
to find out just what had become
of Lord Saltire, son of the Duke
of Holdernesse, and Holmes' rebuke
dissolved the instant such a name
evocative of noble fame
came to his ears, then heard His Grace
would reward anyone who'd trace
his missing son with such a prize
- five-thousand pounds – of massive size
that even Sherlock Holmes was shaken
- all objections overtaken,
current cases placed aside -
as kidnapping and homicide
were on his mind and he perceived
a case worth all reward received.

**Now having,** Holmes' attention, caught
the schoolmaster, though clearly fraught
with consternation, then began
his explanation – why he ran
with manifest exasperation
to the one man in the nation
who could help him – telling that
this missing young aristocrat
had been abducted in the night
and nobody could say who might
have been involved in this disaster
other than the German Master,
Heidegger, who had, it seemed
- thus, worthy of suspicion, deemed -
rushed off half-dressed, descending down
the ivy, clad perhaps in gown,
for shirt and socks, untouched, were there,
but there was not found anywhere
his bicycle, so all agreed
the fellow was involved, indeed.

**Northward**, the men embarked in haste
for Holmes knew time was not to waste
but to employ efficiently,
though use was made deficiently,
for Huxtable's whisker length told
Holmes that they were full three days old
which meant that clues once new and clear
were now degraded, with the fear
that rain and traffic mixed to spoil
the traces of events and foil
the great detective's efforts to
determine what and how and who
had been involved; but came the time
to meet the personage sublime
but found his party intercepted
by someone who'd not accepted
any need for Holmes to be
involved at all and proved to be
James Wilder, a man obsessed
and keen to have the facts suppressed.

**Although his welcome** was unsound,
Holmes said he'd stay and look around
though Wilder and His Grace objected
but, with Holmes being so respected,
could not order him to drop
investigations or to stop
from prying into private matters
although, so far, into tatters
all such investigations fell
and nobody at all could tell
where Master or young Lord had gone,
though Holmes, upon the mystery, shone
the light of reason by suggesting
Heidegger's guilt needed testing
pointing out no second bike
was missing and, rather than hike
behind, the young Lord had to ride
by means another would provide
- someone unknown - and, so, the case
called for somebody else to chase.

**No ransom note** had been received
and Holmes, ever alert, perceived
that Wilder, over-protective
of the Duke, had used invective
any time his master'd been
presented questions which he'd seen
as detrimental to His Grace,
and Holmes, observant, sensed a trace
of some unknown situation
underlying his vexation,
so, Holdernesse Hall, left to find
what clues he could of any kind
about the Moor beyond the School
for Holmes, nobody's dupe or fool,
knew there he'd find the answers to
those questions dodged by Wilder who
held secrets deep and, likely, dark
and so, anew, Holmes would embark
upon his quest for Lord Saltire
and, of the actual facts, enquire.

**Gypsies were seen** but soon discounted,
so, a further search was mounted
finding tyre prints not matched
to Heidegger's, but which were patched,
a feature Holmes later observed
on one of Wilder's tyres, which served
to reinforce the sleuth's distrust
and proved, to be involved, he must,
but then Heidegger's prints were found
and later, dead, upon the ground
that Master too, killed by a blow
which Lord Saltire could not bestow
so someone else of strength had killed
the man, and Holmes, with fervour filled,
went to the local Inn and peered
into an upper window, cheered
a little, then with Watson went
with resolve on his face, intent
- his facts assured - to pay a call
upon the Duke within his Hall.

**Holmes put** it to the Duke that he
was guilty - after saying he
knew Wilder had been involved
and, though all facts were not resolved,
knew, also, the innkeeper struck
and killed Heidegger who had pluck
enough to try to help the boy,
young Lord Saltire, but the ploy
went sour when the man was killed
to which His Grace, great fear instilled,
said Wilder, jealous, made contact
- his first son, illegitimate, in fact -
with that innkeeper to abduct
Lord Saltire, but all such conduct
if not, by the Police, revealed,
Holmes vowed his lips forever sealed
- not to be opened afterward -
then pocketed his large reward,
and Wilder, his anger spent,
to far Australia would be sent.

. . . . . . . . . . . . . . . . . . . . . . . . . . . . . . . . . . . . . . . . . .

## Black Peter

**When Captain** Peter Carey's death
occurred, Holmes heaved a mighty breath
of satisfaction and delight
well knowing that, at last, a fight
well worthy of his talents would
demand his time and, so, he should
get into harness and proceed
- as though a knight upon a steed -
but first would have to glean each fact
about the brutal fatal act
and so it was that Watson spied
a harpoon-wielding Holmes and cried
out in surprise that he explain,
right there and then, in English plain,
what he'd been doing with that spear
and Sherlock made it very clear
he'd been at work attempting to
with massive effort and ado
- while it was hanging from a rig -
transfix the carcass of a pig.

**Holmes said**, in Allardyce's shop,
he tried until he had to stop
and realise, try as he might,
he could not recreate the plight
which, down at Woodman's Lee, befell
- by savage means, as all could tell -
one Captain Peter Carey who
had been a sealer, hitherto,
and was, like insects on a card,
impaled upon a wall so hard
the killer's harpoon clearly must
have been delivered by a thrust
so vicious and ferocious that
his face displayed contortions at
the moment of his savage death
when he expelled his final breath
so loudly that his scream of pain
was such his daughter would remain
so terrified she could not move;
though, of his death, she did approve.

**She blessed** whoever struck the blow
that killed her father, such a low
regard had people for the man,
but, none-the-less, Holmes' case began
by looking at each basic clue
and giving each detail its due
consideration till it proved
quite innocent and was removed
from all contention to supply
the facts about just who and why
had done the deed for reasons yet
to be established, soon to get
attention from one who would look
beyond the crime to what it took
to have a hefty man suspended
on a harpoon which had ended
through his body, bones and all,
into a solid wooden wall
especially when Holmes couldn't pierce
a hanging pig with thrusting, fierce.

**Inspector** Stanley Hopkins called
on Holmes declaring he was galled
and quite bamboozled and distressed
by Cary's case which he confessed
was far too much for him to solve
alone, so asked Holmes to involve
himself in the investigation
so he'd have some explanation
of a most perplexing matter,
so Holmes, never keen on chatter
- such as Hopkins had begun
and Holmes invariably would shun -
said that the newspaper reports
- to Holmes, accounts of poorer sorts -
spoke of a seal-skin artifact
- the man's tobacco pouch, in fact -
although he had possessed no pipe,
then at this, Holmes began to gripe
and say that, with this, he would start
and then, his case, begin to chart.

**Hopkins proceeded** to reveal
what facts he had with stifled zeal
and Holmes was told the man was called
'Black Peter' by all those appalled
by what he'd said and what he'd done
and no good word was there for one
too often drunk and violent,
malicious and malevolent,
a perfect fiend who'd flog his wife
and daughter who'd both run for life,
and, on his ship 'Sea Unicorn',
had nothing but contempt and scorn
to offer with a heavy hand,
and, as at sea, he was on land
where, in his 'cabin', he would sit,
a hut, in fact, which he would fit
out as if he were still aboard
the 'Unicorn', and where he'd hoard
dark secrets from an evil past
which had him, down to Hades, cast.

**Further clues** got Holmes to thinking -
like the rum two men were drinking
though brandy and whisky had been
available which, to a keen
and skilled detective, would infer
the men were sailors who'd prefer
rum's heaviness and sweetened taste;
then Hopkins, moving on in haste,
produced a small book bearing notes
and reams of numbers, cryptic quotes,
and C.P.R. and J.H.N.
which Holmes read, with great acumen,
as Canadian Pacific
Railway but, with such specific
clues at hand, Holmes would admit
he now had trouble making fit
scenarios considered first,
but further clues would whet his thirst
for bloodstains on the notebook told
a story which, to Holmes, was gold.

**More clues** had shown somebody'd been
inside the cabin, very keen
to find some object, so a trap
was set and caught a distraught chap
called Neligan who'd then admit
he'd dropped the notebook in a fit
of panic as he fled the room
where Peter Carey met his doom
and that his long-lost father had,
- though branded falsely as a cad -
his bank's securities, removed
for reasons which, if ever proved,
would show he acted for the best
- for proof, the son would never rest -
but, bound for Norway, disappeared
- lost overboard, so many feared -
but some securities were sold
by Peter Carey, and this told
young Neligan he had to trace
and meet the Captain face to face.

**Yet Neligan** had not the strength
to kill Black Peter so, at length,
Holmes set a trap to catch a man
with strength sufficient, in a plan
to snare a burly ship's harpooner
which, it turned out, was no sooner
advertised than caught the one
who had, the deed so deadly, done
and who was Patrick Cairns who had
once sailed with the evil cad
and, for his silence, would demand
a sum of money, but the hand
of Carey held a knife he'd thrust
at Cairns who, fearing that he must
react with deadly force or die,
and swearing that he told no lie,
had grabbed the harpoon from the wall
and, straight at Carey, struck with all
the strength that he could gather, hence
he'd killed the man in self-defence.

..................................................

89

## *Charles Augustus Milverton*

**Returning home**, Holmes spied a card
upon a table, gripped it hard
then threw it angrily aside,
retreated to the fireside,
while Watson, baffled, had been quick
to stoop down to the floor and pick
it up to find out why Holmes had
- the fellow's face, in anger, clad -
seen fit to throw the thing away
when all the item had to say
was Charles Augustus Milverton,
Agent, of Hampstead, whereupon
Holmes said, in all of London, he
was quite the worst man who might be
encountered for he was the sort
who, by his nature, would resort
to blackmail to enrich his bank
accounts - so, from his presence shrank
for he was well below the class
of snake which slithered through the grass.

**Holmes added** that the man was there
by invitation - anywhere
being preferable to sharing space
with one who threatened to disgrace
a lady who'd been compromised
by letters written, ill-advised -
but he had been engaged to try
to get the fellow to comply
and to accept a lower price
- Holmes saying this was his advice -
for Lady Eva Brackwell could
not meet the fellow's price but would
agree to something lower which
she could afford – not being rich -
and Holmes declared this was the best
of all outcomes, and his request
was that the letters stay unread
to let the wedding go ahead
for, Lady Eva, brought undone,
could never profit anyone.

**But Milverton** insisted he
would profit greatly whether she
paid him or called the wedding off
and, at the words of Holmes, would scoff
by saying he had several more
such Ladies pending who'd deplore
the fate they'd witness suffered by
one such as them who'd dare defy
his foul resolve and, so, would pay
the sum demanded, or the day
would come they'd have to face the same
as Holmes' client, feel the shame
of ill-considered letters bought
by Milverton who keenly sought
to pay disloyal servants or
unworthy former suitors for
a single imprudent remark
on paper, just enough to spark
distrust in those who couldn't face
the thought of living down disgrace.

**Holmes faced** the man, this Milverton,
but failed to move him, whereupon
he called to Watson to assist,
- should Milverton dare to resist -
in using force upon this guest,
unwelcome, to make him divest
himself of letters harmful to
his client, but the man would do
no more than show a pistol, large,
and say that he could bring a charge
against them both, for he was now
the one being wronged, and that somehow
the Lady Eva had to find
the money, so Holmes, in a bind,
allowed the man to go his way
then, when he'd left, all he could say
was that he'd wait till all was dark
then, to the fellow's home, embark
and break in and recover all
the letters and, disgrace, forestall.

**Watson then dithered**, but agreed
upon conditions that they'd need
to only take from Milverton
those letters which were used upon
his victims – those and nothing more -
and then decided that, before
they undertook this risky task,
each man would need a silken mask
and pair of silent shoes, and wear
their evening clothes so they could swear
they'd both been to the theatre and
were walking home and had a grand
night out, though Holmes, before he'd act
would have to make a sound contact
within the house of Milverton
and spoke with Agatha upon
the house's layout, learning much
- though he'd become engaged, as such,
at least in principle – and now,
to so proceed, knew where and how.

**Holmes**, to Watson's great relief,
was not the sort to be a thief
though, had he been, he'd be the best
for Watson, himself, could attest
to Sherlock's skill in breaking in
to houses without fuss or din
which might alert their occupants
to uninvited miscreants;
and so it was, in dead of night,
the soft-shoed pair, masks fastened tight,
approached the home of Milverton
and entered, Holmes descending on
a window into which a hole
he'd cut and crawl through, like a mole,
Watson in tow, and then proceed
- the need for silence, both to heed -
to where he'd learned that Milverton
kept all his documents, and on
arrival saw a fire burn
and heard poor Watson's innards churn.

**Holmes opened** up the safe with ease
but heard a sound which didn't please
the sleuth one bit, for Milverton
was speaking nearby, so Watson
and he, behind a curtain, hid
as Milverton entered, livid
with someone who was running late,
someone he started to berate
and ask what was it she might sell
but then gave out a muffled yell
of stark surprise when she produced
a pistol which had him reduced
to cringing as he recognised
a lady who'd been compromised
by blackmail - and whose husband died
of shock when he had been advised
of letters held – and then the pair
heard six shots ring out through the air
all followed by the man's death throes
in payment for his victim's woes.

**The lady** made a quick escape
and Sherlock Holmes, mouth still agape,
locked both the doors and to the fire
threw everything he could acquire
out from the opened safe, then he
and Watson, wanting then to be
- as fast as they could run - away
gave out a muffled short "Hooray!"
on reaching home at Baker Street
- the rising sun's rays there to meet -
then contemplated what occurred
and how the fellow's death had spurred
them into action which was fraught
with danger, great, if they'd been caught,
but Holmes and Watson, next day, found,
when, on a walk through London, bound,
a portrait of that lady who
killed Milverton, and chose to do
no more than keep her secret, dark,
and, of her act, make no remark.

**Some sought** out Holmes on matters grim
when chances had turned rather slim
for cases to be solved by those
unable to bring to a close
such matters needing special ways
of looking at those vague displays
of evidence; and it transpired
Inspector Lestrade had required
the expertise Holmes brought along
- pursuit of truth, rejecting wrong
hypotheses not matching fact
which, followed otherwise, detract
from finding meaning in the clues
left by the felon and subdues
the logic of a line of thought -
all which Lestrade, in anguish, sought
when busts of great Napoleon
someone had stolen, whereupon,
not keeping them, the thief, instead,
to fragments, smashed the fellow's head.

**Lestrade** had thought no one could hate,
so much, an image of the late
and long-dead Emperor of France
but had no theory to advance
unless the man was raving mad
or was a hooligan gone bad
who'd done the damage just for fun
and, finished, had gone on the run,
but, two more busts, identical
- which made things problematical -
were then destroyed the self-same way
and their destroyer went away
without reward in goods or cash,
Lestrade, though, never acting rash,
had, up to this point, found no clue
sufficient to help him pursue
some over-wrought iconoclast
or anti-French enthusiast,
while Watson, never one to panic,
said he might be monomanic.

**Holmes refuted** Watson's notion
showing no tact or emotion,
just analysis, pragmatic
- confident more than dogmatic -
while Lestrade, though energetic,
rarely could be sympathetic
to the ways of Holmes when he
had not sufficient clues to be
prepared to share his line of thought
- which those around him felt he ought -
although Lestrade had called Holmes in
when his ideas were wearing thin,
but, in the mind of Holmes, there grew
another notion which he knew
would show that hate was not involved
and that the crime would be resolved
not chasing maniacs bombastic
nor strange types iconoclastic
but by thinking thoughts which thrust
the thinker to the actual bust.

**Before Holmes** had the time to act,
Lestrade had news which would detract
from thoughts of nuisance for, this time,
he told all gathered that the crime
of murder, foul, had been committed
and a bust, too, was submitted
to destruction as before
although no one could offer more
upon the matter than the bust
was now the fourth one dashed to dust
and fragments, and they all had been
identical, and that a keen
horn-handled bloodied knife was found
beside the dead man, on the ground,
and, in his pocket, was a map
and photograph of some strange chap
sharp-featured, somewhat simian,
with bushy eyebrows, but a man
who had – this adding to the puzzle -
a profile like a baboon's muzzle.

**Morse Hudson** had a shop which sold
artworks and it was he who told
Holmes of the broken bust he found,
but, when told two that he sent 'round
to Dr. Barnicot had been
destroyed, he vented out his spleen
at senseless acts, though when he saw
the picture of the man whose jaw
protruded, he advised Holmes that
the man was Beppo, who'd worked at
Gelder and Co. who'd made a batch
of six, of which, three, they'd dispatch
to Hudson and the rest remit
to Harding Brothers's shop, to whit,
the source of that smashed on the night
the man was killed and gave such fright
to Horace Harker, Journalist,
and, all of this, Holmes would enlist
to set a trap to snare the one
who theft and murder, both, had done.

**The journalist** was quite obsessed
and had the criminal assessed,
as lunatic and dangerous
with tendencies quite murderous,
which Holmes would use after he'd seen
Gelder and Co. to find who'd been
involved in manufacturing
the busts, and found a blustering
Germanic manager surprised
at all the fuss, who then advised
Holmes they were not expensive, then
gave out an exclamation when
he saw the photograph, for it
showed Beppo whom he would admit
he'd once employed but had been sent
to prison where, a year, he'd spent
for stabbing someone in a fight
though, to have been released, he might,
but still his cousin was employed
at Gelders and, their trust, enjoyed.

**Holmes had learned** Beppo had been
employed by Hudson who'd not seen
the fellow since two days before
the first bust was destroyed, though more
Holmes could not say, except the man
Beppo might well have had a plan
to search the files to see who'd bought
the busts, all which told Holmes he ought
find out, from Harding Brothers, who
had also sold the other two
remaining busts, and this being done
selected from two names just one
and waited outside his address
and were rewarded with success
when Beppo broke in, then emerged
with bust in hand, and then converged
both Holmes and Watson as he broke
the bust to pieces with one stroke,
though nothing in the shards was found,
but still Holmes knew his plan was sound.

**Just one** bust now remained intact
so Holmes paid well so he'd extract
it from its owner, for he knew,
inside, was some object which drew
Beppo to risk incarceration,
so Holmes, in anticipation,
smashed the bust to find within
the Borgia Pearl and, with a grin,
said Beppo took it from the man
he later killed, but made a plan,
to hide it a drying bust
of great Napoleon and trust
he could retrieve it when he'd served
his sentence and, till then, preserved
his secret, though stepped in the snare
of Sherlock Holmes who would declare
he'd solved the case, the killer caught,
a lesson to Lestrade he'd taught,
and in his safe the pearl was thrown,
but then what happened is unknown.

..................................................

**Holmes had**, at times, issued rebukes
but, it occurred that, at Saint Luke's
- a College in a famous town
which was for centuries renown
for its famed University -
the threat of great adversity
caused Hilton Soames' to leave his post
of tutor, for he was most
desirous that Holmes assist
- and would upon that point insist -
him in a quest to find the cad
who, in deceit, shamefully had,
to read some printers' proofs, been lured
- test papers left out, unsecured
and open in the man's domain -
but Sherlock Holmes would make it plain
that he - at this greatly annoyed -
was, for the present time, employed
at studies of his own which no
distractions would make him forego.

**Holmes then told** Soames to notify
Police, which did not satisfy
the man one bit and he retorted,
if the matter was reported
to officialdom, there'd be
a dreadful scandal, one which he
would see avoided like the plague
and, clarifying something vague,
proceeded to relate the fact
that there had been a lowly act
and students may have been involved
and he would like the matter solved
without delay for someone had
- one most definitely a cad -
encountered his door, quite unlocked,
and entered without having knocked
to find upon a table top
- and lacking decency to stop -
examination proofs spread out
then read them, graciousness to flout.

**The printer's proofs** had been supplied
and Soames was keenly occupied
ensuring no mistakes remained
- for none were ever entertained -
in passages of ancient Greek:
Thucydides – not for the meek
but for the scholar well-prepared -
for much was hinged upon who fared
the best in its correct translation
- cheating leading to vexation -
for the winner would be due
the Scholarship of Fortescue,
- a princely sum for any student -
thus, it had been quite imprudent
that the proofs were left exposed,
and, at this, Sherlock Holmes supposed
that Soames had evidence to show
someone had read the proofs to know
their content in advance and, so,
an honest effort might forego.

**Soames told** the sleuth when he returned
that all his insides shook and churned
when, in his door, a key he spied,
a duplicate which he'd supplied
to Bannister, a servant, who
was not the sort of man to do
such things, but on this day it would
have consequences dire should
the word get out, for there were spread
around his table, clearly read,
the proofs, and that there'd been a cut
made in the table's cover, but
the cut was very clean and new,
and then another thing which drew
the man's attention was a ball
of clay and sawdust, and this all
combined to whet the probing mind
of Holmes who said he'd gladly find
whoever had intruded, and
reverse this action, underhand.

**Holmes, energised**, ever alert
to clues, both hidden and overt,
saw in the room the pages strewn,
the sharpened pencil roughly hewn
with 'NN' left upon its shaft
which Holmes, being master of his craft,
could see it was all that remained
of "Johann Faber', he explained,
and then observed the clayey ball
with grains of sawdust through it all
and roughly pyramidal in
its shape, like those Holmes found within
the tutor's bedroom showing that
the intruder had stood or sat
there as Soames had, with Bannister,
discussed the matter, sinister,
though Holmes, on this, was not fixated
but the sleuth had concentrated
- rather than whoever cheated -
on where Bannister was seated.

**The servant** seemed to have evaded
one chair, but this notion faded
briefly, for the prime subject
moved onto whom they might suspect
which fell to students - three in all,
and on whom Holmes would pay a call -
the first being Gilchrist, sporty, smart,
an athlete from the very start
who, at the jumps and hurdles, got
his College Blue and who was not
the highest on Soames' suspect list
but, of the second, would insist
that Daulat Ras, in Greek, was weak
but he was steady, not a sneak,
then moved to Miles McLaren who
was brilliant when he'd chosen to
apply himself but had, of late,
been rather less than passionate
about his studies and, with dread,
must look to the exam ahead.

**Three students**, Holmes had on his list,
but would, on Bannister, insist
suspicion fell, at least in that
the fellow was evasive at
being asked about the chair he took
which Holmes could never overlook
for logic said he should have taken
one much closer, and seemed shaken
far too much when interviewed
and clearly, inside, something brewed
for he was balanced on an edge
and had few answers left to hedge
but Holmes could see, cautiously, that
the odds of guilt had pointed at
McLaren who'd used language stark
and acted with a temper dark
but Holmes, too, found the clayey ball
might well precipitate downfall
for someone else, as there had been
a vital clue which Holmes had seen.

**That clue** was clay and sawdust found
right where long jumpers came to ground
and so, on Gilchrist, Holmes' eye fell
and he, when questioned, came to tell
that Bannister, years past, had served
his father and he was unnerved
when, on the tutor's chair, he found
the student's gloves and with unsound
judgement he hid them, but Gilchrist,
with much remorse would then insist
unfair advantage he'd not take
and full admission, thus, would make
for, all the night, his conscience strained
and so no other thing remained
for him to do but withdraw and
take up an offer to expand
his prospects, after this admission,
taking a police commission
in far Rhodesia, and so
Holmes said this was the way to go.

........................................

**John Watson**, snug against the storm,
looked out upon the sodden form
of Baker Street one dreary night
and strained to see with feeble light,
while Sherlock Holmes, no case to solve,
had taken time out to involve
himself in one historic quest
deciphering a palimpsest
which he said seemingly amounts
to no more than the dull accounts
of some old Abbey long ago
- some four long centuries or so -
when, to the present, he was taken
- thoughts of palimpsests forsaken -
by the grinding of a wheel
- stone yielding to its hardened steel -
against the kerb as, to a stop,
a cab had slowed and, out, would hop
a man, them both to summon, thus,
as Holmes said "What he wants is us."

**There, Stanley Hopkins** of The Yard
ran through the rain, plummeting hard
and drenching all those fool enough
to be outdoors, but any tough
detective took good with the bad
and Hopkins had a rather sad
tale he would tell to Holmes in hope
that he'd find time to help him cope
with finding what had happened to
Willoughby Smith - a young man who
had not an enemy to count -
for suicide he'd not discount
nor accident, and murder seemed
unlikely to Hopkins who deemed
the whole thing as unfortunate
with not much to investigate
though there was doubt to give him pause
and keep an open mind because
the young man died right after he
said "The Professor – it was she!"

**Hopkins continued** giving facts
to Holmes of any artifacts
discovered, and of people who,
at Yoxley Old Place, hitherto,
had any dealings with the Law,
but all, from Hopkins, he could draw
was that all people there were true
though there had been a vital clue
found in the dead man's hand when he
had grabbed it from the one called 'She'
- a set of spectacles, no less -
a golden pince-nez to profess
to Holmes those subtle signs which he
- though no one else - could see to be
significant and would portray
the pince-nez's owner in a way,
with ease, investigators might
identify this 'She' on sight
to then, of liberty, divest
by placing 'She' under arrest.

**Holmes read** the pince-nez like a book
and said to Hopkins he should look
out for a woman, quite refined
and lady-like, although defined
by being rather short of sight
with eyes set close together, tight,
and thick of nose with shoulders round
and forehead puckered, who had found
a recent need to visit her
optician for she'd be eager
to have the nose clips fixed for they
were new and this would, thus, convey
to him she'd had them both replaced
quite recently, and might be traced
because opticians were quite rare
- even in London – and he'd spare,
despite the falling drenching rain,
some time to catch an early train
from Charing Cross – the old Kent line -
and be on site by eight or nine.

**Professor Coram** worked upon
a learned book, relying on
Willoughby Smith and others who
each had domestic tasks to do
but Holmes arrived aware that none
of these could be the guilty one
and found nobody matching the
description of the one called 'She'
had been observed, but tracks were found
which he could see were inward-bound
and saw, from marks around a lock,
someone had made them in some shock
as if surprised and, perhaps, then
had killed poor Willoughby Smith when
reacting out of fear and not
premeditation, and then got
confused – her pince-nez snatched away -
and then escaped without delay,
and Holmes, with many clues to link,
found he had much on which to think.

**And, think**, Holmes did, to good effect,
by focusing his intellect
upon what clues he had at hand
and, of his logic, take command
to rid his mind of notions, wrong,
and come up with a premise, strong,
for he could see the killer could
not have escaped and therefore should
still be inside the house, also
more food to Coram seemed to go
as though another he would feed,
and, suddenly, as though decreed,
before Holmes had the time to speak,
a high bookcase began to creak
as, like a door, it opened wide
and caused all there to look inside
to see a human form produced,
a human form which Holmes deduced
to have killed – taken by surprise -
Willoughby Smith, that young man wise.

**There, in** the light of day appeared
a woman, someone once endeared
to Prof. Coram – his wife, estranged,
and acting, seemingly, deranged -
who stated Coram was, in fact,
a Russian who, in such an act
of treachery had saved his life,
betraying, not only his wife,
but friends of whom some had been sent
to prison, while some others went
- this Brotherhood of Nihilists -
to meet their deaths as terrorists
who fought the regime of the Czar
while Coram sought to run so far
away and change his name that none
would ever know what he had done,
though Anna, his abandoned wife,
regardless of her risk to life,
had tracked him down, a note to send
demanding justice for a friend.

**Anna explained** how she had been
young and naïve but very keen
for reform, though by violence
and Nihilist malevolence,
police were killed and Alexis,
a friend who placed an emphasis
on peaceful protest, was denounced
by him, her husband, who had pounced
on gaining freedom and reward
and lived in comfort afterward,
but Anna, contrite for her crime,
said that she had so little time
to live, for poison she had taken,
notions of revenge forsaken,
pleading that before her end
somebody'd take, to free her friend,
a document, and Holmes agreed
and, to the Embassy with speed,
went off, that friend's freedom to chase,
while Stanley Hopkins closed the case.

......................................................

97

**A great behemoth** of a man
had filled the doorway and began
to tell Holmes of what had to be
a looming great catastrophe
if Holmes could not help him locate
a man who'd chosen to vacate
his lodgings just before the day
he was to run into the fray
and from the Right Wing win the game,
this fleet Three-Quarter by the name
of Godfrey Staunton who, by far,
had no one, in the land, on par
for judgement or for general skill
when, from the scrum, the ball would spill
for he would wait to see the form
of play demanded, then he'd storm
on in and take the ball and run
and, any opposition, stun
as sinewed limbs and muscled joints
would cross the line and take the points.

**But Cyril Overton** did not
seem able to suggest what plot
or circumstance might keep this man,
this crack Three-Quarter, from his plan
of beating Oxford when they met
next day, so Overton would fret
- he being skipper of the team -
until he knew Staunton, the cream
of Cambridge, was there to run out
and then inflict a massive rout
on Oxford, otherwise there'd be,
for Cambridge, a catastrophe,
and Hopkins of The Yard could not
assist but told Overton to trot
around to Baker Street to find
that Sherlock Holmes might be of mind
to take an interest in the case
and have sufficient time to chase
down – being quite a mystery thwarter -
any missing crack Three-Quarter.

**The skipper**, Overton, said he
had no idea of what could be
the reason for the man's absence,
for trickery or violence
would not seem to have been involved
although the mystery evolved
after the players had retired
by ten, for Overton required
that all must have sufficient rest
so each man would be at his best,
but spoke to Overton before
the man turned in, and saw he wore
the look of being bothered and
quite pale, though he would demand
he had a headache, only slight,
and then he turned in for the night
but soon a rough and bearded man
brought him a note which then began
a series of events which led
the skipper, to Holmes, having sped.

**Staunton, pole-axed**, fell right back
into a chair, his muscles slack,
but then rebounded, rushing out,
the bearded man in tow, about
some urgent matter yet unknown
to Overton, though it was shown
that Staunton hadn't gone to bed
and that some matter, in him, bred
such consternation he had not
sufficient time to say what got
him so upset, so Overton,
with few facts then to work upon,
contacted Cambridge, finding none
had seen the man, but then someone
suggested that Lord Mount-James might
have some suggestions on the plight
of Staunton, nephew and heir to
the man's estate and fortune, who
had little fondness or regard
for one so miserly and hard.

Holmes quizzed the porter finding that
the bearded man - not thin, not fat,
but medium in looks – was near
to fifty, plus he made it clear
no worker nor a gentleman
was he, but, as the two men ran,
the word "Time" caught the porter's ear
and both men had the look of fear
about them, then it came to light
a telegram came on that night
for Staunton, who in turn replied
and wrote upon the blank supplied
a message using ink and pen
which Holmes was to recover when
he saw the blotting pad displayed
the final words which said, dismayed
in tone, "Stand by us for God's sake."
which told to Holmes much was at stake
but, before plans could be contrived,
a surly Lord Mount-James arrived.

The fellow had turned up and would
complain as loudly as he could
about Holmes' interference, but
the sleuth's reply in short time shut
the miser's mouth by telling him
his missing nephew posed a grim
scenario for he well may
be held to show some gang the way
to steal the Mount-James fortune, huge,
by force or subtle subterfuge,
then, with the fellow silenced, he
found Staunton's telegram to be
of little help, so caught the train
to Cambridge, there to ascertain
from Dr. Armstrong of the School
of Medicine – nobody's fool -
if he might know the whereabouts
of Godfrey Staunton, but his shouts
of indignation told Holmes he
knew more than where the man might be.

The Doctor said he knew the man
but, rather yielding to the plan
of Holmes, he was antagonistic
making Holmes feel pessimistic
though he pressed on, forceful, and
despite the Doctor's reprimand
insisted that no threat was posed
to Staunton, but the Doctor closed
discussions harshly, then Holmes saw
upon a desk a page to draw
the Doctor out, for it displayed
Staunton's receipt, but then, dismayed,
the Doctor had his butler tell
both Holmes and Watson they'd do well
to leave forthwith, and they obeyed,
but matters had, to Holmes, conveyed
- as thirteen guineas were involved,
a tidy fee – he'd have things solved
by watching where the Doctor went
as if a hound upon a scent.

Armstrong was followed by the sleuth
until, at last, he learned the truth
of Godfrey Staunton's whereabouts,
then, mindful of the warning shouts
of Armstrong, stepped inside to find
his quarry, quite out of his mind,
though this brought Holmes little relief,
for there was Staunton struck with grief
for, on a bed, his young wife lay
dead from consumption just that day
and Armstrong strongly remonstrated
Holmes for having demonstrated
neither sympathy or tact
but would, this stern rebuke, retract
when Holmes swore he'd not acted for
the miserly Lord Mount-James, nor
would he make public any fact
for he, by principle, must act
to keep the truth where it belonged -
to do less would have Staunton wronged.

........................................................

## *The Abbey Grange*

**John Watson's slumber** was once more
disturbed and broken well before
the sun had risen, as his friend
- one Sherlock Holmes – said to expend
no wasted time in rising and
in dressing so they could command
a cab for Charing Cross to catch
the first Kent train with great dispatch
to Marsham where, at Abbey Grange,
there had occurred an action strange
and which Detective Hopkins hoped
- as he in truth just hadn't coped -
might be examined by the one
man who might find what brought undone
Sir Eustace Brackenstall by act
of violence with great impact
upon his skull, though Randalls, three,
were seen but, since, had time to flee,
and, never in a rush to blame,
Holmes knew, afoot, was now The Game.

**Young Stanley Hopkins** knew enough
to call Holmes in when things got tough
and Holmes knew well Hopkins was not
so foolish that he might allot,
without investigation, guilt
but wait with patience till he'd built
a story plausible and sound
with evidence, himself, he'd found
though he, at times, realized he'd need
the eye of Holmes if he'd succeed
for, though the case seemed ironclad,
the young detective simply had
'way back, within his mind, the thought
that something didn't mesh which ought,
and that his skills, though well refined,
- with evidence at hand, combined -
could not make sense of all he saw
and knew that Holmes would see the flaw
invisible to all but him
and solve this case overtly grim.

**Holmes felt** the case was sure to quell
the demons which would come to dwell
inside his brain to tease his mind
unless a mystery of kind
so enigmatic and profound
would have him looking over ground
and chasing inconsistent clues
of false and most deceptive hues
which lesser men would not observe
- nor any credit would deserve -
beset by contradictions, huge,
maintained by subtle subterfuge
and untruths meant to divert blame
in some craftily-maintained game
whose outcome would have been assured
and someone's innocence secured
should he have, back in London, stayed
and not to Marsham, Kent, have strayed
to solve the situation strange
which had occurred at Abbey Grange.

**Hopkins** had called, full seven times,
for Holmes to come and help with crimes
he could not solve, but this one posed,
as Holmes, the sleuth of sleuths, supposed,
some element yet unexplained
which Hopkins had not entertained,
yet, on arrival, Holmes would find
that Hopkins, now, was of a mind
to close his case and put the blame
upon the 'three Randalls' whose fame
was such that all around would know
that one of them had struck the blow
which killed Sir Eustace Brackenstall
on being found inside the Hall
intent on robbery - so told
the Lady Brackenstall with bold
determination on her face
despite the fact that Holmes could trace,
upon her forehead, then her arm,
the evidence of recent harm.

**The injured** Lady Brackenstall
- nee Mary Fraser – could recall
that via the French window had come
an older man – a look fearsome
upon his face – and then two more,
though younger than the one before,
and she'd been struck upon the face
and had passed out, but roused in place
upon a chair, both gagged and bound
- a bellrope, pulled down, tied around
her tightly – then Sir Eustace ran
into the room, but then the man,
the older one, had struck him dead
and she had, overcome with dread,
fainted away, but, coming to,
found all the murderer would do
was take some silver and then fill
three glasses full of wine to swill,
then left her there as all withdrew,
and that, she swore, was all she knew.

**But Holmes** would learn all was not well
between the couple, and heard tell
of frequent violence upon
the Lady by her husband on
occasions of great drunkenness
which took all thoughts of happiness
away for her who had, before
her marriage, led a free, far more
relaxed existence in the land
of South Australia, though the grand
and noble title turned her head,
but Holmes, although alarmed, instead
asked, of himself, why she'd been left
alive, and why was wine and theft
still in the killer's mind when he,
identifiable, would be
most surely hanged if ever caught,
and, thus, the whole matter was fraught
with half-truths and discrepancy
as Holmes could sense a fallacy.

**Holmes. eagle eye,** two clues, perused:
the wine and then the bellrope used
to bind the Lady Brackenstall,
for beeswing in the glasses, all,
told one glass, from the bottle, came,
the next two from that very same
first glass, not bottle – this had been
the pouring order - for he'd seen
no floating beeswing, thus she lied,
and also that cork bits implied
the corkscrew used was rather short
- a common multiplex knife sort -
and that the bellrope had been cut
and then its end had been frayed, but
whoever did the cutting should
have been more than six feet and would
have been quite agile and could cope,
as sailors would, with tying rope
and Holmes, to a conclusion, came:
the three Randalls were not to blame.

**Though Lady** Brackenstall complained,
Holmes had, in short time, ascertained
a ship's captain, whom she had met
at sea, was visibly upset
on hearing how mistreated she
had been, and Holmes found out where he
resided then, a summons, sent
which he obeyed and quickly went
to Lady Brackenstall's defence
and said that he had loved her, hence
he came to help her but engaged
an armed Sir Eustace, full enraged,
and whom he struck dead while defending
life and limb, the matter ending
knowing that he'd likely face
a charge of murder, so, at pace,
a ruse was organised which fooled
Hopkins but never Holmes, well-schooled
in such deception, though he'd not
blame anyone for such a plot.

## The Second Stain

"Oh woe is me, and all is lost
and Britons, all, may bear the cost
such that the nation may not cope."
within him wailed Trelawney Hope
when he discovered that - by theft,
he had presumed, by someone deft
and skilled in burglary at night
who worked with neither sound nor light -
a letter in his trust was gone
and that the light which, on him, shone
would be extinguished, not to be
relit, and great catastrophe
might fall on Britain should it come
into the hands of some loathsome
unprincipled agent who'd sell
it to the highest bidder, well
aware that war might well result
and, to destruction, catapult
the nation, so, with needs, corrective,
sought out London's great detective.

Prime Minister, Lord Bellinger,
had seemed the very harbinger
of death when, with Trelawney Hope,
he met with Sherlock Holmes - to grope
at straws, Holmes felt – for he was not
prepared to trust Holmes and allot
to him all facts pertaining to
the misplaced letter, leading to
rejection by Holmes to be called
to action, leaving quite appalled
this Premier of Britain and
his staunch, reliable right-hand,
Trelawney Hope – the Secretary
for European Affairs – and wary
of the dangers of release
of facts most certain to increase
the risk of war and likely to
result in scandal which would do
much damage to the land's prestige
and Bellinger's noblesse-oblige.

Lord Bellinger, upset, unused
to such rejection, unamused,
begrudgingly conceded to
share all with Holmes if he would do,
with great discretion, what he might
to find this letter lest a blight
descend on Britain such that she,
weakened by war, might cease to be
the greatest power on the globe,
so it was up to Holmes to probe
all nooks and crannies of the land,
search every miscreant at hand,
seek out those who'd do Britain ill,
delve into all such matters till
that errant envelope was found
and was, for Whitehall, duly bound
so none beside those very few
with need to know would ever view
its contents, dangerous and dire,
whose words could set the world afire.

A foreign potentate, Holmes learned,
had sent the letter as he yearned
to increase what prestige he had
forgetting protocols forbad
such action – hasty, ill-conceived -
which certainly could be perceived
as threatening, and Holmes knew well
he'd have to act quite fast to quell
the dangers Bellinger outlined
so Holmes, with matters now defined
and given sanction to proceed,
questioned Trelawney Hope at speed
about his dispatch box and who
might have had ready access to
its contents, to which he replied
- though hating what this had implied -
that he had faith in all within
his household and could not begin
to conceive in his mind just who,
this thing, deplorable, might do.

**Upon departure** of the men,
Holmes took the time to think and, then,
in contemplation, pipe in hand,
considered who might, in the land,
have been involved – knaves premiere -
then Oberstein, La Rothiere
and Lucas all came to his mind,
but Watson said he wouldn't find
Eduardo Lucas helpful for
this possible perpetrator
was murdered on the very night
the envelope was lost, and right
away Holmes knew he was their man
and, so, out to his house began
but, when informed a lady'd called,
Holmes' forward impetus was stalled
for this was Lady Hilda who,
wife of Trelawney Hope, seemed to
have terror written on her face
which certainly seemed out of place.

**The Lady** entered, quite perturbed,
with none of her emotions curbed
but full-expressed - her fear betrayed
with apprehension full-portrayed -
and asked Holmes what the document
contained, and if it might foment
not war but some adverse outcome
upon her husband, unwelcome,
which might destroy the man's career,
but Holmes refused to volunteer
the contents or the dreadful fate
for Europe it might generate
should it, in public, be released
and so the Lady's pleading ceased
and Holmes went to the murder scene,
investigations to convene
there with Lestrade of Scotland Yard
who, knowing he liked problems, hard,
asked Holmes to ponder and explain
the mystery of a second stain.

**One blood stain** on the carpet and
one offset on the floor would stand
as proof the carpet had been turned
and Holmes, with lady Hilda spurned
by him that very day, suspected
her involvement, and expected
she'd been there, and found she had
despite police rules ironclad,
but not to murder, for the man
- the villain in the evil plan -
was killed in frenzy by his wife
who - insane, jealous – took a knife
and stabbed him in a maddened trance
then fled away to distant France,
so Holmes deduced the Lady gave
Lucas this document to save
herself from being compromised
by notes she'd written, ill-advised,
which Lucas held, and felt that she
under suspicion, had to be.

**Holmes sought** the Lady and accused
her forcefully; though, unamused,
she just as forcefully defied
Holmes and indignantly denied
she'd moved the carpet so she'd trace
the letter in its hiding place
but, though defiance, she'd display,
Holmes, unrelenting, stripped away
her frail denials, one by one,
and, when this heavy task was done,
Holmes, in the dispatch box, then hid
the letter and, on being bid
to show results, said, as before,
Trelawney Hope should check once more
his dispatch box, and there he found
the missing letter safe and sound
to great relief and cries of joy
though Bellinger could see some ploy
at work - but Holmes was most emphatic:
"We, too, have secrets, diplomatic!"

# _The Valley of Fear_

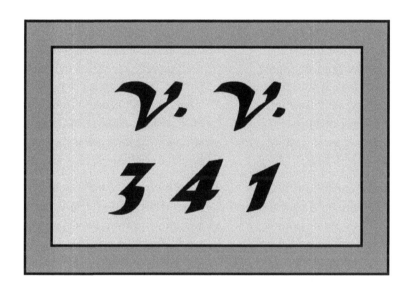

**With breakfast untouched** on his plate
a wistful Holmes perused a late
delivered scrap of paper and
- holding it up high within his hand
to be observed in stronger light
so he, with practiced patience, might
discover any writing form -
he then, with understated scorn,
declared, just from its Grecian 'e',
the letter must, by Porlock, be
and, if it was from Porlock's pen,
as it seemed to have been, well then
the matter must be urgent, so
all other matters he'd forego
for Porlock was the nom-de-plume
of someone, Sherlock would presume,
who had something he felt he must
convey as some encoded trust
for this strange enigmatic party
was in the pay of Moriarty.

**But disappointment** followed soon
for Porlock – though he'd been a boon
to Sherlock as he could be bought
for information Holmes had sought -
the vital key, did not provide,
and so Holmes had no way to guide
him through the coded message but,
Holmes read that Porlock, scared, had shut
of all of his communication
fearful of recrimination,
savage, from his master's hand,
so Sherlock Holmes then took command
and scanned the first letter once more
more closely than he had before
and said that 'five-three-four' would be
the page number - which proved to be
correct - and 'C-two' indicated
'column two' which vindicated
Holmes who then knew 'two-nine-three'
would prove, the numbered word, to be.

**So many pages** in that book
suggested to Holmes he should look
within the Bible, though he mused,
in many forms, that book was used,
so Bradshaw then came into mind
but its words were not of the kind
to be accessed for codes, so he
thought what the very book might be
was Whitaker's new Almanack
but then he took that notion back
and got the old one which would prove
to be correct, then made his move
to decode that which Porlock wrote
and, in good time, could read and quote
that 'danger very soon may come'
perhaps for 'Douglas' who in some
'rich country' seemed to be right 'now'
at 'Birlstone House' and despite how
strange was its manner of expressing,
it added 'confidence is pressing'.

**As if on cue** - in high regard -
Alec McDonald of The Yard
came in and from the cryptic note
read 'Birlstone House', a place remote,
and was surprised – a little shocked
and was, from standing, almost knocked
when he read 'Douglas' – for, that day,
some dreadful news had come his way
of Douglas, killed by shotgun at
this Birlstone House, declaring that
Holmes delved in witchcraft and had seen
that he, to Birlstone house, had been
upon his way but thought to stop
at Baker Street and then to hop
his way upstairs so he might find
if Sherlock Holmes might be of mind
to come along, as surely would
this king of sleuths, who then asked could
Watson come too, and join the fun,
though, if he did, he'd bring his gun.

**The eager trio**, Sussex-bound,
reached Birlstone Manor House and found
their way across the shallow moat
by drawbridge – no need for a boat -
and met with Sergeant Wilson who,
being first on-scene, was ready to
hand over to those more adept
at murder matters, though he'd kept
the scene untouched, then pointed out
the faceless body stretched about
the floor, and bloody footprints on
a window sill, and card upon
which 'V.V. Three-Four-One' in ink
was written, then said they might think
about the hammer lying there
upon the floor, and showed them where
someone, behind the curtains, hid
in muddy boots and, then, amid
a glut of clues, the scene forsook
to give those three a better look.

**Sussex Detective** White Mason,
in formal charge of all upon
arrival, was duly informed
that possibly someone had stormed
across the moat after he'd killed
John Douglas, and - perhaps instilled
with hate-filled vengeful rage - had shot
his victim but, incensed, forgot
to take the deadly shotgun, cut
down short for ease of hiding, but
White Mason saw that 'P-e-n'
remained, though Holmes insisted then
- with, murder means, his mania -
'Pen' had been 'Pennsylvania'
once printed full – and whence it came -
and 'Small Arms Company', a name
well known and which might well suggest
the murderer – though this he'd test -
could be American and may
mean Douglas had some debt to pay.

**New vital clues**, though, would appear
to Holmes who'd make it very clear
a missing dumb-bell from the room
was implicated in the doom
of Douglas, and he saw, as well,
the bicycle from which he'd tell
the murderer had likely ridden
to the house and then had hidden
it from view, but which was not
reclaimed because the evil plot
had, somehow, not gone to the plan
devised, and that the flustered man
escaped across the moat and then
on foot continued on, though when
the bicycle's owner was traced
and was American, Holmes faced
his colleagues with a knowing look,
then, mockingly, his head he shook,
for Watson, meanwhile, had observed
the wife was not the least unnerved

**And Cecil Barker**, friend of old
to Douglas, was seen making bold
and laughing with that widowed wife
as though there'd been no loss of life
which told Holmes something was amiss
- something which he could not dismiss -
and then said he would drain the moat
for clues of type which wouldn't float
and, leaving that idea as bait,
Holmes, hiding in the dark, would wait
until in Barker's hands he saw
wet clothing from which he'd withdraw
the dumb-bell's twin, and Barker knew
the game was up but then, in view,
stepped out John Douglas, quite alive,
and said, if he was to survive
the next few days, he must seem dead
to all the world because, instead
of him being killed, as per the plot,
the killer had himself been shot.

**Unrecognisable**, that man,
that would-be killer, had a plan,
long simmering, of vengeance on
the one all knew as Douglas, John,
but Douglas felt he might employ
the dead man's body to decoy
all others, dressing this would-be
assassin in his clothes so he
would be - thought dead - left quite alone
- an act he hoped Holmes would condone -
and Barker helped for they had been,
in California, friends, and keen
to search for gold at which the two
men found success, but Douglas to
escape from looming danger ran
to Britain's safety and began
his life anew, his riches spend,
but knew his enemies would send,
in time, an agent who would wreak
vengeance upon him, cold and bleak.

**Some ten years** earlier, and more,
away from Britain's misty shore,
America's coal fields, vast,
produced a hard and desperate cast
of hard-worked men prepared to kill
for vengeance and, perhaps, the thrill
of getting back at those they saw
as natural enemies who'd draw
coal from the ground, souls from the men
who toiled beneath the earth and then
received a pittance, just enough
to live, until a miner, tough,
saw promise if he'd organise
those men so he could exercise
great power over them and those
who might, his sole control, oppose
and, thus, emerged a brotherhood
of crime in a pretence of good,
under a Lodge's banner bold -
the Order Of Freemen, of old.

**Vermissa Valley** felt the strength
of Lodge Three-Forty-One at length
and those who could had left, but then
into that vale of desperate men
from far Chicago came a man,
one Jack McMurdo, with the plan
to find a haven from arrest,
but found he'd have to face a test
- a test unlikely he'd forget -
from almost everyone he met
- police and criminal alike -
and found that he would have to strike
accordance with, or have to dodge,
one Boss McGinty of that Lodge
of Freemen bound by oath and fear
of retribution threatened clear,
and so McMurdo - biding time
until he found the moment, prime,
to act - trudged onward through the gloom
to Shafter's house to rent a room.

**At Shafter's boarding house** he met
Ettie, old Shafter's daughter, yet
though finding his attraction matched,
discovered. doing so, he'd hatched
the fearful hatred undisguised
of one, Ted Baldwin, who'd surmised
that Ettie had belonged to him,
and so, began, a time of grim
and bitter rivalry he'd dodge
as best he could for, in the Lodge,
Ted Baldwin was a man to fear
but, still, McMurdo made it clear
that, in Chicago, he had been
a member of the Lodge, now keen
to join Vermissa Valley's men
in brotherhood so he could, then,
look in the eye all those he met,
and asked if Baldwin could forget
their enmity, though Baldwin swore
he hated him like none before.

**McGinty** told them, in despair,
the rift between them, to repair,
for they were brothers, sworn and true,
and if they fought then both would rue
his vengeful fury, but prepared
to check McMurdo who had dared
come to his Valley, brash and bold
as anyone, able to hold
his own, so glib of tongue that he
might prove, some later time, to be
an asset to him and his band
of Scowrers who, though, would demand
his loyalty, and soon that time
would come and, to a life of crime
where discipline merged with brute force
- from which there could be no divorce -
into Lodge V.V. Three-Four-One
- the checks upon him now all done -
entered McMurdo, as a brother,
swearing he would serve no other.

**The weeks went by** and violence
delivered with malevolence
descended on mine owners and
those who opposed the dreaded band
of Scowrers sworn to act with no
remorse, on orders, and to go
to lethal lengths, and although try
as people might, none could defy
such fury and, so, had to pay
out for protection, but the day
was coming when, in firms back East,
shareholders said they might at least
protect their distant assets more
than they had ever done before,
though little did investors know
that someone soon would strike a blow
upon the Scowrers – deadly, hard -
but first that someone would discard
his disguise and emerge effective
as a Pinkerton detective.

**With Ettie told** to be prepared
to move with speed and not be scared,
McMurdo put his plan in play
and, as his disguise fell away,
there stood that Pinkerton man known
as Birdy Edwards who had thrown
the Lodge awry and now would clear
the Valley of its source of fear
and took McGinty and his men
by clever subterfuge and, then,
McGinty, to the gallows, went,
though Baldwin, for his crimes, was sent
to serve ten years and then released
- his hatred not the least decreased -
and sought out Birdy who had fled
to California's gold fields, led
by dreams of riches and to hide
till Baldwin's hatred might subside
but this, to be a false hope, proved
and so, to Britain, Birdy moved.

**Sadly,** the faithful Ettie died
but, still, as John Douglas, he vied
for peace, and lived a quiet life
at Birlstone House with his new wife
but, in due course, saw Baldwin's form
approaching like a raging storm
and struggled with him till one shot,
a shotgun blast, defused the plot
against himself by leaving dead
Ted Baldwin, not Douglas, instead,
which was, in court, deemed self-defence
and all was well till, some months hence,
a message brought Holmes news he feared
for Douglas, at sea, disappeared,
and Holmes saw Moriarty's hand
at work - though at a distance - and
although incensed, Holmes knew that he
at this time had to let things be
but, one day, he'd avenge the wrong -
the fiend had won, but not for long.

....................................................

# _His Last Bow_

*Wisteria Lodge*

*The Red Circle*

*The Bruce-Partington Plans*

*The Dying Detective*

*The Disappearance of Lady Frances Carfax*

*The Devil's Foot*

*His Last Bow*

## *Wisteria Lodge*

**Holmes asked Watson** to construe
the word 'grotesque' and, then with due
consideration, Watson posed
suggestions with that sense enclosed
- those being 'remarkable' and 'strange' -
though Holmes declared the needed range
of meaning must include the sense
of 'tragedy' though much more tense
for being 'terrible' in scope
and, through his memory, would grope
for cases worthy to be called
'grotesque enough' to have appalled
his sensibilities and, then,
recalled those queer Red-Headed Men
and also those Five Orange Pips
with many illustrative quips
then said someone – Scott Eccles - sent
a message like a quarry's scent
- 'incredible' and quite 'grotesque' -
words, to Holmes, quite picturesque.

**Holmes then proceeded** to bombard
his friend John Watson rather hard
with remonstrations on the way
boredom set in, but had to say
the telegram which Eccles sent
and words he used would now prevent
the tedium from setting in
and change his frown into a grin
of expectation and, when hearing
footsteps on the staircase nearing
to the point where Eccles strode
into the Baker Street abode,
Holmes had, before the man could speak,
assessed his form, his type to tweak
from his appearance and his manner
which, to Holmes, would wave a banner
high and proud, but saw his flushed
and reddened cheeks as, in, he rushed
and, with propriety expunged,
right into business, quickly plunged.

**No sooner** had the man arrived,
than fate, perhaps, just then contrived
to have come in, from Scotland Yard,
Inspector Gregson, followed hard
by Baynes, Inspector legendary
- of Surrey's fine Constabulary -
who called on Eccles to shed light
upon a note found in the night
inside a dead man's pocket that
said he would be, on that night, at
the victim's house, so Eccles would,
as only one who'd been there could,
say that, Garcia, whom he met
just recently, said he would let
him stay, though in the morning he
found no one in the house could be
located – so he wisely thought
that Sherlock Holmes, to see, he ought,
but learned, taking away his breath,
Garcia had been bashed to death.

**Decidedly unnerved**, the man,
Scott Eccles, felt some secret plan
had been afoot but could not say
what deviltry had been at play
for prior to Garcia's grief
the men's acquaintance had been brief
but common interest in maps
drew them together seeking scraps
of local information such
that Garcia insisted much
he join him at Wisteria Lodge,
but, there, he'd do no more than dodge
all Eccles' queries, and had seemed
distracted greatly, unredeemed
by quality of food or drink,
and all Eccles could do was think
his visit was a great mistake
then, later, would be brought awake
in darkness by Garcia's knock
to be told it was one o'clock

**So, down** to Surrey, all removed,
for Eccles' story clearly proved
intriguing to Holmes, keen to find
out what exactly was behind
the strange events, but Baynes was not
so keen to share all clues he'd spot
but did declare he'd found a note
which, to all gathered, he would quote
as 'Our own colours, green and white.'
with more directions which were quite
mysterious but written by
a woman signed as "D", though why
or what this meant he could not say
although it seemed to tell the way
along a corridor upstairs
suggestive of secret affairs,
but when, for death, he set the time
at one o'clock, this did not chime
for Eccles who'd, that hour, spoken
with Garcia when awoken.

**Holmes theorised** Garcia might
have tampered with the clocks that night
to give an alibi unto
Garcia from Scott Eccles who
admitted he'd not seen the time
himself and that the deadly crime
might have been done at one o'clock
though, then, there came a mighty shock
for Warner, constable on guard,
declared he'd seen, out in the yard,
a giant with a horrid face
who, seen, had run away at pace
toward High Gable quite nearby,
and Holmes, as was his wont, would pry
then find High Gable housed someone
called Henderson, a man outdone
by none in spirit, rich, with two
young daughters, both attended to
by Miss Burnet, and secretary
Lucas, huge and very scary.

**Baynes, keen** for kudos, had announced
that, on the culprit cook, he'd pounced
but this, he said, was just a ruse
to put at ease and to confuse
the culprits, true, who Holmes would hear
intended they should disappear
and, to that end, drugged Miss Burnet
for she'd not aid, nor would abet,
their plan, but as the group approached
the train, a rescuer encroached
and helped the lady to escape
which left them all with mouth agape
but, though the sleuth and police tried
arrest, the culprits had defied,
evading each capture attempt
with sneering arrogant contempt
and it was found, the man thus sought
and who, tenaciously, had fought,
was, as one Don Murillo, shown -
the Tiger of San Pedro, known.

**This beast** of San Pedro had fled
his country after he had bled
its treasury, of funds, bone dry,
but Miss Burnet was one to try
to bring him justice for, in fact,
she, with Garcia, made a pact
to kill this tyrant in disguise
for he had murdered - from surmise
he posed a threat – her husband who,
Victor Durando, hitherto
had been San Pedro's minister
in London when the sinister
event took place and she was left
distraught and widowed and bereft
but, though Murillo got away,
to him would come a judgement day
and, some months later, in Madrid
where he and all who'd helped him hid,
the word came through that he had got
his just deserts by being shot.

........................................

113

## *The Red Circle*

**A frightened Mrs. Warren** came
to Sherlock Holmes – she knew his fame
and his great capability
and charmed infallibility
when on a case, for she had need
for him to come and to proceed
to find out why her lodger might
vacate his rooms in dead of night
and not be seen after that day
he'd offered double rates to stay
on his own terms, the first to be
a front door key, and then that he
must not be troubled or disturbed
or have his privacy perturbed,
and, in print, he'd communicate
his needs to her - like "soap" of late -
and he was bearded, fully, and
his clothes were dark and smart, not bland,
and he spoke with an accent, slight,
and all, to her, did not seem right.

**Not over thirty**, she professed
about his age, and she confessed
he'd never given her his name
since that first morning when he came
to lodge with her ten days before
- though she knew not what was in store -
and somehow Sherlock Holmes could see
a mystery to some degree
intriguing due to her insistence,
perseverance and persistence,
and the fear which she expressed
which dissipated when he pressed
his fingers to her shoulder to
give reassurance he could do
what she had asked for and had hoped,
for she, most surely, hadn't coped
and would, her waking hours, spend
in worry, though that now would end
- her heartbeat now a gentle throb -
for Sherlock Holmes was on the job.

**A cigarette butt** on the tray
and match the lodger threw away
inferred he had no beard, for it
would be much seared if he had lit
and smoked a cigarette, and there
was no mark of a holder where
a holdered cigarette goes flat
and crimped a little, also that
the burnt end of the match was short
and Holmes, from that clue, could report
no pipe or cigar had been smoked
for, by his logic full invoked,
such items take some time to light
and so, for burnt match ends, he might
expect they should be longer, so
the man who seems to come and go
and has a beard is not the one
residing there, though he had done
nothing to justify intrusion,
thus there could be no conclusion.

**Undaunted,** Holmes would then surmise
the lodger's printing would disguise
his handwriting, and seeing 'match'
upon a note, the sleuth would hatch
the notion that the lodger could
not speak good English as he would
have written 'matches' had he been,
then pondered on what he had seen
in advertisements newly placed
in newspapers in which he traced
a code of sorts which seemed to say
that some relief was on its way
and, in a window, soon would glow
a signal light which then would show
some action was to, soon, begin
but Mrs. Warren then rushed in
and said her husband was abducted,
beaten roughly then conducted
well away and then was freed
on Hampstead Heath to, home, proceed.

**But those abductors**, Holmes declared,
must have erroneously snared
the husband, not the lodger, so
- mistake discovered - let him go,
but Holmes, too, saw, as advertised,
the signal house, clearly described,
then he and Watson hid within
the Warren house to, there, begin
their wait to see who would collect
the lodger's lunch tray, and expect
a man, clean-shaven, it would be
but then discovered 'he' was 'she'
and, so, felt danger, great, must loom
to keep the woman in that room
which Holmes now knew to be in line
of sight, direct, to see the shine
of any lights which emanate
out from the signal house and, late
that evening, sensing what it bode,
read off the flashing signal code.

'**Attenta**' then 'Pericolo',
said to the long-patient duo
Italians must be implicated,
words which Holmes roughly translated
as 'Beware' and 'Danger' but
the message was abruptly cut
mid-word, and so, off, they began
to face the unknown as they ran
toward the signal house, but met
Gregson of Scotland Yard all set,
himself, to enter, aided by
a Pinkerton man – never shy -
who had been, both, upon the trail
of one who never seemed to fail
to kill a quarry as assigned
by those within the dread maligned
'Red Circle' and, as up they rushed
and in the signal room all crushed,
they saw there, as each gasped for breath,
Black Gorgiano stabbed to death.

**The lady** in the lodger's room
also saw signals through the gloom
and rushed but found Black Gorgiano
dead and not husband Gennaro
who had joined - when young of age
and, from injustice, in a rage -
the Red Circle, though sought to flee
to New York where he might be free
to live a long and honest life
together with his faithful wife
Emilia but, there, they were found
by Gorgiano who would hound
Gennaro to kill one he knew
or else be killed himself, which drew
a quick response as off both fled
to London to avoid the Red
Circle's revenge, though it was lust
for which Black Gorgiano thrust
himself upon Emilia who,
with him, would have nothing to do.

**All this**, and more, Holmes was to learn
for all the couple did was yearn
for peace and safety in their lives
but vengeful hate sometimes survives
despite it being detrimental
to the hater with a mental
state pushed on to great extremes
such that the most intense of schemes
is manifested, though desire
for one's self-preservation, dire,
brings hated people to strike back
and so, countering an attack,
Gennaro struck, through fear and dread,
the mad Black Gorgiano dead,
then feared a charge against him, but
the Pinkerton man said to shut
the case as all New Yorkers would
say that he acted as he should
in fear which justified the deed,
and Gregson, more or less, agreed.

...................................................

**With only petty thieves** about
on London's streets, his urge to pout
saw Sherlock Holmes bemoaning all
of Britain's criminals who'd fall
below the standard which would make
him, any sort of interest, take,
but when a telegram arrived
from Mycroft Holmes, his hope revived
as Sherlock's brother stated he
was on his way and soon would be
at Baker Street, there to discuss
some as-yet enigmatic fuss
for someone called Cadogen West
and Sherlock sensed a looming quest
for, from experience, he knew
that only urgent matters drew
his brother from his Whitehall post
to visit him with haste, utmost,
and so prepared himself to face
the prospect of a chase apace.

**His nerves alert**, his brain afire
and stimulated with desire
to be upon the scent, he stalled
and then, from memory, recalled
accounts that this man West was found
deceased beside the Underground.
but Arthur had been his first name
followed by Cadogen, the same
as Mycroft indicated in
his telegram, then said "Begin"
to Watson who then read, complete,
the article with facts replete
which told him West, a clerk, had been
at Woolwich Arsenal; and, keen
on finding West, an employee
of Government, Holmes could foresee
a case ahead to test his mind,
a challenge of a greater kind
than chasing down some petty thief
which brings his boredom small relief.

**And Mycroft** - as Sherlock advised
his friend and comrade - exercised
authority unseen by most
but felt by many from his post
to which the flow of information
from all points across the nation
permitted him to focus all
- though keeping every fact on call
while he retained, quite circumspect,
those diverse matters which affect
the nation and the world at large,
so, in a way, he was in charge
and was, himself, the Government,
so something quite important sent
him seeking Sherlock's special skill
about this fellow, West, whose ill-
fated train journey - worrisome
to all but Sherlock Holmes - had come
to find him, so made Mycroft time
for he could sense a major crime.

**Mycroft, himself**, was furious
- though Sherlock, merely curious -
and had to make the grim confession
that West had, in his possession,
seven top-secret documents
which should, by rights, and all intents
and purposes, have been well locked
away, and he was greatly shocked
for they were highly secret plans
the nature of which clearly bans
any release of their details
for doing so, in fact, avails
nobody but the naval foes
of Britain, so if, on his toes,
Sherlock got up, got moving on
to find how plans Bruce-Partington
prepared were found on this man West,
he would protect the very best
of all designs, for this machine
was Britain's secret submarine.

**The dead man's body** had been found
beside the tracks upon the ground,
his skull, quite plainly, badly crushed
as if he'd fallen or had rushed
mistakenly or, maybe, had
been pushed, though nothing ironclad
could be determined on that score,
but Sherlock Holmes required more
and learned all trains upon that track
ran west to east, though never back,
and that no ticket had been found
to say where West, that night, was bound
nor where he'd boarded, and the blood
from such an injury should flood
the ground where he had struck, but none
could be discovered, so someone
had moved the body after death,
so Holmes declared, then drew a breath
of quiet determination and
said West was not Mycroft's brigand.

**Two pounds fifteen** were found on West,
cheques and two tickets for the best
seats at the Woolwich Theatre, so
to robbery, the facts said 'No'
but West's fiancé said they'd been
upon their way when he had seen
something which made him leave her side
- no reason, though, could she provide -
then heard next morning he was found
near Aldgate past the Underground,
but Woolwich Arsenal was close
to Woolwich Theatre, grandiose,
and Holmes considered West saw, near
the Arsenal, a colleague, clear
through wafting fog, so he approached
that colleague and perhaps reproached
him for some great imprudent act
which clearly had some great impact
upon the truly loyal West
who had, quite surely, done his best.

**Two further facts** would now combine
so Sherlock Holmes could then refine
his theory – firstly, being that
a foreign agent left his flat
and went abroad just after West
was killed – coincidence, at best -
and secondly, an Underground
clerk said he'd seen West, shaken, bound
for London Bridge, so Holmes assisted
eagerly by Watson listed
Hugo Oberstein to be
that foreign agent, and when he
broke in his flat and found bloodstains
and saw that many east-bound trains
stopped right beneath his window, he
knew that the story had to be
that, here, West died – he had the proof -
and then was placed upon the roof
of any train which stopped, then fell
somewhere the killer could not tell.

**One, Colonel Walter** – traitor, thief -
from Oberstein received relief
for gambling debts but was required
to steal the documents desired
but Arthur West confronted him
and went to where this agent, grim,
was living but, avoiding strife,
Oberstein took the hero's life,
looked out the window at the trains,
stuffed seven plans on his remains
kept three, then placed West's body on
a train's roof, then it went upon
its way as Sherlock indicated -
Arthur West was vindicated,
the secret plans were all recovered,
the perpetrators were discovered,
and Sherlock would, in gratitude
for his resolve and fortitude
and all the help that he had been,
receive a tie pin from the Queen.

**Long-suffering**, his landlady
knew Sherlock's doubtful guests - shady
and undesired visitors,
those brash Police inquisitors,
those unwashed children of the street,
those women she'd not wish to meet,
those men who seemed, from prison, sent
and on, no good, presumed intent -
although she was, of Holmes, quite fond
for there'd developed quite a bond
between them as she saw the good
within him and she understood
the passions driving him along
to battle with the evil throng
within the precincts of the land
in which she lived, and saw the brand
of 'errant knight', the noble crest
emblazoned on his soul – the best -
so when she said Holmes was near death
Watson responded in one breath.

**"Yes, Mrs. Hudson."** then away
John Watson rushed into the fray
of London's streets to save his friend
of old from some unworthy end
for he had, for three fevered days,
not drunk nor eaten, though his ways
were often thus, but Watson sensed
catastrophe ahead and tensed
his mind to meet what he feared most
and hoped that he'd not meet the ghost
of Sherlock Holmes, but found his friend
in his appearance, near his end
as he was gaunt and fever-flushed
and as, instinctively, he rushed
to treat his friend, Holmes told him "Stay"
and said that he should keep away
for he might catch his dread disease
though nothing, truly, could appease
Watson's concern and, help, would get
for he'd not lose his friend just yet.

**Watson continued** to implore
his ailing friend but, on that score,
Holmes ranted with hostility,
deriding his ability
in medicine beyond the norm
of practice of a general form
and that, no confidence, he had
in Watson whom he had forbad
to touch him or, even, come near
for he had made it very clear
that Watson's lowly rated skill
was quite inadequate but, still,
despite the hurt he had endured
Watson said he would have him cured
and that, an expert, he would seek
- perhaps he'd try Sir Jasper Meek
or Penrose Fisher, London's best,
or Dr. Ainstree he'd suggest -
to treat a tropical disease
but, still, this left Holmes ill at ease.

**Holmes said** he'd have no one engaged
 - despite the fact his fever raged -
and then asked Watson if he'd stay
two hours after which he may
contact a man Holmes nominated
- Culverton-Smith - estimated
greatly for proficiency,
his knowledge and efficiency,
and who had, in Sumatra, been
a planter who had often seen
and treated such diseases to
the point where he knew what to do
more than the lettered experts could
profess, and Watson said he would,
then heard Holmes give a dreadful yell,
- as if some demon out of Hell -
when, on the mantlepiece nearby,
an ivory box, Watson would spy
and pick up to examine close
then put back with Holmes so morose.

**No explanation** was supplied
though this reaction had defied
all Watson's reasoning beyond
the sickness of one held so fond
despite that friend's remorseless scorn
which, on the doctor, deep, had worn,
but came the hour Watson would
see if this Culverton-Smith could
attend to Holmes and then, perhaps
- with knowledge of how fever saps
the mind and body of all strength -
provide a treatment which, at length,
would put health back into his friend
- a friend near, seemingly, his end -
and though no love was lost between
Holmes and the fellow, Watson's keen
and forceful nature was invoked
- the fires in him fully stoked -
to have Culverton-Smith attend
to Holmes to have him on the mend.

**Culverton-Smith** had sealed, in jars,
like prisoners locked behind bars,
the worst microbes which he had caught,
those tiny agents fully fraught
with lingering and painful death
for those infected – tortured breath,
tormented bodies, days on end,
as, downward, sufferers descend -
and, though no sympathy he'd hold
for Holmes, the fellow duly told
Watson that he would come to see
Holmes quickly so that he might free
the sleuth from agonies which racked
his fevered body and attacked
the greatest intellect Watson
had ever known, and whereupon
he'd done his duty, he returned
to find Holmes worse, although he burned
with keenness, and bade Watson hide
behind his bed, his time to bide.

**Before Watson** went seeking aid,
Inspector Morton duly paid
a visit to Holmes, though the man
in Watson's eyes, would, rather than
show sympathy to Holmes, he had
acted, perhaps not like a cad,
but quite unsympathetically
and far too energetically,
but when Watson returned, Morton
had disappeared and, whereupon
hearing Culverton-Smith arrive,
he acted quickly to contrive
a hiding place so he might hear
his observations, loud and clear,
then listened to Holmes' laboured tones,
the clicking of his pain-racked bones,
as Culverton-Smith gazed upon
the sick and fevered paragon
who, strangely, said he might forget
the death of Victor Savage, yet.

**Culverton-Smith**, haughty and smug,
just gave to Holmes a careless shrug
then said, the ivory box, he'd sent
contained a sharpened spring - potent
with microbes, dire – meant to pierce
through Holmes' finger bringing fierce
reactions which would rise and ravage
Holmes just as with Victor Savage,
then, in his pocket, placed the box
and, like a sly and wily fox,
told Holmes there was no evidence
to show with any confidence
that either man was murdered, but,
just as the man began to strut,
Inspector Morton said "You're nicked!"
and, thus, the man knew he'd been tricked
as Watson, too, emerged to say
this was the fellow's last free day
and Holmes recovered instantly
though Watson cursed indignantly.

......................................................

## The Disappearance of Lady Frances Carfax

**As Watson's boots** disclosed a clue,
Holmes went to some pains to construe
that his friend had, that day, enjoyed
a Turkish bath, though this annoyed
John Watson just a little bit
for he could not see how to fit
his boots and Turkish baths together
but then was asked by Sherlock whether
he would like to know what clue
he'd seen – what mark or residue
revealed that fact – and then supplied
the fact that, in a trice, he'd spied
his laces were tied up to show
a well-constructed double bow
suggesting - to one highly trained -
a bootmaker, though he explained
the boots were new and would not need
repairs as yet and so, at speed,
knew who had tied that bow, appendant -
it was a Turkish bath attendant.

**Preliminary** sparring done,
Holmes told his friend that anyone
could see he might prefer a change
and asked if he would care to range
- first-class with all expenses paid,
looked after, princely, by a maid -
to Lausanne, high in Switzerland,
where special skills were in demand
to help a woman of the class
as strong as iron, brittle as glass,
- lonely, friendless, vulnerable -
with modest means, though tolerable
that she might travel state to state,
city to city, sleeping late
then moving on, susceptible
and sometimes imperceptible
to all but types who prey upon
the lonely, then Holmes told Watson
that, there, the very worst was feared
for one such lady'd disappeared.

**Lady Frances Carfax**, though not
a rich woman, could well allot
resources such to pay her bill
at Hôtel National and still
leave fifty pounds more to be paid
to Miss Marie Devine, her maid,
after, for several weeks, she'd been
a guest, though often there'd been seen
a large and bearded unknown man
who had arrived and then began
to badger Lady Frances to
the point where all that she could do
was move location weeks before
Watson arrived, though he'd explore
the circumstances of her move
and why that she'd so disapprove
of that strange man, then found that she
at Baden-Baden now might be
located, though he was to find
a mystery of a darker kind.

**Watson's arrival** lagged behind
the lady's trail, for he would find,
from Baden-Baden, she'd departed
from there too, and so he started
questioning those who might know
of any matter which might show
some hint of Lady Frances' fate
and hoping he was not too late
if some unknown disaster loomed
for he felt she, somehow, was doomed
but found, there, that she had befriended
someone looks had recommended
- Dr. Schlessinger who'd been
debilitated by his keen
and holy Christian mission to
attend unto the needy - who
had left in company with her
and his good wife, though he'd prefer
to pay her bill – she'd little cash -
but did display her jewellery, rash.

**Watson did learn**, to his surprise,
that asking questions was unwise
as that strange bearded questionee
attacked him, though he did break free
when onlookers rushed to his aid
though, then, he found the man had paid
attention to the lady in
his youth and sought to rebegin
their long-delayed relationship,
though she'd now given him the slip
on two occasions showing that
he should stop his advances, flat,
and that the fifty pounds she'd paid
her tearful, though now absent, maid
had been a parting wedding gift
and, so, there was no angry rift,
but Watson, with more tasks to cram,
to Holmes sent off a telegram
in which he made a statement clear
concerning Schlessinger's left ear.

**That telegram** from Baden-Baden,
although short, to Holmes was laden
full of dire warnings, for
it marked a nasty predator
for it told of a jagged ear
on Schlessinger, which made it clear
no doctorate, had he, scholastic
nor any post, ecclesiastic,
but was a fellow Holmes knew to
be 'Holy' Henry Peters who,
back in Australia in a fight,
had half his ear chewed off one night
and now preyed on a trusting sort
of pious woman who'd exhort
the friendship of this living saint
- as he, himself, would often paint -
and feel the need to help this man
with some evangelistic plan
which was, for funds, forever short -
funds he would readily extort.

**From Baden-Baden** Watson fled
and, back to London, quickly sped
for Holmes felt Holy Henry would
return, forthwith, for there he could
blend in and, secrecy, enjoy
to go about some wily ploy
which bade Lady Frances no good
and, timeliness, Holmes understood
was of the essence, though a week
would pass before the one they'd seek
would come to light – a pendant, fine -
and Holmes, his forces, would combine
then, with a simple stratagem,
determine who had pawned the gem
then follow that person to where
Lady Frances might be and, there
at once rush in to save her life
but gave a shudder when the wife
of Holy Henry made a stop
outside an undertaker's shop

**The wife** stepped in and there she bought
a coffin - oversized, they thought -
and then Holmes' agent followed her
back home and, though he would prefer
to bust on in, reported back
to Holmes who, keen upon the track,
made way at once to that address
provided and, under duress,
the wife let Holmes come in to meet
with Holy Henry whom he'd greet
by asking where the coffin lay
and, to it, rapidly made way
to find a body, dead, within,
but knew there was more space, therein,
but, with no warrant, were restrained
but this they, in good time, obtained
and found Lady Frances alive
but chloroformed, and they would strive
successfully to save her life,
though Henry escaped with his wife.

## *The Devil's Foot*

**Holmes had a change of heart** , or so
it seemed to Watson when, with no
apparent reason, Holmes had sent
a message which seemed to relent
upon his great aversion to
having the least of things to do
with public praise for doing good
- a duty known and understood -
for he told Watson that he might
consider writing of the fright
and terror posed when they had faced
the Cornish Horror, long displaced
by newer cases, although he,
this Sherlock Holmes, could never be
immune from weakness and fatigue
from too much work and great intrigue
and Dr. Agar said he'd need
- to which Holmes grudgingly agreed -
to spend some restful time away
on Cornwall's distant Poldhu Bay.

**Holmes settled down**, long days to spend
in private study near the end
of Cornwall's windswept promontory
sorting out the long-told story
of Chaldeans trading tin
and language, it would seem, wherein
the ancient Cornish tongue was born,
so it was claimed, though Holmes was torn
away from study and from rest
when strange events drew forth the best
detective that had ever been
- recovering, but ever keen
to take a case of great intrigue
regardless of his great fatigue
and solve its mysteries by means
by which the trained observer gleans
what others overlook or miss
or, unforgivably, dismiss -
to have his special skills revived
because the Devil had arrived.

**A call to action** such as this,
with all its deadly emphasis,
was something Holmes could not ignore,
for, now, being summoned to the fore,
the man, for action, was prepared
- despite how formerly he'd fared
from his exertions, great and dire -
for all the fellow would require
would be a case in which he'd see
a challenge - not a vulgar fee -
and when the Vicar Roundhay came
- the work of Satan quick to blame -
with Mortimer Tregennis, he
knew something dire had to be
afoot in Cornwall, so he bade
the men explain just what had made
them come to him and to involve
him in some matter and to solve
some mystery of evil brand
in which the Devil had a hand.

**A tragedy**, they said, occurred,
and from which they had quickly spurred,
in which, after an evening's whist,
it seemed some evil demonist
- after Tregennis left that night -
had worked, as only demons might,
to leave his sister, Brenda, dead
and brothers, George and Owen, lead
to lunacy, with fear displayed
upon each face, all which dismayed
Tregennis when he next arrived,
so Holmes, as he was yet deprived
of first-hand facts, put questions to
the man and found that, hitherto,
there'd been a falling-out between
him and his siblings, although keen
to mend the rift, he'd gone that night
to put unpleasant matters right
and left with ill-will nullified,
he claimed, and siblings satisfied.

**To Holmes**, Tregennis then described
an incident which he ascribed
to something moving in the dark
outside and which had left a mark
of apprehension on his brother
George, although he made no other
mention of the strange event,
so Holmes – the hound upon a scent -
arose to check the scene first-hand
- investigations, take command -
and saw, himself, grossly contorted
faces Tregennis reported
though the housekeeper would swear
that, though the sight she could not bear,
no noise she'd heard throughout the night,
no trouble to have caused such fright,
to which Holmes nodded, giving thought
to why, on such a warm night, ought
there be a fire, to which he
knew, some connection, had to be.

**Holmes' musings** recognized a flaw
and he, outside the window, saw
no footprint made upon soft ground
so, in Tregennis, he had found
an inconsistency to make
him so suspicious as to take
himself away to ponder more
upon the matter set before
him as an act of deviltry
though Holmes considered chemistry
to be more likely, for some drug
might be considered, for the smug
Tregennis caused the sleuth to wince
for he, too ready to convince
all others that Satan had been
at work – too eager and too keen -
but, at the house, when he returned,
Holmes found the fires in him burned
intensely when Dr. Leon
Sterndale's form he gazed upon.

**No sooner** had Holmes seen the man
than Vicar Roundhay, to him, ran
with news Tregennis, too, had died
in dreadful fear, and then Holmes spied
a lamp which someone used to heat
some substance on a plate placed neat
above its flame – for smoke, a guard -
so Holmes thought on this long and hard
and, in the fellow's room, had found
a substance, to a powder ground,
and which, upon the lamp, he'd heat
but then begin to rant and bleat
until Watson took him outside,
lungfuls of fresh air to provide,
but Holmes knew then Tregennis killed
his siblings, but the highly skilled
mind Holmes possessed knew he had not
destroyed himself, but saw a plot
quickly devised, and Sterndale may
have something vital he might say.

**Brenda he loved** but could not wed
for, though his wife had long-since fled
from him, he could not be divorced
and, so, with Brenda killed, felt forced
to kill her killer in the way
that she'd been killed and, thus, repay
Tregennis with the fumes of death
inducing great fear with each breath
he'd take – a more-than-fitting fate,
he thought, for such a reprobate -
for no proof was there to affix
the means unto the plant 'Radix
pedis diaboli - known as
the Devil's Foot because it has
a dual shape, human and goat -
a deadly poison made to float
about in air when heated, but
Holmes saw the justice and then shut
his case and told Sterndale return
to Africa and, Cornwall, spurn.

**Two Kaiser's men** on Britain's shore
discussed events just days before
the deadly guns of August brought,
upon the world, a war which wrought
such misery that all would think
God's curse had pushed them to the brink
of mutual annihilation
- nation violating nation -
although those two men, at that time
had, on their minds, a plan sublime
to neutralize the British who,
they hoped, would think it best to do
no more than keep a watch, sincere,
on war with France, not interfere,
but first they had to ascertain
if Britain was prepared for pain
and suffering and loss of life
on such a scale that its strife
might spread across its Empire, wide,
and, revolution's spark, provide.

**Von Bork**, an agent, and a spy
for Germany would prod and pry
for information - vital facts,
that detailed knowledge which attracts
opponents and their agents paid
who scoop up data unafraid
and unconcerned of who might pay
with life or limb one future day -
though this man was a patriot
and loved his country, hating not
the British on whom he had spied
but still considered, justified,
his actions, for he was the best
and knew there was a coming test
of strength upon the Continent
and that his actions could prevent
an ignominious defeat
and, so, he'd lie and steal and cheat
to place into Von Herling's hands
such knowledge of how Britain stands.

**Baron Von Herling** was in haste
for he had little time to waste
- he being Germany's Legation
Secretary, Chief, on station
in a land which might declare
war on his homeland which would fare
his countrymen no end of grief -
and met Von Bork in the belief
that Britain was, in many ways,
defenceless in these final days
of peace in Europe as his man,
within a heavy safe, began
to show his bulging files contained
those secret details which explained
'Egypt', 'The English Channel', and
'Harbour defences', 'Ireland',
and 'Aeroplanes', and 'Portsmouth Forts',
and more, though, of all these reports,
his 'Naval Signals' were, he'd found,
now out of date and quite unsound.

**The agent,** to Von Herling, then
revealed he'd have things sorted when
his contact, Altamont, arrived
that very night, for he'd contrived
to say in code he'd managed to
obtain the 'sparking plugs' to do
a job of work upon his car
but then said this particular
expression told him he'd acquired
new 'Naval Signals' and desired
to be away without delay
and, at that time, was on his way
- this brash Irish-American
who hated Britain like no pan-
Germanic Junker ever could -
and so the waiting Von Bork should
have full five-hundred pounds prepared
for Altamont would not be snared
in Britain with war looming near
for prison was a thing to fear.

**Von Herling**, confident and smug,
then gave an apathetic shrug,
impatient to begin the fight
but, in a window, saw the light
of Von Bork's servant, Martha, glow
- she being old and rather slow -
then said they'd meet back in Berlin
and bade 'goodbye' while stepping in
his huge Mercedes motor car
but hadn't gone so very far
when Martha's shining light went out,
and Von Bork quickly went about
destroying evidence which might
show what he knew after his flight
back to Berlin was finalised,
and then rechecked and organised
his safe crammed tight with every file,
but one, of Britain's secrets while
he waited till he heard the sound
of footprints on the gravelled ground.

**Those footprints** sounded soon enough
as Altamont – his manner rough -
arrived, having obtained with guile
the missing 'Naval Signals' file
but spied the safe and with disdain
- as if to von Bock to complain -
claimed he could see by just one look
it could be forced by any crook
but Von Bork showed the man the lock
in which he had placed so much stock
for it, he said with animation,
had a double combination
of six letters set around
four inner numbers to confound
the best safe-crackers in the land,
but then he overplayed his hand
by telling Altamont that he
had set the six letters to be
'August' – the month he'd long foreseen -
then four numbers, 'Nineteen-Fourteen'.

**While Altamont's** chauffeur relaxed,
the agent had the German taxed
on how close now were Britain's men
on closing in on him, and when
demanding that he hand to him
the 'Naval Signals', quite a grim
Von Bork was told "First pay the cash!"
and he complied but thought it brash
and, then, the 'Naval Signals' took
but, in the package, found a book
on Bee Culture which signified
that Altamont had clearly lied
about the secrets and his name
- and quickly, Sherlock Holmes, became -
as he and 'chauffeur' Watson grabbed
Von Bork and told him he was nabbed
and all his efforts were in vain
which clearly gave the man great pain
for every file which he possessed
was useless leaving him distressed.

**Martha appeared** – it seemed her light
had been the signal on that night
to say Von Herling had departed
after which Altamont started
- now as Sherlock Holmes - the end
of two years' work to apprehend
this master spy after he'd spent
such efforts, only to have sent
false information to Berlin
to which Von Bork, quite in a spin,
responded saying Holmes could not,
in law, restrain him but forgot
that Sherlock Holmes sometimes ignored
the rules – something Von Bork deplored -
in favour of the greater good
and, so, Von Bork then understood
it was of no use to complain
but, still, Holmes had to say it plain
to Watson that, about to blow,
was such a wind they'd yet to know.

# _The Casebook of Sherlock Holmes_

**September Third**, Nineteen-O-Two,
both Holmes and Watson needed to
relax and to recuperate
- their pains and stresses to negate -
and so, after a Turkish bath,
they smoked - as in an aftermath -
two fine cigars, then Sherlock stretched
his arm out to his coat and fetched
a message to which he'd replied
- its sender being dignified -
one Sir James Damery who'd been,
upon a mystery matter, keen,
and would arrive at half-past-Four
and who'd, upon that matter, pour
out his concerns of future crimes
to be committed at such times
one man of infamy decides
they should occur, one who resides
in Britain, one more evil than
Colonel Sebastian Moran.

**Sir James**, Watson said, all could trust
in situations when one must
keep scandal-fed publicity
- exposing one's complicity -
at bay so it would have no chance
of any great significance
to ruin one's reputation and
one's future prospects, great and grand,
so, as he'd made contact, Holmes knew
an awkward case, toward him, drew,
and when Sir James, on time, arrived
Holmes learned somebody had contrived
by use of his romantic flair,
to lure a lady, young and fair
and gullible and clearly fooled
by his appeal, though poorly schooled
in dangers of the type he posed,
and for whom, now, behind doors closed,
Sir James to Holmes would indicate
a colleague's daughter's looming fate.

**Sir James** named Baron Gruner but,
before his lips had even shut,
"The murderer, an Austrian."
Holmes shouted, for he knew the man;
but, so surprised, Sir James ought not
have been, for Holmes was always hot
upon the trail of evil sorts
and kept abreast of all reports
of crime upon the Continent
and, presupposing his intent,
said he was far too busy to
help out at that time but would do
his best to listen and advise
Sir James on which way might be wise
to thus proceed, and he agreed
though telling of the need for speed
of action on the matter which
concerned this lady, young and rich
and innocent, who'd fallen for
this fiend all women should abhor.

**No one** could act officially
for this was not, judicially,
a case in which a broken law
was obvious, and such a flaw
would render matters delicate,
but Sir James would not indicate
the person represented so,
Holmes said, this case, he must forego
for he had need of facts, complete,
if ever he was to compete
with one such as the Baron who,
with reputation foul, might do
his worst but still escape his due
deserts and use his revenue,
ill-gotten from an unseen crime,
to spend at will until the time
another victim he would seek,
a victim timid, rich, and meek,
so Sir James felt he must relent -
a crime, in making, to prevent.

"**Miss Violet** de Merville is
in love with Gruner, despite his
bad reputation which he claims,
and she believes, stem from the aims
of those who'd wish to do him harm,
and, so enamoured by his charm,
she will not listen to the calls
from family who see the falls
ahead for her." and Holmes concurred
someone of spirit must be spurred
to action, for the two would be
wed soon, and then catastrophe
for Violet would loom ahead
- perhaps with her being left for dead -
so Holmes said he might have a plan
to try to reason man-to-man
with Gruner, then report results,
be they successes or insults,
which Sir James could, without delay,
unto his client, then relay.

**Holmes sought** to meet with Gruner who
said there was nothing Holmes could do
which he, for then, had to accept,
though, being someone quite adept
at dealing with setbacks, would ask
a colleague to accept a task,
he being Shinwell Johnson, who,
a reformed criminal, would do
whatever Holmes cared to request
which was to do his very best
to find out if the Baron had
an enemy who'd hate the cad
enough to bring the man to grief
and so it was, with great relief,
he found Miss Kitty Winter who
said what the Baron loved to do
was ruin women and notate,
within a hidden book, their fate,
and that book of his deeds unsound,
in Gruner's study, could be found.

**Kitty was one** who held such hate
that she would bring Gruner a fate
such that he would regret the day
that she, by him, was cast away,
but Violet would not accept
what Kitty said and firmly kept
her loyalty to Gruner, so
Holmes knew that he would have to go
and steal the book and, to that end,
John Watson, to the house, he'd send
as a diversion with a Ming
ceramic saucer, pretending
to be one seeking out a sale,
while Holmes, reflected on the scale
of such illegal methods but,
to such a complication, shut
his mind and crept into the home
of Gruner looking for the tome
and found it quickly, although he
would almost, caught by Gruner, be.

**As Holmes ran off**, Kitty advanced
and, at the angry Gruner glanced,
then threw into his grimaced face
a vial of vitriol at pace
then heard the fellow scream in pain,
and, pleasure, she could not contain
as acid burnt through flesh exposed
as she ran from the scene, composed,
and Holmes showed Violet the book
exhorting her to take a look
at what Gruner had written down
and, on her face, a dismal frown
appeared as she saw how she'd been
deceived, but Holmes could never screen
Kitty, avenged, although her crime
would see her serve short prison time,
while Holmes, with guilt felonious,
had his client, illustrious,
to back him and ward off the Law
so he, its wrath, would never draw.

## The Blanched Soldier

**The Boer War**, finished and concluded,
soldiers returned – some excluded
from rejoining former lives
by memory which long survives
the dreadful battles straining nerves,
the fear of death which long preserves
itself in ever-damaged minds
as on and on it crushes, grinds -
but one consulted Holmes upon
a matter - after friend Watson
departed when he took a wife
abandoning the thrilling life
of crime detection, consultive -
that soldier visiting to give
a grim account of what might prove
to be a crime – should Holmes approve -
against a dear comrade in arms
who shared the dangers and alarms
but, injured, was from danger cleared -
and now, somehow, had disappeared.

**James Dodd** - a man of virile form
though troubled by an inner storm
of worry for a comrade, good,
one Godfrey Emsworth who had stood
with him upon the battlefield
and was the sort who would not yield
without a fight, and was the son
of Colonel Emsworth who had won
the V.C. when he, too, stood fast
outside Sebastopol, being cast
into the battle, boots and all,
and rose up when he heard the call
to duty sounded, as did he,
Godfrey his son, but who would be,
in battle, wounded grossly and
sent homeward with a dismal band
of injured soldiers but, in spite
of having often written, quite
a curt response had been received
and James felt he had been deceived.

**The Colonel** told him Godfrey had
set off like some drifting nomad
around the world, not to return
before one year, and he would spurn
all visits, but James was his friend
and he'd stand by him to the end,
and set off to the family seat
- Tuxbury Old Place – and would beat
upon the door and then demand
to be admitted indoors and
be told just how his comrade, old,
might be contacted but was told
to go away but, though he did,
of him, no one could long be rid
when he, to battle on, decided
till his victory was provided
and that he knew, alive or dead,
was Godfrey Emsworth, though ahead
were difficulties unforeseen
which might dissuade one far less keen.

**Holmes listened** eagerly but would
not comment greatly for he could
not, at that stage, have facts enough
to fathom out more than a rough
assessment of the case at hand
but told James he should understand
his method was to listen, then
confirm his facts and, only when
those facts converged coherently,
he might theorise efficiently
and come up with a working plan
to test; but, still, the missing man
suggested much he could not prove
as yet, but said James ought to move
with caution for the Colonel might,
if pushed too far, decide to fight,
for something there was clearly wrong
and, although James did not belong,
he had been Godfrey's comrade, true,
and surely, some account, was due.

**To Tuxbury Old Place**, none too slow,
went Sherlock Holmes with James in tow
and also someone whom he thought
might clarify things more, so ought
to be included, but when they
to Colonel Emsworth would convey
their feelings and concerns, he would
threaten the lives of all and could,
he said, shoot with impunity
them all and have immunity
from prosecution as they'd not
stay off his land, but Holmes then got
the man's attention as he took
command and ripped out from a book
a single page, produced a pen,
surprising everybody when
he wrote one word then handed it
to Colonel Emsworth who it hit
so hard that, although agitated,
the Colonel's bluster dissipated.

**Holmes' thinking** he would then explain,
in language confidant and plain,
that three main possibilities
- in rising probabilities -
he'd list: the first being that some crime
had been committed, though the time
had not come when his guilt was proved
but, if so, he would be removed
to foreign parts, so this was wrong;
then, secondly, there was a strong
suggestion of his lunacy
though this, too, seemed a fallacy
as, though at home he stayed contained,
he had not been the least restrained
and roamed about the property
suggesting no insanity
had been involved; and so, at last,
Holmes had his final option cast
and that involved that dread disease
which left the Colonel ill at ease.

**What Holmes** had written on the note
- a single word, one to denote
a life foreshortened, segregation,
disfigurement, degeneration
of the body, "better dead" -
the word itself, a term of dread
for "Leprosy" – to most quite vague -
was feared far more than any plague
for, once contracted, no relief
could be expected, only grief
from which escape was only found
in death and burial in ground
far from one's family and friends,
but James' loyalty commends
him for, as Godfrey stepped into
the light, all that his friend could do
was offer him his hand to shake,
a hand which Godfrey wouldn't take
for, as that friend towards him loomed,
Godfrey declared that he was doomed.

**But Holmes** announced that, on that day,
a colleague had come all the way
to pronounce on that diagnosis,
hopeful of a new prognosis,
and Sir James Sanders - specialist
and noted dermatologist -
examined Godfrey and could see
that he, of Leprosy, was free
and that the Ichthyosis he
contracted was something to be,
in time, completely cured, and
shook Colonel Emsworth by the hand
and told him that the news was much
more pleasing than he'd hoped, for such
scale-like afflictions of the skin,
in looks, seemed very much akin
to Leprosy, and Holmes declared
that 'subtle forces' clearly spared
young Godfrey Emsworth who now might
live life unblanched and clear of blight.

**As Watson,** to old haunts, returned,
his memories, long-buried, churned
as images came to the fore,
- some to extol, some to deplore -
when page boy Billy came in sight
which gave to Watson great delight
though Billy said that he held fears
for Holmes' health - holding back tears -
for not one bite in many days
had passed his lips, and though the ways
of Sherlock Holmes had always been
irregular, that vital sheen
had left his face; but there was more
- a situation to deplore -
for Billy pulled the window drape
back, leaving Watson's mouth agape
as he saw a facsimile
of Sherlock Holmes dressed up to be
as lifelike as the actual man -
a decoy in a deadly plan.

**When Watson asked** Billy what had
Sherlock been working on, the lad
- expressing confidence, complete -
responded in a voice replete
with great respect and much concern
that he was able to discern
that he'd been looking for the Crown
Diamond, but it could not be found,
and that this highest-profile crime
deeply affected Britain's Prime
Minister, and Home Secretary,
and also, as was customary,
greatly upset Lord Cantlemere
who, as a critic, was severe
and unrestrained in language cold
on Sherlock Holmes on being told
the great sleuth was to be involved
in hope the matter would be solved,
and Billy – confidence unbounded -
spoke of Cantlemere confounded.

**Billy told Watson** Holmes had been
in costume ranging in between
a worker out job-hunting and
an aged woman to expand
his range of roles so he could blend
in easily to comprehend
what ordinary people knew
and, of course, to get the view
of those who sat outside the Law
and, from detectives, would withdraw
but might let something vital slip
or even give a useful tip
to one like them, though this had strained
the form of Holmes who had abstained
from food to hone that mind so keen
that it could fathom clues unseen
by others, making Watson think
that his old friend was on the brink
of something quite extraordinary,
something of which to be wary.

**The sight of Holmes** came as a shock
to Watson who, though, like a rock
showed no surprise and spoke to show
Holmes that he had great need to know
just what caused him to seem dejected
to which Holmes said he expected
to be murdered that same night
- which seemed to generate delight
in Holmes, though Watson was alarmed -
but Holmes soon had his fears disarmed
by telling him he had a plan
to catch a very clever man
- the Count Negretto Sylvius -
a veritable genius
who'd stop at nothing to stay free,
so Holmes asked Watson to agree,
should he be murdered when off-guard,
to give that name to Scotland Yard
so it could make the man atone
for that and stealing such a stone

**That stone**, that yellow diamond
of which King Louis was so fond
- bequeathed by Cardinal Mazarin -
and, until now, held safe within
the Tower of London with the Crown
Jewel collection of renown
for its security, so much
that no one ever thought that such
a stone could ever go astray,
and so it was with some dismay
it was discovered to have been
removed in stealth and never seen
again, though Holmes suspected that
the Count – a mental acrobat
of some distinction at that time,
quite capable of any crime
and quite a marksman with a gun
who killed wild animals for fun
and for excitement of the hunt -
was guilty, in terms rather blunt.

**Holmes said** the Count now hunted him
helped by Sam Merton, hard and grim,
but hoped that his facsimile,
not him, the victim, soon would be
for it was placed so it would throw
its shadow on his front window
and draw the Count's unerring fire
- which, of course, was Holmes' desire -
but there was danger just the same
though it turned to surprise when came
a note which said the Count now sought
a meeting with the sleuth who thought
he must prepare to face a trick
by someone whom he knew would stick
at nothing to remove a pest
like Sherlock Holmes who'd get the best
of anybody, given time,
so Holmes, to him, would be a prime
target, though one quite hard to hit
for Holmes would trust him, not a bit.

**The Count**, with Sam Merton, came in,
a trace of smugness and a grin
upon his face, but Holmes, prepared
to have this haughty fellow snared,
told him Police were on their way
so here was not the place to stay
and he should leave the stone with him
for his prospects were getting grim
but he would give the Count a chance
to get away – a desperate stance -
and while the villain remained seated
Holmes, into his room, retreated
playing on his violin,
and, though complaining of the din,
the Count relaxed and dropped his guard
- all his precautions to discard -
took out the stone so Sam could see
what all claimed was the apogee
of gems, as Holmes leapt up and grabbed
the stone and said they both were nabbed.

The Count saw the facsimile
of Holmes, but there was no way he
could know Holmes secretly would take
the place of this fine waxwork fake
while, on a gramophone, he'd play
his tune, then deftly sneak away
and listen to the men discuss
the stone and trust that, without fuss,
he'd take the stone and both the men
but have his pistol ready when
the time came to enact his plan
for Holmes knew well than neither man
would give in easily, but fight,
as if possessed, with all his might,
but, in good time, Watson arrived,
Police in tow, and Holmes derived
the satisfaction, most sincere,
of besting that Lord Cantlemere,
then tucked into, at last, with zeal
an overdue and welcome meal.

## The Three Gables

**A visitor** to Baker Street
was one Watson cared not to meet
as, like a mad bull, through the door
he burst and stood, huge, on the floor
- an African, Steve Dixie called,
born of the Deep South, now installed
in Britain with his 'Bruiser' brand -
and gave a warning, a demand,
with clenched fist under Holmes' nose
to which Watson, by impulse, rose
and took a poker to defend
his otherwise unruffled friend
and saw the Bruiser drop his tone
- though still display his fist of stone -
and tell Holmes that, out Harrow way,
there was a man who said to stay
away from matters which did not
concern him, although Sherlock got
a jab in - to Steve Dixie's loss -
with "Barney Stockdale" - Dixie's boss.

**From many punches**, Dixie'd swerved
but this one left the man unnerved,
more so when Sherlock took a stance
to follow through and to advance
to strike his self-assurance hard
and keep the fellow off his guard
by mentioning a murdered man
called Perkins, saying Dixie can
explain things to the magistrate
and think about his likely fate,
so Dixie rapidly backed-off
proceeding awkwardly to scoff
and say that he, that day, had been
elsewhere and was, by many, seen,
but Holmes knew well this pugilist
was beaten and would now desist
and tell whatever facts he knew,
and thus, Holmes, by such tactics, drew
more from him using words and bluffs
than any might by fisticuffs.

**To Watson**, Holmes told of a note
from Mary Maberley who wrote
begging advice on strange events
- some most peculiar incidents -
at her 'Three Gables' home, for she
remembered Holmes had proved to be
useful to Mortimer, her late
husband - though this was of a date
before Watson had ever known
of Sherlock Holmes and had been shown
those powers, observational,
and interests, occupational -
as, off, both went to catch the train
to Harrow Weald, there to obtain
the case's facts but found, instead,
the woman's son, Douglas, was dead
- a young man full of life and zeal
who'd died in Rome from an ordeal
involving what the lady called
a fiend – which left Sherlock appalled.

**But Mrs. Maberley** cut short
her sad and heart-rending report
about her son and said she'd been
approached to see if she'd be keen
to sell her house, and had replied
that she might be, and then supplied
an over-valued asking price
which only acted to entice
acceptance, though the realtor
then made a princely offer for
her furniture if she would just
sign now, though afterward she must
take nothing from the house unless
it had been checked, and she could guess
that, though the offer made was good
and that, the terms, she understood,
those terms were so absurdly strange
that she thought that she should arrange
to seek out Holmes for what he thought
and what the matter truly wrought.

**Holmes listened** on intently and,
as if by some unseen command,
he grabbed a doorknob, pulled in fast,
and there, eavesdropping, stood aghast
Susan the maid - newly engaged
but now affronted and outraged -
who then confessed that she had read
the contents of Holmes' note ahead
of posting it and then was seen
to speak to someone very keen
for knowledge he might pass along
and Holmes told her it would be wrong
to keep the fellow's name repressed
and was surprised when Holmes expressed
the name of Barney Stockdale who,
Susan admitted then, would do
the bidding of one very rich
- a woman – little help, but which
put Holmes upon the scent he sought
and gave the great sleuth food for thought.

**Holmes quizzed** his client patiently
while analysing stringently
each statement, though it came to nought
until he noticed items brought
from Italy – her son's effects -
in which Holmes said that he expects
to find some hint, some vital clue,
perhaps some unknown residue
which Douglas left behind in Rome
- though recently transported home
and corresponding with the time
of purchase offers – and that crime
must be involved for Stockdale to
send Dixie threatening to do
Holmes harm and keep him far away
although, the sleuth, he could not sway,
but, next day, he was quite perturbed
- the son's effects had been disturbed
and just one page was to survive -
page two-hundred and forty-five.

**Holmes read** the writing on the page
penned in a wild pathetic rage
declaring that revenge was all
remaining after some downfall,
and Holmes could see a man cast out
of some romantic tryst about
which he proposed to have involved
someone about whom men revolved
and fell like moths too near a light
compelling him to say it might
involve a Spanish beauty, one
who'd brought so many men undone
- one Isadora Klein by name -
a name in which intruders came
to 'Three Gables' by night in stealth
though not for treasure, nor for wealth,
but to possess a tale complete,
a story, lurid, and replete
with details of a woman, cold,
a fickle beauty to behold.

**Holmes found** and faced the woman who
said she did what she had to do
but Douglas was a man possessed
and, when rejected, was distressed
for he had wanted marriage but
found prospects for that soundly shut
but was persistent, so she had
him cast out and she, then, forbad
him to return, and Stockdale's brutes
of evil violent reputes
beat him so much he swore to write
his story, which he did in spite
of dying slowly, and in pain,
to Isadora's great disdain
but Sherlock warned her she must pay
or he would give her game away -
five-thousand pounds he would require
for Mrs. Maberley's desire
to be fulfilled – a wish profound -
and she would sail, the world, around.

## The Sussex Vampire

**Holmes read** the letter, chuckled wryly,
then, of Watson, asked him dryly
what he'd make of fancies, wild,
then went on in a manner mild
to pass the letter to his friend
who read it loud from start to end
incredulous on its content,
for what the writer, to Holmes, sent
was a request to be advised
- their lack of knowledge undisguised -
upon a matter for which they
had no advice they might convey
as Morrison and Morrison
and Dodd to Robert Ferguson
of Ferguson and Muirhead,
tea brokers, so, they thought, instead,
of Sherlock Holmes of great repute
- that master thinker, absolute -
on what to do when it transpires
that one's confronted by vampires.

**Holmes took his Index**, then perused
its contents under 'V' and mused
about old cases, solved and not
- recalling every tangled plot -
but found his quest to be unkind
for under 'Vampires' he'd find
a reference to the living dead
and how they walked about instead
of lying quietly in graves
and that one might destroy such knaves
by driving hard stout wooden stakes
into their hearts which then unmakes
their pacts with Satan, so he cried
"Pure lunacy" though Watson tried
to reason with him saying some,
within their fevered minds, become
convinced that drinking blood revives
their failing youth, and each survives
by sucking blood from victims found -
their minds convinced, although unsound.

**A second letter** Holmes perused
though, with it, he was less amused
than captivated by the thought
that, listen to the man, he ought,
for, from that letter, Holmes could sense
a situation getting tense
domestically for, though they'd been,
for five years, happy, ever keen,
it seemed towards his wife he'd found
a lessening of love, once sound
despite her being foreign-born
and, from her native Peru, torn,
and, to him, always loving and
affectionate, he'd felt the hand
of doubt and reservation sweep
away the closeness, fond and deep,
which he, since they'd been wed, had felt,
as, day by day, his love would melt
away for she, in anger, had
attacked his son, a troubled lad.

**That lad**, her stepson Jack, had been,
since very young, and now fifteen,
afflicted with a twisted spine,
a situation to confine
the lad somewhat, though for one year
a new stepbrother made it clear
that his needs now were paramount
and Jack's seemed less and less to count,
but still he seemed a gentle boy,
so why the mother should employ
a stick to strike the lad and bring
out massive welts, no single thing
but jealousy this might suggest
from loving her own son the best
though, then, the infant's nurse declared
that she was horrified and scared
on hearing screams and then to view
her mistress bending low, askew,
above her infant son to bite
him on his neck as if in spite.

**Though Ferguson** denounced it all,
he and the nurse both heard the small
defenceless infant scream and yell
and in both rushed, his cries to quell,
but saw, upon his neck and sheet,
the signs of blood, but then would greet
with great revulsion and disgust,
blood on the wife's lips, blood which must
have come from sucking from the bite
- as by some human parasite -
made on the crying infant's neck
and, only taking time to check
the infant's wound and have it dressed,
he locked his wife, herself distressed,
into her room and then sought out
help from those who would know about
how madness might affect the mind
and bring about this most unkind
of maladies which makes one think
one must have human blood to drink.

**Watson had** known the man from school
and knew the man was not a fool
nor given to exaggeration
but, in his exasperation
leading to near full despair,
might be so stressed as to impair
all judgement and, as Holmes began
to interview the Sussex man,
he learned that he had paid the nurse
to remain silent on this curse
and found the older son, Jack, had
pined for his mother, though the lad
seemed happy with his stepmother
and kindly to his young brother
but Holmes, too, saw a spaniel try
to walk, though in a way awry,
and heard a vet had diagnosed
paralysis, then saw exposed,
all from Peru, upon a wall,
weapons displayed, and deadly, all.

**Holmes' focusing** upon the dog
left Ferguson somewhat agog
and to consider Holmes to be
quite off the track, but Holmes felt he
should reinforce instinct with fact
and check the infant's neck with tact
and question nurse and maid apart
to see if either might impart
some explanation, and then saw
the elder son, Jack, quickly draw
himself toward his father then
embrace him lovingly, though when
the father felt the lad's embrace,
he pulled away with little grace
and asked to see the infant who
he loved so fondly Holmes could do
no less than say Ferguson's wife
was no threat to the infant's life,
and called her, leaving all confused,
a loving woman, much ill-used.

**Holmes sensed** Jack sent a poison dart
first at the dog - a test to start -
then at his despised infant brother
but, enraged, the infant's mother
struck Jack with a stick then bent
to suck the poison out and vent
blood from the infant's neck and save
its life and, though she wouldn't crave
that blood to drink, onlookers saw
a woman, mad, desiring raw
blood from her son, and with this known,
the truth, to Ferguson, was shown
so he'd accept the reason why
and Holmes could pen a curt reply
to Morrison and Morrison
and Dodd: "re Robert Ferguson
of Ferguson and Muirhead
on matters of the living dead"
informing them the case was solved
and vampires were not involved.

· · · · · · · · · · · · · · · · · · · · · · · · · · · · · · · · · · · · · · · · · · ·

**Holmes, in a flippant mood,** appeared
one morning and, to Watson, neared
with foolscap folder in his hand
- the look upon his face not bland
but somewhat mischievous, in fact,
though not devoid of friendly tact -
and of his friend, a question, asked,
a question which would have him tasked,
so Holmes told him that he should try
the phone book on his desk nearby,
and Watson, as Holmes had insisted,
checked if 'Garrideb' was listed
which it was - as 'Nathan' - but
not for the man who soon would strut
to Baker Street and who soon came
card-bearing - 'Garrideb', by name -
who hailed from Kansas - Counsellor
at Law called 'John' - and looking for
just one more Garrideb to make
a trio and, a fortune, take.

**John Garrideb** was made aware
that Nathan Garrideb – so rare
in surname, both – had just engaged
Sherlock's assistance which enraged
the legal man and left him taxed
though Holmes soon had the man relaxed
by saying that he was involved
to have a single matter solved
by finding any other man
in all of Britain of the clan
of Garrideb – should one exist -
and, when he had, he would desist
from prying further - just report
success, or that he'd fallen short
of his objective - then retreat
to Baker Street, there to entreat
another case and then forget
the one just solved - or not - and let
his mind adjust, new facts command
about some new case now at hand.

**So, Holmes**, while focused on the case
of finding Garridebs, would chase,
down, as a consulting detective,
matters only an objective
man of facts had need to know
then, to a paying client, show
and then discard, but never share
with others, for he was aware
that trust was what his clients sought
and what their proffered fee had bought,
so, when this latter Garrideb
appeared, Holmes felt a sticky web
of scheming and intrigue being spun
and knew, by it, there had begun
a game to trap unwary prey,
but Sherlock Holmes would not obey
the rules a predator might make
but well-tried rules held for the sake
of those who'd come to him in need
then, for their benefit, proceed.

**His patience** put hard to the test,
Holmes sat and listened to his guest
tell of how surname-sakes were sought
by A. H. Garrideb who'd fought
his way to riches, vast, around
the western U.S.A. but found
no other 'Garrideb' but him,
the councilor, so, in a grim
and desperate moment, felt he must
make out a will which would entrust
full fifteen million dollars to
the safety of his bankers who,
to just three Garridebs, would pay
five million dollars, each, the day
that those three Garridebs were found
- and all identities proved sound -
and, so, this Garrideb called John
from Kansas had set out upon
a quest – two Garridebs, his aim -
a mighty fortune, theirs to claim.

**Suspicious,** Holmes began to chatter
on a quite fictitious matter
of his friendship with a man,
a made-up Dr. Starr who ran
Topeka as its mayor, devised,
and when John Garrideb advised
Holmes that he knew the fellow, he
could see his visitor, to be
a liar, but did not disclose
his thoughts, though later would expose,
with help from Scotland Yard, the man
as one James Winter who began
a U.S. criminal career
but fled to Britain, there to steer
a course, illegal though diversive,
violent and quite subversive,
but, for then, Holmes had in mind,
a Nathan Garrideb, to find
who was, discovered, found to be
eccentric but bonafide.

**James Winter**, someone also billed
as 'Killer Evans', once had killed
a man called Prescott - served his time -
but both had been partners in crime
when Prescott was a forger, keen,
and Winter, at the time, had been
a confidence man quite adept
at getting people to accept
whatever he said to be true,
such people who would come to rue
the day they'd met this trickster, vile,
this conman with an honest smile
but lying heart, and Holmes could tell
he must act fast if he would quell
some crime about to unfold at
the house where Garrideb had sat,
a fixture, for years, every day,
for Holmes knew Evan's motive lay
in having Garrideb removed
out from his room as, soon, it proved.

**As Holmes** and Watson waited in
the room alone, they heard the din
of someone entering, and saw
that Killer Evans sought to draw
away a rug and open wide
a hidden trapdoor to provide
access into a room below,
a room apparently to stow
something of value, quite unknown
to Nathan Garrideb who'd shown
great interest in a fortune, huge,
invented by the subterfuge
of Evans as a trick to make
this genuine Garrideb take
himself away and, so, vacate
the room he'd never contemplate
abandoning, but had, that day,
gone off to Birmingham to pay
- for fortune, starry-eyed, ambitious -
a visit to a man, fictitious.

**With Nathan Garrideb** now gone,
the light into the cellar shone
and showed a printing press and stacks
of banknotes, counterfeit, on racks
where Prescott left them long before,
so, Holmes and Watson quickly bore
down upon Evans who produced
a pistol Holmes had not deduced
which discharged striking Watson in
the leg – quite to his friend's chagrin -
which caused that friend instinctively
to react quite emotionally
and strike Evans upon the head
in fear that Watson could be dead;
and, when Evans was led away,
Watson was ever pleased to say
his wound was worth the pain that morn,
as it, Holmes' stoic face had worn
away and left a countenance
of friendship of true resonance.

## *The Problem of Thor Bridge*

**A month had passed** - a month unkind
to Sherlock Holmes whose eager mind
had hungered for a case to solve,
a case of worth which would involve
his intellect and give him pause
to think and ponder on a cause
quite monumental - or quite small -
for either one would sound the call
to action for his idle brain
and put it back to work again -
but, when a plea came in a letter
seeking help, Holmes thought it better
that two eggs, before him, cooked
should - neither one - be overlooked
but eaten, forthwith - not in haste
but slowly so as not to waste
the effort in their preparation -
then, at breakfast's termination,
read the letter, faced his friend,
a question to him to extend.

**Holmes would**, to Watson, often pose
a question which might well disclose
how much the doctor didn't know
(perhaps, Holmes' cleverness to show
or how much he'd come to rely
upon his friend – no one knew why)
but Holmes, that morning, asked Watson
if he knew of a Neil Gibson
known as the 'Gold King', far and wide,
and Watson struck back – showing pride
to counter his provocator -
"The former U.S. Senator?"
to which Holmes, in turn, responded
he, that day, had corresponded
with Holmes on a matter dire
asking, if he'd so desire,
to come and to investigate
a death and rescue from a fate
quite undeserved, a lady who
had nothing, with that death, to do.

**The lady**, Grace Dunbar, was not,
the letter said, one who would plot
to kill a fly, much less someone
- not man nor woman - and had done
nothing in this confounding mess;
though it admitted an excess
of clues had pointed to her guilt
and had a case against her built
for the deceased was Gibson's wife
described as well past prime of life
and Grace Dunbar, young and attractive,
might have found herself a captive
of this Gold King's riches plus
his handsome virile form and, thus,
thought she'd have both, this governess
and house-hold manager, no less,
if Gibson's wife, somehow, would die;
so, stealthily in wait, she'd lie
then point a pistol at the head
of Gibson's wife and shoot her dead.

**The telling evidence** discovered
was a pistol soon recovered,
from Grace Dunbar's wardrobe and
the fact that she could not command
an alibi of any sort
and that there'd been a clear report
she'd been nearby about the time
of the commission of the crime
upon Thor Bridge, which told Holmes she
might well be innocent while he
made comment on how waters, deep
and long and narrow, slowly creep
beneath the stone bridge which provides,
within two balustraded sides,
safe passage, but was interrupted
when a man called Bates disrupted
thoughts still gelling in his mind
and Holmes felt that he ought to find
some time for this man as he had
been shouting Gibson was a cad.

**A villain**, an infernal brute,
a fearful tyrant, absolute,
were terms used by Bates to describe
Neil Gibson in his diatribe
which told Holmes of brutality
toward one whose vitality
and looks had faded, though that wife
still loved her husband and, for life,
would do so, then in haste Bates rose
and brought the meeting to a close
as Gibson would, quite soon, arrive
but Holmes, forewarned - his mind alive
with notions of the man's abuse
and of the woman's sad misuse -
meant Gibson would be unprepared
and Holmes would have the fellow snared
and struggling before admitting
Grace Dunbar, a most unwitting
object of his new affection,
may have caused his wife's dejection.

**Such proved true**, so Holmes, of Bates
- who managed Gibson's vast estates -
asked of his master's arsenal
of weapons - quite phenomenal -
and was informed a box of two
pistols was empty, leading to
the fact that one which had been found
in Grace Dunbar's wardrobe was bound
to have been one and, so, the other
missing pistol - its twin brother -
might have been the one which killed
Neil Gibson's wife and, thus, had stilled
the tongue of one so poorly used
and verbally, at least, abused
but there had been a message sent,
presumably from Grace, which lent
more credence to suspicions she
decoyed the victim so she'd be
upon the bridge's stony span
and then succumb to Grace's plan.

**Holmes spoke** with Grace within her cell
and, from the start, the sleuth could tell
she wasn't guilty, not at all,
but hadn't evidence to call
for her release, so back he went
within his mind upon the scent
of something stirring, something wrong,
a notion forming, stark and strong,
and off to Thor Bridge he set out
- the court's assessment he would flout -
for he would show Grace Dunbar's guilt,
upon a stack of lies, was built
- such lies so venomous they'd kill
without being spoken loud and shrill -
but Holmes would need a length of string
and Watson's pistol if he'd bring
the facts to light and free the one
on whom injustice would be done
as Holmes set up a simple test
on which Grace Dunbar's life would rest.

**Holmes tied the string** around the grip
of Watson's pistol, then he'd slip
a sturdy knot around a stone
dangled above the water, prone
to drag the pistol, when it fell,
into the water, there to dwell
forever, as had been the aim
of Mrs. Gibson to proclaim
- being so insanely jealous and,
not, of her full mind, in command -
Grace Dunbar as her killer so
up to the gallows she would go,
but Sergeant Coventry would drag
the waters and, in time, would bag
two pistols – to a stone, each tied -
one being Watson's, one supplied
from Neil Gibson's matching pair
and Sherlock Holmes, with ample flair,
declared the gods of justice sent
word Grace Dunbar was innocent.

...............................................

## The Creeping Man

**"Come at once,"** the note dictated,
"if convenient." - then stated
"If inconvenient, come all
the same." - a message which might gall
all but the stalwart Doctor who
had campaigned with and listened to
demanding calls from one called 'friend',
one Sherlock Holmes, whom he'd defend
from threats of every type and kind
but knew 'a whetstone for the mind'
of that same friend was all that he,
at times, could ever hope to be,
but this time Holmes, the great detective,
was insightful and reflective
upon matters which pertained
to dogs, unleashed and unrestrained,
and asked this man of medicine
and military discipline
if he thought dogs, perhaps, detect
our human moods and, these, reflect.

**Watson expressed surprise** for he
knew well that Holmes would always be
prepared to use a bloodhound's nose
to solve a case and would suppose
a bloodhound might mimic the one
who owned it, though if one had done
so, he'd not heard, in all his days,
of dogs with imitative ways,
but Holmes asked Watson, now agog,
why would Professor Presbury's dog,
a wolfhound he called 'Roy' attempt
to bite him, to which, with contempt
for such a question, Watson groped
for a reply, then said he hoped
such would be better asked of him,
this Presbury, for facts were slim
about the matter, and he should
seek first-hand knowledge, if he could,
to which Holmes, quite prepared, replied
such knowledge, soon, would be supplied.

**But it was** Trevor Bennett who
- being private secretary to
this hound-harassed Professor - had
contacted Holmes, though felt a cad
for doing so, but also knew
Presbury's mind had gone askew
and that the fellow was in need
of help, preferably at speed,
for Bennett was betrothed to wed
Presbury's daughter, Edith, led
to apprehension and distress
for actions she had to confess
were far from normal for the man,
this great Professor who began
quite recently to display traits
of strange expressions, awkward gaits,
and that upon his hands and knees
would sometimes walk and, by degrees,
began to act as though he'd been,
as man and monkey, set between.

**From standing tall**, this creeping man,
had hunched himself down low and ran
about at all times of the night,
and gave to Edith such a fright
when she awoke at two o'clock
one morning to receive a shock
on seeing in her window, near,
her father's face, though it was clear
there'd been no way to scale the wall
outside – two storeys, full, the fall -
except by water pipe and creeper
which suggested to the sleeper
she'd been dreaming, although she
well knew the fearful sight to be
quite real, so Holmes decided to
proceed with little more ado
to see, first-hand, the situation,
though it was with indignation
he would be received by him,
the great Professor, very grim.

He was erratic, fierce and rude
towards the sleuth who'd dared intrude
without an invitation given
such that Holmes found he was driven
back, though Bennett's intervention
brought about the circumvention
of this nasty confrontation,
though the man's gesticulation
and his raging fury showed
a drug within him may have flowed,
but Holmes would need to gather more
than possibilities before
he could construct a theory, sound,
and then, from Bennett, duly found
that all had started on the day
the man had, from his time away
in Prague, returned an altered man,
a man who, like some primate, ran,
and Holmes, by careful observation,
saw a nine day separation.

Nine days between each strange attack
was clear and, so, Holmes returned back
the next ninth day to be in-place
with Watson and Bennett to face
the man-to-monkey transformation
filled with fear and fascination
of the spectacle to come,
an exhibition unwholesome
but mesmerising for a sleuth
determined to uncover truth
not just of source, but of intent
behind the actions which had sent
a wise Professor on a path
toward, perhaps, an aftermath
of non-reversibility
of mental instability,
although, behind it all, Holmes knew,
was something barely out of view
behind the actions so uncouth -
the man sought to renew his youth.

This, Holmes deduced on having learned
Professor Presbury had yearned
to wed a lady very much
his junior in her years, and such
was his desire to be fit
in body that he would submit
to treatments, radical, received
in Prague where Lowenstein conceived
of taking serum from a man-
like anthropoid, though other than
this source, a Langur monkey might
be substituted, though hindsight
showed monkeys rarely walked erect
and, so, Lowenstein should expect
its serum introduced to men
would not be beneficial when
it took affect; and, thus, it proved
when Presbury emerged and moved
and clambered, monkey-like, around
then teased poor Roy, Presbury's hound.

Human in form but now disposed
to foolish acts, Presbury closed
on Roy who, frantic, struggled for
the chance to reach his tormentor
and slipped his collar, breaking free,
then set upon the man with glee
and tore his throat, but Bennett's shout
and rapid action brought about
the man's release, and Watson ran,
with Bennett helping, to the man
and bound his wounds, his life to save,
and morphia, the fellow, gave,
though all kept silent on the matter
fearing that unbridled chatter
would, great reputations, spoil,
though Holmes would quickly act to foil
the work of Lowenstein who'd been
quite irresponsible, too keen
to take his fee without regard
for clientele impacted hard.

**Although the Downs** of Sussex claimed
the later years of Holmes, he aimed
to keep John Watson as his friend
and, often visit, recommend
though Watson had, in later years
- as such a long friendship endears
friends to each other fondly - found
his constitution more unsound
than once it was, but still he came
to keep alight that dimming flame
of comradeship which danger wrought
and lingered on with every thought,
but, on his own, Holmes had to solve
a local case seen to revolve
around communities nearby
and, without Watson, Holmes would try
to have the matter's truth supplied
and find out why McPherson died
before his eyes in great distress -
a sight he'd not wished to witness.

**His bees** gave Holmes, not only honey,
but, at market, extra money
which would supplement his needs
though he was of the type which heeds
the doctrine that 'less can be better'
which he followed to the letter
living frugally, enjoying
life and Nature, still employing
- although, crime-fighting, he'd decried -
those gifts which Providence supplied
- a stroll or swim for exercise -
and it was never a surprise
to meet a neighbour while about
to whom one always gave a shout
and greet - by chance or as arranged,
always with pleasantries exchanged -
like Harold Stackhurst, local coach,
who made a most friendly approach
to Holmes and said he'd come to seek
Fitzroy McPherson, sound and sleek.

**McPherson lived** for exercise
though he would never compromise
his heart condition which he kept
controlled, and had learned to accept,
would always pose a limit to
those robust sports which would undo
the strides he'd made which were admired
by all around; though it transpired
that, as Stackhurst and Holmes had met,
they saw a sight they'd not forget
as young McPherson seemed to sway
and stagger and then, in dismay,
threw up his hands and gave a yell
of agony and then he fell
as Holmes and Stackhurst raced apace
to help their friend but had to face
a dying man whose final breath
comprised three words just before death
enveloped him – they seemed insane -
they heard him say, 'The Lion's Mane."

**What he had meant**, neither could say
but, as they tried to help that day,
they saw, as his coat fell, great strips
of red as though thin wire whips
had scourged his body leaving scars
as bright as red hot iron bars,
and soon - it seemed no time at all -
a shadow fell, a gloomy pall
of darkness from a man they knew
but little liked, as did so few
of those who lived upon the Downs
who, for his grimaces and frowns,
distrusted him – their distance, kept -
this Ian Murdoch, grim, inept
at all but surds and conic sections,
transformational projections,
but who seemed quite sympathetic
and ran off at a frenetic
speed from that scene so troublesome
to summon the Police to come.

**Holmes**, from a vantage point quite high,
then scanned the beach but gave a sigh
of disappointment spotting just
three far-off figures he knew must
be 'way too distant to have been
involved and, so, with senses keen
to be observing what they might,
he moved in close, not with delight
but with determination to
find out what sort of fiend might do
such things upon a man so liked,
but saw that only one had hiked
along the track down to the sand
then back again, although a hand
and knee print told Holmes that the dead
man raced and stumbled both in dread
and pain for help, but there was not
a clue at hand he might allot
to anyone of any guise
who'd caused McPherson's sad demise.

**In quick time**, at Murdoch's behest,
a constable - the burliest
man in the force – called Anderson
duly arrived and, whereupon
he was the man in charge, he sought
the facts, though listened well and thought
that any observations made
by Sherlock Holmes were of a grade
exceptional, and as both read
a letter written to the dead
man from Maud Bellamy - sincere
in her affections - saw a mere
suggestion of a clue emerge
but could not make the facts converge
to build a theory which would hold
together, so went dead and cold
that line of thought, and alternate
suggestive matters learned of late
had Holmes directing thoughts suspicious
straight at Murdoch - strange, capricious.

**But, too**, the lady's brother had,
considered McPherson a cad
despite most liking the deceased,
but such suspicion, too, decreased
and, for a week, enquires stalled
till locals – horrified, appalled -
had found McPherson's missing dog
quite dead and still as any log
with signs of agony quite plain
- the dog, too, died in fearful pain -
and something stirred in Sherlock's mind
as he observed the knotted kind
of whip-like marks upon the skin
of Murdoch, too, fast ushered in
when rescued from the beach near death
but managed to, with heaving breath
and pounding heart, relate to all
that he, such pain, could not recall,
and Holmes – excitement to subdue -
now felt he held the vital clue.

**For Murdoch's pain** had much to teach
and, so, returning to the beach
- his eagle eyes no longer blind -
Holmes, with the others, sought to find
McPherson's murderer, which hid
within a rock pool, deep amid
the waving fronds, and Sherlock, thrilled,
in quick time had the creature killed
for there it was – the Lion's Mane -
Cyanea capillata - bane
of all it touches with its whip-
like tentacles which leave a strip
of painful paralysing welts
on predator or prey whose pelts
cannot withstand the poisoned punch,
the venom from the mane-like bunch
of tentacles which trail behind
the creature – living food to find
and kill to eat; and Holmes, for one,
sought out his bees, his work now done..

**What type of face** might one possess
to make one's landlady confess
to horror and complete disgust
on seeing it; and what type must
be kept behind a veil so thick
that, if it ever dropped, a quick
and fleeting look was sure to cause
a milkman passing by to pause
and look and suffer shock so much
he'd lose his self-control at such
an apparition that his grip
around his milk bottles would slip
and they would shatter on the ground
then splatter outward all around;
and what face would bring to a head
a situation, one of dread
and such foreboding, that it brought
to Sherlock Holmes someone who sought
his help, beseeching him to trace
the secret of that veiled face?

**That face**, that landlady explained
to Sherlock Holmes was such it pained
her to describe the horror felt
on seeing every scar and welt
on what was once a handsome form
but now, by some satanic storm,
was so disfigured, she could not
endure it long and could not blot
its image from her memory,
forget the human tragedy
which hid behind that veil so
its owner, ever, might forego
the shame and dread and self-disgust
should others view her face and thrust,
instinctively, their gaze away,
but her landlady had to say
that lodger, Mrs. Ronder, now
yells out at night – a mighty row -
with loud shouts of "You cruel beast!"
then "Murder! Murder!" twice at least.

**The landlady** continued on
and made an offer to summon
a clergyman, if such she'd need,
or else, perhaps, police at speed
if there was some threat to her life,
some portent of some coming strife,
to which her lodger shouted "No!"
and that, such help, she must forego,
at which point the landlady thought
that Sherlock Holmes was one she ought
approach, to which the lodger lent
support, complete, and said present
unto the sleuth the tragic fame
of Abbas Parva and the name
of Ronder's Wild Beast Show which he
would know – being who he was - to be
a case whose facts were never known
in full, and that, though time had flown
full seven years, she thought the sleuth
might like to learn the hidden truth.

**Holmes did**, indeed, recall he'd read
about this Ronder - savaged, dead
by lion attack – though little more
could he recall upon that score,
but, delving deep into his files
long dormant, he broke into smiles
which dissipated as the grim
accounts of how - though rather slim -
Sahara King - a lion, trained,
who had, for ages, entertained
the eager crowds – escaped somehow
and with a dreadful roar and row
attacked its trainer and his wife
and left him dead and her, to life,
just clinging on, but fiercely clawed
so much it left her face, unflawed
and beautiful, disfigured so
much those who saw it would forego
attempts to describe what they saw -
a face destroyed, ripped red and raw.

**Ronder's** Wild Beast Show, it seemed,
had been, at one time, much esteemed,
- a caravan of fun, exotic,
for the masses, most hypnotic -
but, when tragedy had struck,
was in decline, though not by luck
or failed fortune, for the man,
the leader of this caravan
which masses would anticipate
from year to year, would generate
such vile hatred for the way,
toward his wife, he would display
such cruelty, despite the fact
that she was vital for his act
consisting of them entering
a cage which held Sahara King,
a fearful beast whose trust they'd win
by feeding it each night within
its cage, assuming this would make
them safe – a terminal mistake.

**Then Holmes** and Watson went to see
the veiled lodger, forced to flee
from company for seven years,
perhaps with shedding many tears
about her now-disfigured face,
so Holmes would give the lady space
to tell her 'truth' which she'd withheld
and then the 'true' full story meld
together as a new-spun whole
and find, exactly, just what role
she may have taken on the night
Sahara King, perhaps in fright,
got loose and killed her husband, vile,
and, though she dithered for a while,
she told of love which she had found
with Leonardo who'd expound
the need to be, of Ronder, rid
so made a steel claw and hid
as he passed by the lion's cage
and struck the fellow in a rage.

**Ronder's skull** was crushed below
the might of Leonardo's blow
and Mrs. Ronder loosed the beast
assuming it would charge to feast
upon her husband but, instead,
it grabbed the lady by her head
and, as she screamed, her lover ran
and left her there, his daring plan
reduced to tragedy and farce,
the chances he would help her, sparce,
but Leonardo did come back
with others, and the lion's attack
was thwarted, though too late all knew
to save her face, and then withdrew
that lover to some place away
and she'd not seen him since that day
but learned he recently had died
and, with that great relief, supplied,
she wailed loudly for the truth
to now be told to Holmes, the sleuth.

**Holmes understood**, and sat reserved;
he knew that justice had been served,
far more than full, to her and saw
the man who made that lion's claw
and struck down Ronder passed beyond
the reach of justice, and what bond
remained between the lovers now
was fractured, and would now allow
the veiled lodger's final act,
justice upon herself, exact,
but, though the woman sorely sought
escape from life, Holmes said she ought
not take her life, despite her pain,
and should, from such ideas, refrain,
for life was such a precious gift,
one we must keep, not set adrift,
then, in a package, through the mail,
came news her courage would prevail -
her deadly Prussic acid bottle
declared that such ideas, she'd throttle.

**As Watson was**, as Holmes well knew,
the type of fellow who would view
the Turf Guide with impartial zeal
for what its content might reveal
about the prospects of a horse
performing well - without remorse
being showered on those people who
are drawn to bet with great ado
and can't resist as others can
to give their money to the man
who makes the book and keeps the cash
of punters foolhardy and rash -
the sleuth reasoned that his friend John
would know Sir Robert Norberton
- at least know of him from the days
spent at the track, and of his ways -
and quickly Watson answered back
and said all knew him at the track
for violence and talk, unseemly -
the man was dangerous, extremely

**Watson went on** with more about
Sir Robert, neither thin nor stout,
residing at Shoscombe Old Place
who was a man who loved to race
his horses at a break-neck speed,
and had, for riches, avid greed,
and loved the ladies and a fight
so much that people said he might,
have, as possessed of nerve and pluck,
in Regency Days, been a Buck
one wouldn't ever care to meet,
for he was so far down Queer Street
he'd never find his way back out
and often had to fight to flout
his creditors who, in the main,
were moneylenders trading pain
for moneys owed, one of whom he
flogged shamelessly and had to be
- unstoppable once he began -
pulled off before he killed the man.

**From Shoscombe Old Place** - occupied
some years, since old Lord Falder died,
by Lady Beatrice, Falder's wife
and widow, for her term of life -
a man, John Mason, came to call
on Holmes about the strange downfall
of his employer, brother to
the Lady Beatrice - Robert - who
Holmes heard had traits, redeeming, few,
on asking Watson if he knew
the fellow's character, though now
John Mason could not explain how
or why Sir Robert Norberton
had changed and now seemed bent upon
his sister's isolation, full,
where once no one could ever pull
the two apart, and why he'd sent
her dog away and, thus, prevent
that happiness which she enjoyed
which now her brother had destroyed.

**As well**, Holmes learned, the Lady would
drink heavily, since then, but should
not do so as her health was not
as it once was, but here the plot
for Holmes would thicken much as he,
Sir Robert, in stealth, seemed to be
drawn to an ancient crypt by night
in company with one who might
assist him in some rite, perhaps
- though, of this, Mason had but scraps
to offer Holmes, now much intrigued -
but when, upon that man, fatigued,
Mason and Butler Stephens came
quite suddenly, they would inflame
such fear that he'd run off so fast
he'd not be caught, and then the last
thing from John Mason's strange report
which, Holmes' to action, would exhort,
was, in the crypt, there all alone
was one small piece of human bone.

**A mummy's bone**, he thought, though it,
John Mason stated he'd admit,
had not been seen by him before
- this, he and Butler Stephens, swore -
and, furthermore, another bone
burnt in the furnace, hard as stone,
was found at Shoscombe Hall and brought
to Baker Street, a bone Holmes thought
Watson might well identify,
and Watson hastened to supply
its type, asserting it to be
a human femur part which he,
its upper condyle, would declare,
though Mason made Holmes well aware
the furnace was scraped, every day,
of cinders which were thrown away,
so this bone had been burnt anew
and distrust of Sir Robert grew
but was dispelled with quick hindsight -
Sir Robert, was away that night.

**So, Holmes**, with Watson, travelled fast
to Shoscombe Old Place where he cast
his knowing eyes 'round Shoscombe Park,
the facts of 'Shoscombe Prince' to mark,
for such a horse was set to win
the Derby from which would cash-in,
Sir Robert, who could then escape
the moneylenders and then drape
himself in riches quite sufficient
- funds of which he was deficient -
to live his life in comfort and
continue in a manner, grand
and great, for life, at Shoscombe Park,
but Holmes could see a meaning, dark,
emerging from the facts he had
and knew Sir Robert, though a cad,
was not the type to panic when
accosted by demanding men
so there was something else behind
his manner, something Holmes must find.

**The crypt** was key to what had made
the Shoscombe siblings' fondness fade,
Sir Robert, to his sister, show
reduced affection, far below
that shown before, and why, indeed,
did Lady Beatrice see the need
to keep the maid loved by her brother
Robert who had, to another,
sent her dog, her pet, away
when, to that crypt, it tried to stray,
and why would Robert spend much time
within that crypt when time was prime
for preparations for the Race,
the Derby, so Holmes, at a pace
went to the crypt determined he
would find why Robert chose to be
diverted to that place of death
when he would need his every breath
to keep the 'Prince' in peak condition -
Holmes had to trust his intuition.

**Sir Robert** followed Holmes to find
his ruse was starting to unwind
for, there, was Lady Beatrice, dead,
but she must seem to live, instead,
until the race was won so he,
Sir Robert, out of debt, could be,
for, on his sister's death, the 'Prince'
and all within the whole province
of Shoscombe Park reverted to
Lord Falder's younger brother who
might stop the 'Prince' from running in
the Derby which would then begin
Sir Robert's ruin – perhaps death -
for creditors would not waste breath
on such as he, and he would find
the fate of defaulters unkind,
but fate, this time, would look away
and let Sir Robert win the day
and take his winnings, huge, and keep
his life and not, in failure, weep.

......................................................

**Holmes quite moody** – melancholic -
turned to being philosophic
challenging friend Watson to
characterize a fellow who
had exited as John came in
and see if, from once glance, he'd spin
the tale of this unknown man
- as quickly and as best one can -
and Watson said 'futile, pathetic,
broken, old, unenergetic'
to which Holmes eagerly agreed
but added that we all have need
of realization of the fact
that, should we reach his age intact,
we'll all be like him in the end,
when all our life force we expend,
and typing him should not be hard
for he'd been sent by Scotland Yard
when it had failed to solve his case
so Sherlock Holmes had facts to chase.

**Josiah Amberley** that day
upon a quest was sent Holmes' way
for him to find the whereabouts
of two who'd done what clearly flouts
the decency which all expect
- an action one would not suspect -
both from a well-kept wedded wife
who'd never known a day of strife
and from a friend, a doctor keen
on chess and who was often seen
to visit Amberley to play,
but who, it seems, had run away
with both that well-kept wedded wife
and money saved throughout a life
of useful work and honest toil
by Amberley who'd now embroil
the great detective in a case
to find the pair who'd done this base
and shameful act upon one who
was at wit's end for what to do.

**Josiah Amberley** had been
in business, and his name was seen
upon paint-boxes purchased by
artistic persons who'd rely
upon the colourmen who'd make
their coloured paints without mistake,
though Amberley, his pile made
by sixty-one, had left the trade,
retiring from the ceaseless grind
to Lewisham in hope he'd find
a peaceful and an easy life,
and, in a year, had found a wife
- one twenty years his junior – who,
as younger wives subjected to
their older husbands' habits, might
find boredom was a common plight,
but Amberley declared she'd been
looked after well, and he'd been keen
to treat her very well, he'd beg,
despite his artificial leg.

**Entrusted** by Holmes, Watson saw,
within that story, was a flaw
and that his property was kept
in such a state that weeds had crept
throughout the gardens such that he,
John Watson, said that it would be
unlikely that a woman might,
in such arrangements, take delight,
nor would she think the house a prize
to show off, though a pot of size
containing green paint, he observed
- although the smell of paint unnerved
his sense of smell – had been employed,
though this may have left her annoyed
for having been an afterthought
which, much sooner sorted, ought,
but then heard of the wife's deceit
and also a good friend's conceit,
but Holmes, in such deception schooled,
was not amused nor was he fooled.

**For Amberley**, a player, keen,
of chess, it seemed, had always been,
and often played an evening game
with Dr. Ray Ernest who came
to pay a visit frequently
and was enticed, apparently,
by Mrs. Amberley - now bored
by being, probably, ignored -
and, to the Doctor, had responded
favourably, and then absconded
with her lover, far away,
not being heard from since that day,
and they had taken all he had,
his savings and his ironclad
securities kept locked within
a strongroom for, with great chagrin,
he'd given, to his wife, the key
and access to all his money
which now was gone, as was his wife,
and he was destitute for life.

**The pair** had planned a cunning theft
and stole the money as they left
the house, as Amberley enjoyed
a theatre show when she deployed
a simple ruse to stay behind
- a headache of persistent kind -
and he showed Watson where he'd sat
- a theatre ticket showing that
his seat was thirty-four, B-row -
which wasn't quite enough to show
to Holmes he'd been there, so he sought
proof from the theatre, and which ought,
if found untrue, declare the man
to have devised a deadly plan
of vengeance, undeserved, on those
who, love together, gladly chose
and had run off, and then Holmes found
that version of events unsound
and, at the theatre, found the truth -
a effort worthy of the sleuth.

**Seat thirty-four** and one each side
in Row-B, Holmes checked to provide
the facts, and found that, on that night,
the man had not been there and, right
away, Holmes knew foul play had been
enacted, so the sleuth was keen
to search the house and, therefore had
- though feeling something of a cad
toward a good friend - Watson take
the man in question on a fake
and lengthy journey where he'd find
red herrings of annoying kind
to give to Holmes the time he'd need
to search the house, he being keen
to prove that paint, freshly applied,
had proved or had, at least, implied
that it would cover up the scent
of death and, for a time, prevent
discovery of victims, two,
who had been murdered, hitherto.

**With Watson**, Amberley returned
and then the fear within him churned
as Holmes asked of him where he hid
the bodies, while then, all amid
the man's demands of innocence,
Josiah Amberley's defence
collapsed as Scotland Yard arrived
and officers en-masse contrived
to search for disturbed soil close
unto the house where this morose
and jealous man intombed his wife
and former friend after the life
of each was taken using gas
pumped to the strongroom where, alas,
the pair was lured to be trapped
until the gas around them sapped
them of their air till they were dead
and Amberley could say, instead,
they had eloped – betrayal bad -
though Holmes declared Amberley mad.

# Conclusion:

**Thus ends the saga** of this man,
this Sherlock Holmes, whose tale began
before friend Watson happened by
and sought to ask the question "Why …."

"Why was I chosen, out of all
those on this Earth, to pay a call
on one whose talents were the sort
to cause rebuttal and retort
on the impossibility
of such infallibility
for finding analytic clues
of subtle shades and muted hues
by looking at what others saw
but overlooked - the tiny flaw
which told this man of insight he
had noticed what would prove to be
the vital clue to solve a case
and then embark upon the chase
to bring to justice anyone
who'd have the people's peace undone
like felons who'd not seen the cleft
to logic which each one had left
unnoticed, unrecorded, till,
with unsurpassed detection skill,
Holmes had those felons in his sights,
prevented from escape and flights
to places of proximity
to seek safe anonymity
quite unaware the hounds were on
their scents and soon would come upon
them in their hiding places and,
their quick surrender, would demand

so that they would regret the day
that Sherlock Holmes had come their way
with prowess and ability
to show the grim futility
of more resistance to this man,
this Sherlock Holmes, whose only plan
was to out-think the felon, vile,
and temper, only for a while,
that boredom raging like a torrent,
boredom his brain found abhorrent
such that grim crime, alone, could cure
by being solved by thinking, pure,
for crime was the antithesis
of order, and it was for this
that Sherlock would exist at all
and, so, would answer to the call
so that his brain, restored, could be
reset to face the challenge he
alone could recognize and meet
from Two-Two-One-B Baker Street
where he might study and prepare
to make the felons full aware
of their grim situation which,
rather than making them so rich,
would bring them to meet justice and
submit and face the harsh demand
of punishment within the walls
of prisons, stark, or hear the calls
to mount the scaffold, pay that price
which one pays once, and never twice,
to leave the ledger balanced so
a harshly-maintained status-quo
was reached and order was restored
and Sherlock Holmes, for being bored,
could claim the credit - tribute keep -
and London, peacefully, could sleep?"

..... though fate, alone, can answer true
and give to Watson what he's due
for being there when Holmes had need
of one – stout-hearted, lacking greed
and all those vices which infest
the human race – Holmes got the best -
and two would, London's darkness, fight
and bring, to people, hope of light
and, so, for doing all of this,
within the great metropolis
their legend and their fame live on
in Watson's stories based upon
the exploits of a man who rose,
the face of evil, to oppose
- where-ever it might choose to hide -
and retribution, full, provide
with all its agents overthrown
for where in London wasn't known
the soft tread of the Great Sleuth's boot?

Well, readers know that question's moot.

......................................................

Milton Keynes UK
Ingram Content Group UK Ltd.
UKHW030659081123
432193UK00012B/517

Many
have been the retellings
of Sir Arthur Conan Doyle's
intriguing accounts of the greatest
of all sleuths, the world's first and,
in his day, only consulting detective,
Mr. Sherlock Holmes, but occasionally
there comes along a new rendering of the
man's adventures and his moments of
insightful brilliance.

**The Saga of Sherlock Holmes** is one such
retelling, though so different in its format that
the great ACD (and his, then, and still very-much-
alive, creation) might well have been momentarily
taken aback.  This re-teller, Allan Mitchell, with his
habit of rendering thoughts into verse, has taken
the Holmesian Canon tales and retold each in a
series of rhythmical rhyming stories.

Less a poetic snippet than a succinct mini-
saga, each retold story takes the reader
romping through the convolutions of Doyle's
literary creation in such a way that each
can be enjoyed (somewhat in brief, but
also while remaining faithful to the
original) for its ability to stir the
memory of those exploits, often
long neglected by the reader
but forever
enjoyed.

ISBN 978-1-80424-304-6
90000
9 781804 243046